D0176459

HARD TO DIE

NEW YORK TIMES BEST SELLING AUTHOR
ANDRA WATKINS

WORD HERMIT PRESS LLC • USA

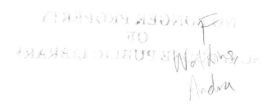

WORD HERMIT PRESS LLC • USA

Copyright © 2016 by Andra Watkins. All rights reserved.

Printed in the United States of America.

For all inquiries, Word Hermit Press LLC, P.O. Box 21849, Charleston, SC USA

Front cover photo: Word Hermit Press LLC

Back cover photo: Robert S. Johnson Photography

Hard to Die: An Afterlife Journey of Theodosia Burr Alston is a work of historical fantasy. Apart from the well-known actual people, events, and places that figure into the story, all names, characters, places and incidents are products of the author's imagination or are used fictitiously. Any resemblance to current events or locales, or to living persons, is entirely coincidental.

ISBN-13 978-0-9908593-7-6

ISBN-10 0-9908593-7-1

Library of Congress Catalog Number Applied For

FOR COOPER

BOOKS BY ANDRA WATKINS

Fiction:

To Live Forever: An Afterlife Journey of Meriwether Lewis
Hard to Die: An Afterlife Journey of Theodosia Burr Alston

Nonfiction:

Not Without My Father: One Woman's 444-Mile Walk of the Natchez Trace

Photography:

Natchez Trace: Tracks in Time

PRAISE FOR HARD TO DIE

"*Creativity abounds in this expertly crafted fictional story woven with historical figures whose deaths were a mystery. With a brilliant first sentence, it was merely seconds before I was hopelessly engrossed. Complex, memorable characters, and a smart, riveting plot that stayed ten steps ahead of me. I LOVED it.*"

–Beth Teliho, award-winning author of *Order of Seven*

"*Steeped in history, espionage, and just the right amount of longing,* Hard to Die *is a steam-powered thrill ride of a novel that will keep you guessing until the very end.*"

–Meghan O'Flynn, author of *Famished*

"Hard to Die *is one of the most imaginative books I've ever read. Andra Watkins is an expert storyteller who has no problem melding history and fantasy.*"

–Jen Mann, NYT best selling author of *People I Want to Punch in the Throat*

"*Where did Theo go? That's the question I kept asking long after I finished the story. When a piece of historical fiction can send me down the rabbit hole of research, I know it's good stuff. Watkins took an obscure character from history and turned her into a fascinating, powerful, and relatable character. I loved this book.*"

–Nicole Knepper, author of *Moms Who Drink and Swear: True Tales of Loving My Kids While Losing My Mind*

"Hard to Die *grabs you from the first sentence and doesn't let go. It's smart, moving, and completely unique. You'll never want it to end.*"

–Mary Widdicks

Death, be not proud, though some have called thee
Mighty and dreadful, for thou art not so;
For those whom thou think'st thou dost overthrow
Die not, poor Death, nor yet canst thou kill me.
From rest and sleep, which but thy pictures be,
Much pleasure; then from thee much more must flow,
And soonest our best men with thee do go,
Rest of their bones, and soul's delivery.
Thou art slave to fate, chance, kings, and desperate men,
And dost with poison, war, and sickness dwell,
And poppy or charms can make us sleep as well
And better than thy stroke; why swell'st thou then?
One short sleep past, we wake eternally
And death shall be no more; Death, thou shalt die.

–John Donne

Hard to Die

ONE: THEO

The train jettisoned me into a Grand Central corridor a few yards from the man who killed my son.

General Wilkinson steamed toward a bank of stairs, and what mother wouldn't follow? I huffed past glassed-in shops flanked by acres of marble and crashed into fedora-clad, wool-suited travelers, but I never lost him. Whenever someone shot me a disapproving look, I used the manners my father praised. "Pardon me. I'm so sorry. Excuse me."

The General strolled into the Grand Concourse. Amidst throngs scurrying from place to place to place, he paused and looked up. I followed his lead and gasped. The night sky twinkled on the soaring ceiling, lit by arched windows near the top. I traced the outlines of Orion, Aries, and Gemini, friends from my childhood.

Wilkinson was my godfather before he lost the privilege. He introduced me to the stories of the sky. I hovered outside my father's study whenever Wilkinson was inside, hoping he'd emerge early enough to trace a new character in the heavens. To study starlight was to travel through reflected time.

I swiped a stray tear before it ruined my mascara. I couldn't recall when I lost the luxury of weakness. Perhaps it died with my boy.

I twisted the ends of my knitted scarf and awaited the General's next move. His fat fist grasped a buttery croissant, procured from a passing cart. Flakes clung like dandruff along the front of his coat as he munched his snack and studied the schedule board. It twinkled with places I remembered. Ossining. Cold Spring. Beacon. Poughkeepsie. Towns perched along the glaciated shore of a river that echoed with my son's laughter.

Until his last summer. He perished before we could head north to escape the heat.

I would confront Wilkinson, even if it meant following him on a haunted tour of every agonizing memory. I would—

Damn. He chewed his last bite of pastry and watched me. My breath pulsed a hurried soundtrack for our stare down. Grand Central was too public for a miscalculated scene. Why didn't I stop to consider where I was before I rushed after him without a plan? Still, I prepared to knock him senseless with my purse as he closed the space between us. His leer never wavered. "Theodosia Burr Alston. I thought that was you, tiptoeing after me. You've grown even more ravishing since I last saw you. I'd know you anywhere."

"General Wilkinson. You always were short on sincerity."

"Oh, I think that's unfair. Why can't I point out how kind the years have been to you?"

"Too bad they haven't smiled on you."

He brushed crumbs from his coat, his smile fading. "I saw you on the platform, hiding behind posts and tripping through doorways. I started to speak to you then, but ignoring clumsiness in others is often the most thoughtful approach."

"You're still masking your selfishness with exaggerated charm. Don't be so predictable."

"Funny how this place delivers unfortunate gifts to my doorstep. You're like a spray of flowers. Only desiccated and dead."

I pretended to kiss the air around his head. "I'll remember how much you like rotted bouquets when I order one to mark your grave."

"Please, dear Theo. Hysterical, murderous threats are unbecoming to a lady."

"When one of your many enemies finally kills you, nobody'll call it murder."

"As much as I'd love to watch them fail, I don't have time for fantasy. Let me give you a little advice since you haven't seen me in a while."

"You think I'll follow your advice? Come on, General. Your advice cost me my son."

"I had nothing to do with your son's death. My condolences, by the way."

"Too late. I won't accept insincere sentiments from the architect of my son's death. And my father almost died because of your misguided counsel."

"Misguided? Really? He's the one who failed. The man ran for president and almost won. Anybody who can get that far ought to know how to assemble a team to carry out a simple plan. We needed a few thousand men to defeat our enemies. I knew how many men they had, remember? But he botched it. He barely found fifty."

"Because you wouldn't give a written guarantee of what they were promised."

"Smart people never put anything of consequence in writing. Besides, he was big-headed enough to believe he could recruit others to the cause."

"You testified against him in a trial for his life."

"Pointing out his misdeeds was my patriotic duty."

"I waited for lightning to incinerate the courtroom when you touched the Bible and swore to tell the whole truth."

"And in the end, the truth didn't matter, did it? Your father walked free."

"I don't know why he didn't challenge you to a private meeting of honor."

"You mean a duel?" He moved closer. "I wouldn't mention such things here if I were you. People don't resolve grievances that way anymore."

"Someone needs to make you suffer."

"Oh, I suffer. You have no idea."

"Then why are you still alive?"

"I know this disappoints you, but I've found it hard to die."

"I'm certain hell is ready to admit you anytime."

The General's eyes bored into me. "You don't understand where you are, do you?"

When I attacked, my purse's brass clasp raked a bloody gash along his hairline, but it wasn't enough to fell my father's arch enemy. Wilkinson always outmaneuvered his foes, especially those with the last name Burr. He seized my arm and steered me through an arched doorway. A subterranean labyrinth harbored a jumbled series of tracks. Pain broiled through my shoulder in my fight to remain upright.

"Don't worry, Theo. Dying doesn't hurt much when you're already dead."

"I'm not dead yet."

He dragged me to the far end of an abandoned platform. "It's 1950, Theo. You've been gone for 137 years. Don't you remember what happened on the ship?" He heaved me into the path of an oncoming train and shouted, "You disappeared. You're dead. And so am I."

TWO: THEO

I flapped my arms through air that couldn't hold me and plummeted toward the rails. Soiled newsprint and cigarette butts rose to greet me. I didn't have time to rebut his ludicrous claims. Both of us, dead? Impossible.

The General's laughter mingled with the squeal of brakes. I tried to climb the side of the concrete canyon, to grab his ankles, to pull him into the abyss beside me. He waited beyond my grasp.

"Hey! Give me your hand!"

Familiar glasses glowed on the opposite platform. My Conductor? Why was he still in Grand Central?

I reached toward his outstretched palms. When I grasped them, I groaned at the pop in my shoulders. He yanked me from the tracks and pulled me to the safety of the far platform. The train bulleted in front of us, but I was safe. I collapsed and lay panting on cold concrete. Every time a gap appeared between the cars, I saw Wilkinson waiting. He wouldn't leave until he knew I was finished.

I couldn't stay there, not with Wilkinson lurking across the divide.

My Conductor helped me to my feet and handed me my purse. I rummaged through it and found my wad of hundreds. At least, Wilkinson didn't rob me. Last time I counted, almost three thousand dollars remained to get me home.

I shifted my gaze to my Conductor. "Why are you still here?"

"Let me take you to another train."

"But you didn't answer me."

"We don't have time. Wilkinson is still over there, waiting to waste your life. Let's go."

A stitch tore through my side, another reminder I was alive. I held my ribs with one hand and followed him along the platform. I couldn't argue with my Conductor's urgency. Any train would give me a chance to escape.

Commuters streamed around us, and we fell in step with them. Perspiration puddled along my woolen waistband, but I kept my eyes on my Conductor's narrow shoulders. How did he always know what to do?

"This is your line." My Conductor led me through an open door and settled me onto a bench in an empty car. He took the one ahead of me. When he turned toward me, I recalled how his freckles always glowed against his pale skin. He didn't smile. "I'm not surprised to see you again."

"Didn't I just leave your train?"

Before he answered me, the train lurched to life. The General ran along the platform and pounded on various doors, but he was too late to board our train. When he stopped, bent over and heaving, I relaxed. I won this time. His sagging frame scrolled by my window. Our eyes locked, and my lips curled into a victory smirk. He failed to obliterate my DNA.

If I saw him again, I was sure he'd try to kill me.

Despite everything I ever learned about appreciating life, I had to be prepared to kill him first.

The train hiccuped along the tracks. James Wilkinson—the General— how could he be back in my life, spinning stories about us being dead? If anyone deserved eternal hellfire and damnation, the General did. He was the reason I lost my father, my son, even my home and the better parts of my memory.

My Conductor cleared his throat. "Why do you think you almost failed this time?"

"I'm sorry? I found my way back to the city, didn't I?" I wanted to get off at the next stop and head back there, not sit in an empty train car discussing failure with him.

"Why do you believe the city is part of your assignment?"

I studied my Conductor's face. His glasses magnified his dark eyes to three times their size, and wrinkles crisscrossed their periphery. "How many times have I ridden your train?"

"Four. It's your fourth time on my line, meaning you've failed three other assignments."

"Assignments? Why don't I remember anything about them?"

"Every time I say your name within these walls, I erase what you did before."

"Before?"

"Your other Nowhere outings."

"Nowhere? What other outings?"

"You're dead. You've been dead since 1813."

Hearing him say it was like drowning. I saw my grief-stricken self boarding a wooden ship. We churned through a hurricane off the Carolina coast. But we survived, only to be felled by a band of Spanish pirates. "Everyone walk the plank!" they cried, but I outsmarted them and persuaded them to take me to New York. I was reunited with my father, Aaron Burr, six months after my son died.

Wasn't I?

No. That wasn't right.

My Conductor tapped his temple. "Do you remember what happened?"

"I drowned. I never made it to my father in New York. Is that why I'm here?"

"No one knows how you died. Until someone solves the riddle of your death or you complete a Nowhere assignment, you can never fully pass on to the next thing and experience a true afterlife."

"So the General wasn't lying. Do you know how he died?"

"Poisoning. Mexico City. 1825."

Fitting Wilkinson died of poisoning. People warned my father not to eat or drink anything Wilkinson offered him, but we always laughed off such admonishments. Wilkinson was our ally, my father's friend, my godfather.

For five years, my father and Wilkinson plotted their invasion of Mexico. Their big land grab, they called it. It wasn't treason to take land from the crumbling Spanish empire and turn it into a country where it was illegal to own other human beings. They envisioned a government where geographical factions didn't write laws to enrich only themselves. In his heart, my father wanted every person, male or female, to have a chance at success. He even believed a woman like me could lead.

In the United States, Aaron Burr was known as the murderer of the great Alexander Hamilton, but he didn't want a single act to define him. My father would rule a new nation with Wilkinson as his second. And I supported them, because they would make this a world of equality and fairness for my son and me.

The General was practically family, until he sent a letter to Thomas Jefferson accusing Aaron Burr of treason. He claimed my father wanted to invade New Orleans, a city Napoleon sold to the United States. Jefferson was apoplectic. That vengeful man never forgave my father for almost beating him in the presidential election of 1800. Aaron Burr should've claimed the prize.

Jefferson made sure Dad was arrested and tried for treason, starting the sickening spiral that led to my son's death at our home in Charleston.

I turned to my Conductor. "Why didn't I remember my actual life before now?"

"Why are you focused on your past, when this life, this assignment, is what matters?"

"But you say I've lived three other Nowhere lives, and I can't remember them, either. My father made me study eastern religions. Is it like reincarnation?"

"Sort of. Nowhere is the only place where one gets repeat chances at life. You don't get to live the same life, but if no one solves the mystery of how you died, you get thirteen opportunities to complete an assignment and move beyond Nowhere."

"Beyond Nowhere? To heaven or hell?"

"What do you think lies beyond Nowhere?"

"Nothing? Eternal rest? My son? I don't know."

He patted my arm. "I don't know either, because I'll never get out of here."

"Why only thirteen chances? Because I'll somehow turn thirteen into a lucky number if I succeed?"

"No more time. I always give you too much information, even though I'm not supposed to."

"But you haven't given me anything. You sat there and asked questions like some sort of therapist charged with leading me to my own conclusions." Would I ever grasp the full extent of Nowhere? I searched his impenetrable face and wondered how many times we had the same conversation. What was the point of revealing how a world worked when failure made its inhabitants forget?

He squeezed my hand. "Maybe that's what I am. Now, Garrison is your stop, right across the river from West Point."

"West Point?"

"Yes. I'll let you know when we're approaching."

Foggy images swirled inside my head. Aaron Burr was vice president when President Jefferson signed the order to turn America's oldest fort into a military academy. I always marveled at how the stone promontory defied the river's march to the sea. Whenever I rode with my father from Manhattan to Albany, he didn't waste an educational moment. Outside, snow-covered mountains framed ice water, a landscape that echoed with his voice. Rocks, trees, and water were the recipe of memory.

As the train slowed into Garrison, my Conductor touched my shoulder. I grasped his fingers and let him guide me to stand. "How will I recognize my assignment?"

"Loads of people find themselves at a crossroads, but some need a nudge toward the best choice. Your assignment needs your help. You'll know it when you find it."

"But what about Wilkinson?"

"What about him? Revenge doesn't yield a better life for anyone, does it?"

"Who said anything about revenge? You saw him try to kill me back there. If he crosses my path, he'll try again."

My Conductor did up the top button of my coat and knotted my scarf at my neck. "Does killing ever result in a better life?"

"It does if I'm saving my own Nowhere life to finish my assignment."

"Lives are so much simpler than we make them. Don't go out there and get sidetracked. There's a life you're meant to have, a soul you're meant to save. Finish your assignment and find out what comes after Nowhere. Understand me?"

Wilkinson's threatening face flashed through my mind. He was out there, beyond the frozen edges of night. Would he find me before I completed my assignment? If he did, I would be prepared to do the unimaginable, because self-defense wasn't murder.

I met his eye and nodded. "I understand, Conductor."

THREE: RICHARD

Everyone called me Dick. Guys in the Army and Germans on the other side of Berlin's communist no man's land and even my superior officer at West Point. Never thought I'd be Dick in any of those situations, you know? Dumb smack, maybe. Or Dunderhead.

January 7, 1950. We got back to campus from Christmas break and our S.O. waited to torture us, because we might have gone soft over the holidays, what with Mommy's food and no curfew and endless screwing. A couple of weeks is a long time to enjoy life on the outside. And as much as I didn't like to admit it, my S.O. was usually right.

So the S.O. met us at the guardhouse that day. A blizzard was howling up, but he marched us across campus with our full duffles and everything. Had us strip to our skivvies, plant bare hands-and-feet in snow up to our elbows, and do push-ups until we were on the verge of frostbite. I tell you I was never happier than when my S.O.'s spit steamed off my cheeks. Helped me remember I was still disciplined and alive, a West Point cadet, not some damn ice cube on a windswept rock in New York State.

I was no pansy. I mean, no mealy-mouthed softies got into West Point.

I grew up in Ohio, meaning I knew what I was getting into. Snow and ice and all that stuff. But sophomore year, I still hated the West Point wind, because it roared down the Hudson Valley and squashed our rocky outcrop with its damn icicle fingers. Nothing like a chill that seeped through every opening when a guy was drilling outside in his underwear.

Couldn't let on, though. No respectable cadet allowed weakness to be the last thing anyone remembered about him, even when his secret wish was to quit. Go home, you know? We all had those fantasies sometimes, ones where we walked away from the Corps and blended into civilian life.

Ha. Almost laughed at my own joke, because everybody knew the service was like prison. Nobody ever forgot his time on the inside. It marked us, you know?

So I was busy thawing body parts under a hot shower when I got the first message, the one that started it all. I stood under the hellish stream and willed myself not to yowl, because I knew a thing or several about handling torture. If I didn't look up to him, I could show my S.O. some misery, give him a little taste of what it was like to want to die. I lived in the shadow of the Soviets for two years, after all. Signed up for the Army right out of high school and stayed until West Point invited me to come on over. Lots of guys used the military to save cash for college, but I was drafted. I didn't have a choice.

I never talked about my enlisted days or demonstrated my favorite torture moves or let on when my Russian professor goofed with a vocabulary word. Discretion was the spy's salvation. I was a damn fine spy. Even after I left active duty and entered the Corps, folks only saw what I wanted them to see and found me when I wanted to be found.

Except that first night back from winter break.

My roommate Joe followed my trail of steam to the basement. Everybody in our barracks showered down there, but I timed my forays to grab a few minutes to myself. Joe was a good guy. Never asked too many questions and pretty much left me alone.

That night, he stood next to the toilets, a respectable distance, his bulk ghost-like in my showery fog. His voice clinked along wet tile. No small talk or anything. Always liked that about Joe.

"You got a message. S.O. just delivered it to the room."

"Yeah? Can it wait? Almost done here."

"S.O. was gonna bring it to you, but I told him I'd take care of it. Figured you'd owe me."

"Drinks. Sure. Wanna sneak out after curfew? Maybe head to the Green Room in Newburgh?"

"Nah. Got too much studying to do."

"Later this week then." I rinsed my mouth out with fire water, spat it down the drain, and shut off the flow, fantasizing the whole time about what kind of drink I'd order and whether I'd get fries with my burger. Why was it people were always thinking about stupid, meaningless shit when real shit came along and smacked them into the rest of their lives?

"Anyway. Your message. George called."

"George?"

I stuck a towel over my dingy blonde hair and rubbed.

"Yeah. Said you'd know him."

"I don't know anybody named George."

"Says he was your friend in West Germany. You know, when you were in the Army?"

"Didn't know any Georges in West Germany, in the Army or out."

I balanced on a wet towel and fought to pull on tightey-whiteys.

"Well, this guy you don't know wants you to get a mess pass and meet him at Hotel Thayer for dinner. Got it all written down. Right here with your pass."

"Damn S.O. Always so efficient."

"Musta known you were craving a night out. Want me to leave it with your stuff?"

"Nah. Throw it here."

Joe flicked two slips of paper my way and strode toward the door, but he always had poor ass aim. Last guy I wanted on any team, the prissy schmuck. Paper stuck to water drops along my right bicep. Pen-and-ink bled together, but it was too late to claim I couldn't read the thing.

I wadded George's request into a soaked ball and aimed it at an open toilet. Best place for George and his instructions, the shitter. So I flushed George and kept my mess pass and finished with my winter dress uniform, smug in what I knew to be fact: George couldn't tell me what to do, not anymore.

Not like when I got to West Germany. I was scared of everything, including my old-ass superior officer George, trolling his temporary post for fresh, decades-younger meat to slap around. He made me patrol the freezing gray wasteland between East and West Germany, all barbed wire and trenches and whatnot, way before anybody used the term *Cold War*.

Damn, I hated his stories from the world war. Real psycho bullshit like how he cut the balls off dead Nazis and collected bones from their middle fingers. I mean, the saps deserved it, but I didn't really see the point of hoarding demon relics from enemy dead.

One time, the bastard even offered to show me his Nazi bone collection. We were on a street next to the Soviet occupied zone, with East German soldiers on the other side of some barbed wire with sub-machine guns they could use to mow right through us, and the guy started bragging about his cache of German finger bones. I couldn't say much to my superior officer, but I sure picked up my step to put some distance between him and me. You know, to make the target clear.

George stayed right on my tail, though, his story bouncing from brick to stone to metal. Last thing I heard was him calling me a wuss, before a barrage of gunfire chewed into the street. I cowered in a doorway and hoped like hell George bit it as I counted to a hundred, a thousand. My ears still rang as I took out my pocket mirror and reconned the area around the corner. Damn, I wanted to find George's meaty pulp chewed all over the cobbles. A single bullet shook a rock loose somewhere above my head, and I forgot George and fell into the lane, my position exposed. Pebbles stung the back of my scalp, my neck, my hands, as I scrabbled for my sub-machine gun.

"Never drop your weapon, Soldier."

George's voice ghosted into the night. When I looked up, he stood over me, the tip of his Luger trained on my head. Never figured the bastard would carry a German handgun, but there it was, about to snuff out my still-young life. We locked eyes, and I braced myself for the popping sound that would end me.

Instead, George aimed his opposite index finger at my forehead and cocked a thumb.

"Pow. Got any cigarettes?"

"Huh?"

Cobblestone dug into my chin while he stood on the sidewalk, laughing at my ass with the East German patrol.

"Smokes, Dickwad. I promised these gentlemen I'd trade smokes in exchange for scaring the shit out of you. Only I don't have any. Guess it's up to you to save your own skin, Private Dickie."

First time I ever savored the thought of cutting off someone's balls, the sadistic prick. I tried to keep my hand from shaking as I pushed to my feet and gave my last pack to the ringleader.

"Life or death, Soldier." George lit a cigar to pair with the Soviet's cigarette. He blew smoke rings into my face and whispered, "Every breath is life or death."

That's how he was and is. And here's another thing about people like George: They're persistent fuckers. I wasn't in my room fifteen minutes before I was summoned to the hall phone.

"Dick Cox!"

My footsteps echoed with chants of *Dick's Cock Dick's Cock Dick's Cock*, as fellas opened doors and wagged their hairy penises my way. They were still going at me when I picked up the phone and listened to the sentry tell me I had a guest in Grant Hall, the on-campus building where we cadets were allowed to meet civilians.

I buttoned my winter coat and headed into a vortex of sub-zero wind chill, figuring I could make an appearance and get rid of George and use my ill-gotten mess pass for my own purposes. My nostrils froze together as I hoofed it across campus, but I hustled into the warmth of Grant Hall, hung up my coat, and scanned the place, all lit fireplaces interspersed with wood and plaster and uniformed blowhards.

My spy skills might've been rusty, but I marked my guest from outside, through a window, before I even entered the place. I wasn't surprised when a hand slapped the back of my shoulder. A snout full of Pinaud Clubman cologne and Jack Daniels was a bad combination in the stealth department, you know? I wheeled on my caller and stuck out my palm.

"George! What're you doing here, Old Man?"

FOUR: RICHARD

"Have I got a story for you, Dickie." George's Cuban cigar fogged the inside of his woodie wagon, all maple and leather and enough room to cart ten people around the valley in style. The thing was a perfect make-out vehicle, not a ride for a goof like George to trash with his cigar ash.

All I could see of West Point was its gothic crown twinkling across the water from where he parked at a riverfront spot in Garrison, New York. Trains rumbled through spindly trees behind us, mostly hauling stuff to the city. No witnesses, you know?

I coughed and noted the glowing clock face near the steering wheel: 18:00. Whatever George's bullshit story, I wanted to be back at the barracks by 18:30. Twenty minutes of George's foul air and ten minutes to get back to my room, where I'd pretend to study for my Russian exam. Damn, I should have been an actor.

I hacked again when George knocked my leg with his fist and blew more smoke. "Wanna hear it? My story?"

"Aw, come on, man. You dragged my ass all the way over here to

Garrison. Must mean your story's too sick for the nosies at Hotel Thayer."

"Suit yourself. I'm just trying to help you, Dickie, but we can sip booze and admire the view."

"Bullshit, George. Why're you here?"

"What's this George shit? Awfully familiar for a subordinate to his superior officer, isn't it?"

"You're not my S.O. Not anymore. So why don't you spill your yarn and quit wasting my time? Because I sure don't wanna succumb to hypothermia with the likes of you."

I coughed into my hands, but my breath froze by the time it hit my skin. "Could you at least crank the car back up? Dammit, I should've split as soon as I saw you. I could've taken my mess pass to Newburgh for a big time."

"You're not happy to see me?"

He unscrewed the cap on a bottle of Jack Daniels and sucked its head. Amber bubbles reflected in the clock's light. He belched and wiped his pout on his sleeve before shoving the bottle my way. "Come on. Quit playing the goody-goody and pick a vice here. Celebrations aren't the same without a little liquid confetti."

"You can shove your celebration, okay? When I said so long to you in Europe, I meant goodbye forever."

"Well, here's the thing about forever, Dickie: It's a nice ride, but it takes a while. Especially for peevish guys like me. I like a little here-and-now with my someday."

"And I told you West Point is the only path to the rest of my life."

"Yeah. Right."

Bastard blew a plume of smoke toward the ceiling and side-eyed me. "What's that thing they say about sex? Be careful where you stick your dick, because everybody you screw becomes part of you."

Eighteen-year-old fellas from Ohio didn't grasp forever. I mean, what teenager did, right? I wasn't any different. My first year in West Germany, I snapped to it and did everything the Army asked. I was always better than the next guy, because I wanted the higher-ups to pick me for plum assignments instead of pissing my time on menial crap.

What a dunderhead.

I snatched the bottle and gulped enough firewater to douse my memories. Hell, I could ace my Russian exam after downing a whole bottle of Jack, but I didn't need people thinking I knew more than I let on. I was hell bent on following my own path and young enough to believe it was possible.

I reached for the bottle again and winced as liquor sparked through my gut. George leaned his beefy head against the driver's window and disgorged more smoke, and I slumped against my door and shut my eyes to ward off his fresh assault. Guess my posture read resigned.

"That's more like it, Dickie. Take another hit. You'll need a buzz for the story I got."

It was 18:10.

"You don't have much time, George, so you'd best make it count."

George created an ash cloud when he stubbed his cigar in the ashtray. The stuff rained on my overcoat and stuck to my eyelashes and probably even snaked into my undershorts. I batted flecks of ash onto the floor while George lit another stogie. Smoke seeped between his rotten teeth. I imagined him guarding the very gates of hell.

Would he trap me with some stupid ass riddle? Or could I outwit him and gain my freedom?

"Your country needs you, Dickie. The damn Soviets are gaining ground. Yeah, we know they exploded their first atomic bomb, but the bastards are working on a super bomb."

Different start than I expected, especially from George. I leaned forward. "How do you know that?"

"Classified, but I'll tell you we caught a mole. One of ours. Name of Fuchs, if you can believe it. He was passing details of our program. They've penetrated our organization, both in Europe and stateside. Nothing is safe, not our country, our citizens, or our freedom."

"So duck-and-cover drills aren't wastes of time. And I thought it was just a bunch of fear-mongering."

"The Soviets are gaining on us, Dickie. The politicians in Washington are hesitating, but the guys at Los Alamos are determined to beat the Soviets to a super bomb. We need to know how close the Commies are to building it, so we can convince the damn politicians to give our boys the green light. We need spies like you, agents who've proven they can penetrate the Soviet system from the inside. You'll be saving your country, making it safe for its clueless people to sleep at night. Isn't that an honorable life?"

"Plenty of other guys were better than I was, George. Get one of them."

"I've got specific orders. You're the one everybody wants."

"And if I don't go with you?"

George took a drag on his cigar and studied the mountains across the river. After what felt like an interminable time, he spoke. "You remember that agent we shared? German girl. What was her name?"

I took another swig of Jack and pretended to recall our two years in West Germany. Buying time to figure out his game. Funny how my defenses all came back, just like riding a bike. The spymasters said I'd never forget my training. Bastards. All of them.

Especially George.

"I didn't share any girl with you, German or otherwise, because hell, I couldn't keep track of the dolls you slept with. No way I'd risk your string of diseases."

"Oh, we shared one young lady. Her name was Alice."

"I never slept with Alice, and neither did you. She would've told me, given she was my partner and all."

He clucked his tongue and stuck his cigar between his teeth. "A shame she's not here to settle the question of her reputation. I guess you'll always wonder, because she's dead."

"What the hell?"

Burning ash clouded his face when I swung for his chin and landed a right on his cigar. A brimstone avalanche down the front of his trench coat, it burned holes in the fabric. I wished George and his story would go up in flames, not just his stupid jacket.

He brushed the mess onto the floor and laughed at my weakness. Spies weren't supposed to mourn a colleague's death, even retired spooks like me.

Alice supervised my descent into the agency, and who better? I mean, she fled the Nazi atrocities and joined up with the Allies during the war, even helped the Americans pinpoint some key Third Reich strongholds. The only reason I was a living, breathing cadet at West Point was because she schooled me well.

But I was at West Point to forget that existence, those deceits. Everybody I met was a possible Soviet, even my apple-pie-eating, red-white-and-blue mother. All those execution-style killings they forced me to do. And always, always I was hiding in plain sight. Alice vouched for me when I begged to get out. I didn't want to spend my life as a spy.

George mopped his face with a handkerchief and reached inside the front of his trench coat. I braced myself for a gunshot, but George wasn't holding a gun. He waved a thin manila envelope and chuckled. "Want to know what happened to Alice?" He slapped my coat sleeve with the envelope and put it between us on the seat. "The Soviets were onto Alice. Official word is they killed her. It's all right here."

Ignoring the envelope, I grabbed the bottle of whiskey and swigged until I hit air, while George shaved another cigar and stuck it between his lips. A fiery circle moved with his voice. "I knew you cared for her more than you let on."

"Of course I cared for her. I mean, my God, she was a person, and she was on our side. I did every lousy mission into Soviet territory with her as my cover, and I came back alive. Hell, don't you love every operative who saved your worthless life?"

I spat words and whiskey. A drop splattered the clock face. 18:22.

George saw me marking time. "Well. I guess I'd better get you back to the barracks. You can study that envelope and get ready for your big test."

"What'd you do to her, you bastard? I bet you ratted her out to the Soviets, didn't you?"

"Doesn't matter now, Dickie. We spies have no time to be softies."

"I'm no spy. Not anymore."

George blew soot in my face, and his belly jiggled when he laughed, a creepy Santa Claus minus the white beard. "We're like the mafia, Dickie. A family you'll leave in a black plastic shroud or with your feet in a pail of cement. You're out when we say you're out. Just ask Alice." He cocked his finger against his temple and shuddered, a threat I knew he meant. "And we have another assignment for you."

"No. I won't do it."

"Remember our cipher code?"

"Look, George. Escaping the life of a spy was the whole fucking point of coming here, because it's no kinda life."

"Like I said, that's the whole point of fucking. Once you take on somebody else's essence, they'll always be part of you. No escape."

He cracked open another bottle of Jack and passed it to me. As alcohol rained into my mouth, I hoped it would make the whole George encounter disappear. I couldn't act if I couldn't remember.

"She wanted out, but she was too valuable. That's why I had to kill her."

I threw the bottle at him. It smashed against his door and soaked him with brown water and glass shards. I lunged, until the appearance of his Luger stopped everything but my voice. "You? You killed her?"

"Strangled her, shot her in the temple, and dismembered her. Once I took off her head, the rest was easy."

I knocked his gun wide and found his throat before he could react. I wrung his flesh until my fingers turned numb, until his leer turned blue, until I chickened out and released his sorry ass. I always believed George's stories were fantasies, things he made up to give himself a sense of swagger he didn't own.

I knew his Alice story was true. Every word was gospel.

His voice rasped into the night air. 18:35. The time shone from the center of the dash as he whispered, "America's in danger, Dickie-boy. I need you to see that. Hell, your country needs you to see it. The best spies want to be on the front line, and you're one of the best."

"But I don't want any part of that life."

"We were afraid you'd feel that way. We're under the gun, Dickie, but I'm giving you a few days to think about it. You're a smart guy. You'll come around."

"And if I decide not to join you?"

"You'll end up like Alice. I'm here to escort you to your new job behind Communist lines or kill you myself. Your choice, Dickie-boy. You've got until the fourteenth to get your affairs in order. And don't think about running. I know how to find you."

Hard to Die

FIVE: THEO

The Conductor pushed me onto the arctic platform at Garrison and closed the door. I shivered and breathed boreal air, molecules and atoms from the land of my birth. I wasn't ethereal. The rules of the living still applied to me.

I muscled into Garrison's gabled station hall. It was too cold to stay on the platform. I squared my shoulders and spoke to the rafters holding up the station's vaulted ceiling. "If I go back to the city, maybe the General will find me, only I'll be prepared. When he makes his move, I'll kill him and come back here to find my assignment. I have plenty of time."

Before I reached the ticket booth, I was knocked sideways by an unseen force. It spun me like a child's broken toy. I crunched into the floor and groaned when muscles ground against bone.

"Excuse me. Miss? Are you okay?"

A gray-clad young man stood over me, with buzzed dark blonde hair and unfocused blue eyes. I gazed into those eyes a few seconds too long before he offered me a hand. "I'm sorry. Did I hurt you?"

I blushed and looked away. "I'm all right."

"Let me help you stand."

Heat nibbled up my arm when I grasped his palm and creaked to my feet. I shook my head to banish the fact that I was thrown off-kilter by his very essence. A man with those eyes was a mirage in the desert, offering water that wasn't there. I tightened the belt on my coat and stepped away from his aura. "Really, I'm fine."

"You sure? I think I knocked you pretty hard."

"I'm not as dainty as I look."

"You staying in Garrison?"

"No. Headed back to the city."

"You already have your ticket then? For the city-bound train?"

"I'll buy one now. Won't take me five minutes to be on my way." I indicated a dark window across the room, topped with a *Tickets* sign.

"Look, I'm sorry to be the one to break it to you, but you can't get a ticket into the city until morning."

"What?"

I squinted into the empty ticket booth and willed someone to appear, while he whistled whiskey fumes and pulled me onto a wooden bench beside him, ready to linger. He flopped one arm over the bench's back and grazed my shoulders with more infernal electricity. I avoided his eye and leaned forward, but if he noticed my agitated state, he didn't say so. "Place closed at 17:00. I mean, 5:00 p.m."

I played with the ends of my scarf. I couldn't spend the night in a small town train station. "Where's the nearest inn?"

"I don't know what's here in Garrison, but Hotel Thayer's just across the river. I'm a cadet over there. Hence the costume."

"Cadet? You mean at West Point?"

He winked and my cheeks burned anew. "No other cadets allowed in this valley, miss."

"This Hotel Thayer. Can I get a ride across the river? A boat or something?"

"River's too frozen for a ferry, but the bus back to West Point's due here in less than a minute, and my ass, I mean butt, better be on it."

My eyes climbed the chiseled lines of his face. God, he was attractive.

He twisted an envelope between his palms and smiled. "If you're sure you're all right, I really need to get moving. But you can join me if you want. You know, take the bus to West Point and get a room at the Thayer."

"I can take the bus back over here in the morning?"

"Yeah. Here or Peekskill. If you're headed to the city, might be easier to get off the bus at Peekskill."

West Point. What ghosts would shriek at me there?

I followed the cadet through a heavy wooden door. Staying at Hotel Thayer would be easier than scouting an unfamiliar town for an available room. Plus, I sort of knew someone there if I counted the cadet.

Outside, winter flung icy darts into my chest. I thrust my hands into my pockets and fought to breathe. How did I ever survive winters in this place?

The cadet fell in beside me. "Here. Maybe you should use my overcoat until we get to campus, miss. It's wicked out here tonight."

Before I could thank him, I was engulfed in a gray mass of whiskey-and-cigar-scented wool. Grateful for his chivalry, I shivered beneath its bulk and watched a bus hurtle through an obstacle course of snowdrifts. It slid to a stop a few feet from us. Gold paint reflected the words *West Point.* I waded into knee-deep snow behind the cadet, my boots sinking into his footprints. Inside the bus, he pushed me past a couple of other uniforms and sank into a seat next to me.

"At least you didn't make a rookie mistake."

"I'm sorry?"

"Best side of the bus. If it were light out, you'd be able to see the river during the whole ride. Pretty amazing, that view." He plundered through his coat pockets and held up what looked like a quarter. "I always snap pictures when I ride across this bridge."

"Pictures?"

"Yeah. This thing?" He cradled the quarter in his palm. When I looked closer, I realized it was more like a pocket watch with a tiny hole to peer through. He shoved it back in his pocket without letting me inspect it further. "It's a Petal camera. Smallest camera ever made."

Of course, I had so many questions about the whole process of freezing images from life, but I bottled them up and asked something I considered benign. "Sounds like you enjoy being here, mister . . . I'm sorry, what's your name?"

"Richard. Richard Cox. And you are—"

"Theodosia Alston, but everyone calls me Theo."

"Nice to meet you, Theo. You in college around here?"

"No, but I'm sure I'm not much older than you."

Why did I say that? He ran his blue eyes over my face until my flesh burned. "I'm sure you're not."

I shifted in my seat and trained my gaze to the world beyond the window. It was easier than blurting, "Do you know what it feels like to have you look at me that way?" I gazed into his eyes and lost my mind. West Point cadets probably had scores of girls vying for their favor. Whatever his liquor-fueled attraction, he'd forget me by morning, and if he didn't, my disappearance would seal it. I had to go back to the city and let the General find me. Only then could I stop looking over my shoulder and complete my Nowhere assignment, whatever it was.

Soft moonlight penetrated snow clouds to reveal an ice-choked river, reminders of the glacier that formed the entire valley. Snowflakes sugarcoated everything, a trick of nature to ease us humans into thinking the world was perfection and purity. I'd been around long enough to know better, but I still enjoyed the view. "We used to climb mountains for days to see the river like this. How long has the bridge been here?"

He shot me an unreadable look before answering. "Couple of decades, I guess. Next one's not until Poughkeepsie. It's kinda weird to have to drive so far to reach places I can see from my window."

The bus motored toward a rocky outcrop, George Washington's prized knot at a bend in the Hudson River, once the fort at West Point. I shivered and turned away from memories, only to find Richard aiming his camera at me. He pressed the button and slipped the contraption into his coat pocket. "Hope you don't mind. I wanted to capture the way your skin reflected the light. Maybe I can show it to you when I develop it."

My lips formed words before I could stop them. "Maybe I'd like that."

SIX: RICHARD

I didn't wanna leave her. Sure, I had stuff to do and even more shit to think about, but nothing got between a guy and his dick, especially when that guy was a spy. Hell, I showed her my camera so I could snap her picture. When I walked her into the lobby at Hotel Thayer, I hung around until they handed her a room key, not because I intended to follow her upstairs. I wasn't a total jerk. But if I manipulated my sign-in for morning mess, I could sprint over to the Thayer. I'd set up a city date before she checked out and make it look official. Believable.

I liked that idea, because I planned to be around West Point a while. The way her chocolate curls brushed her scarf . . . well, I wanted to see the skin under that thing. Run my fingers over it, you know?

Imagination warmed the trek along icy pavement. It passed the time until I pulled up at my barracks. Better than dwelling on George and his ultimatums, because we spies existed to bridge the gap to the impossible: Kill this target to rid America of duck-and-cover drills; take this poison if you're cornered; return to espionage.

Or die.

When I headed inside to my room, light and shadow tripped me up, and the stairwell spun. I huddled on the bottom stair, a blurry mix of drunk and scared. "Focus, dickwad," I whispered. "Focus on what's important."

George and his blasted envelope. God, I wished I'd never met him. I intended to serve my twenty-one months, time every drafted male was required to give to his country. Afterward, I wanted college, a family, and a respectable career.

But when my sergeant insisted I try out for a *special Army program*, I was eager to please. Bastard said I was perfect for it, and since I always did my best, surprise! I got the job. Me. I climbed over every other enlisted man and penetrated East Berlin. Working with Alice, I ferried messages to and from informants behind the Iron Curtain, classified details encoded into my gray matter and transmitted to theirs. No notes. No evidence. No trail.

And when some goof gave misinformation or squealed to the enemy?

It was my job to assassinate them . . . and other stuff. I didn't want to relive my own torture sessions behind enemy lines or remember what I did to other men in the name of patriotic duty. The higher-ups said we must defeat the Soviets at any price, but some of the things they ordered me to do defied humanity. I carried my camera everywhere to record my surroundings. Pictures might help me piece my life back together if I was captured or brainwashed or whatever.

Anyway, Alice cleaned the scene. Three times, she saved my life. Once, I saved hers. I still saw the flash of gunfire before I knocked her into a Polish alley. We sprawled together in an icy puddle, legs and arms tangled, and listened to retreating footsteps. Instead of being scared shitless, she bit my ear.

"Hey, Cox. Do that again, and I might sleep with you."

"Can I throw you in a stinking puddle and rough you up first?"

She untangled one arm and looked at me. "Maybe."

"Yeah, but that makes me a dick. Besides, I'd rather not risk losing you in the first place."

She ran her index finger along my cheek, and my skin sizzled. "We'll just have to take our chances, won't we?"

Alice teased her way through a male-dominated world, and most of us took her seriously. Nothing intimidated her, not even death. I wanted to be like that at first, until Alice rescued me from my first torture session. To clarify, I was the torturer. We were supposed to pour our venom on every Commie bastard we caught. But I couldn't do it, you know? It was barbaric to throw a guy on a board and ply his nose and mouth with a water hose until he almost drowned, Soviet or not. Alice took over and even gave me credit when we got a confession.

We completed almost a dozen successful operations before I decided spying was no life for a guy who wanted a family. I couldn't imagine dragging a decent girl to the armpit of the Soviet Union to start life anew, or worse, marrying a fellow spook. Higher-ups wouldn't permit serious entanglements anyway. A spy wasn't allowed emotional baggage. I wanted out.

Without asking anybody, I applied to West Point and was accepted on my merit. No meddling from my congressman, no favoritism. The Corps accepted Richard Colvin Cox, because they believed I deserved a spot. How often did that happen, huh? I considered it a sign, turned in my orders, and started packing.

But here's what was funny: Nobody from my former life blocked my next move. Alice introduced me to couple of suits who walked me through a briefing. What to say about my Army days. What was classified. Stuff like that. After everything I did as a spy, from the killings to the lies, I couldn't believe how easy it was to resign.

Stupid me.

I stumbled downstairs to the shower, perfect place to slough off most of my night. As I stood alone under the hot stream, I let my mind wander over different terrain. Brunette curls and rosebud lips and a hint of experience. I bet Theo was one of those girls who took charge. I soaped up and imagined what she might be like, you know, underneath piles of winter wear. I was almost ready to go when another cadet thwacked my ass with a towel.

"Hey, Cox. Ready for your Russian exam?"

"Piece of cake," I bragged and let water wash thoughts of Theo down the drain. I might not know much about her, but I intended to find out.

Upstairs, I stalked past my roommate Joe and rested my head on my desk. Joe didn't see me slip George's envelope into my notebook for later. I couldn't open it in front of anyone. I needed to read it when I knew I could sneak off someplace and burn it without attracting attention.

Joe cleared his throat and threw his skinny legs on his desktop. "Hey, Dick. How was the Thayer? You sneak an extra shot or several?"

"I must stink like a damn distillery."

I might've gotten the spins, but I never slurred when I drank. Spooks controlled their tongues, because they learned what to avoid. I was a solid beer guy. No pussy-ass wine or hard liquor and I was good, but a shot of spirits turned me into a hopeless narcoleptic. George knew it. I belly-flopped onto my mattress and replayed for myself one of the last times I saw Alice.

She was a few years older than me, like Theo, I suspected. She always got the orders for our next assignment, meaning I always followed her when she called. I didn't know where we were headed, but whispers indicated Moscow itself.

I walked to meet her on our usual Berlin street corner near no-man's land. The war ended three years before, but it was still some scene. Construction crews buzzed between bombed-out buildings, but if they worked around the clock for another three years, they couldn't heal the scars.

I waited for her to slip me my instructions in our usual cipher code, but she threw me a curve. She cooed at me in German any eavesdropper could understand. "Come. Next door."

Spies weren't supposed to trust anybody, but I would've tailed Alice anyplace. I already mentioned wanting to nail her, but she wouldn't let me. Ancient male-female horse shit dynamics. We never outgrow them, do we?

Turned out, 'next door' was the shell of a cathedral, a place we'd never used to rendezvous. I wondered what she was up to, but in a celebratory sort of way. I thought I'd finally worn her down. Clouds scudded across the roofless sky. It was the perfect place for a farewell screw.

But when I went for her hand, she rolled her eyes and slipped through a crack in the wall. Of course, I followed her, still convinced it was my lucky day. Together, we stood inside the bombed-out reminder of holiness in the unholy Nazi regime.

"Private Dickie-boy." George's voice boomed across rubble.

I wheeled to find him standing on a remnant of the altar, his arms stretched wide. "You make a lousy crucifix . . . sir."

"Tsk-tsk. I'll always be God to you."

Alice slipped back to the street the way we came. There I was thinking we were finally going to get busy, and she delivered me for my apparent reckoning with George. Spies were ordered to do all kinds of shit we didn't like. She was following orders. I never held it against her, mostly because George let me go.

But if George was telling the truth tonight, her face didn't exist anymore. I vowed to find out what happened. I still had contacts on the inside. Wouldn't be easy, but maybe I could get a coded message to somebody. I mean, I couldn't make a decision about the rest of my life without all the facts, right?

Joe stood up and stretched his gangly frame until his back popped. "Hey, Cox. I'm gonna hit the showers before I call it a night, okay?"

I waved and settled into the mattress. Soon as I heard the door click, I bolted to my desk and slipped my fingers between the sealed flaps of George's missive, expecting to find the usual coded meeting location. Maybe directions to a clean vehicle for my expected getaway.

Instead, a black-and-white photograph fluttered to my desk, but two tones didn't matter. I knew the color of blood.

A woman's mutilated body filled the frame, torso knifed to shreds and meaty stumps where her limbs and head used to be. I'd witnessed some gruesome stuff in my time, you know? But I couldn't stop acid from stinging my tongue, and I swallowed chunks to keep from spewing all over my desk. Whoever the woman was, George wanted me to think she was Alice.

Did he take me for some sort of lightweight?

I snapped a picture of the whole mess, tore up George's photograph, and stuck it in the envelope. I needed to get out of the room after lights out. Joe never ratted on me. I knew where I wanted to burn the bloody mess.

Same place I'd throw the pieces of George when I killed the bastard.

SEVEN: THEO

I couldn't sleep. Wind crashed down the valley and rattled the Thayer's windowpanes. An undercurrent of menace whispered in its wake. Everything about West Point was haunted and wrong, but maybe I was confusing it with my not-life.

Was that what I should call Nowhere?

After all, how often did a person find out she disappeared almost 150 years earlier? What a twisted form of punishment, to inhabit a world between life and death over something I couldn't control. What happened if I squandered my thirteen tries? Would I vanish from life's timeline? Would my son?

I rubbed my eyes until light popped behind my lids. Damn what my Conductor said. Everything about this life hinged on the General. He watched me escape. I couldn't spend time looking over my shoulder, wondering when he would scream from the haze and finish me.

I padded to the bathroom and splashed water on puffy eyes. I needed sleep to retrace my steps, I lectured the woman in the mirror, translucent skin and hair all askew. If I found the General, I maintained the advantage of surprise. He would certainly try to kill me again, but I would be ready. People were murdered in New York every day, I told my image as she bit her lip and avoided my eye.

Could I finish someone, even if he deserved it?

Whatever happened, I'd burrow into the labyrinth of the subway. I'd ride back to Garrison and complete my assignment, to help someone at a crossroads make the best choice. And when I did, would another train take me to whatever came after Nowhere?

My father made sure my tutors taught me to be a critical thinker. I could speak and write in five languages, and I won debates with the most educated men of the day. While I didn't believe in heaven, I hoped to see my son again.

The oval face of the bedside clock glowed 4:30 a.m. No point trying to sleep, not with Wilkinson hovering beyond my window, an appointment I was compelled to keep. I sank into cotton sheets and cradled the phone on my shoulder. Somebody at the Thayer ought to be able to help me.

"Front desk." A male yawn dragged through my ear.

"Yes. This is Theo Alston. Room 223."

"Would you like to order breakfast?"

"No. Thank you, though. I was wondering . . . "

"Yes?"

"What time does the West Point shuttle start service to the train stations across the river?"

"Weather permitting, the first trip will be at 5:00 a.m."

"I'll be down in ten minutes."

I forgot to thank him in my zeal to pull on day-old clothing. Did I always wander Nowhere in the same outfit? I flicked on another lamp and dumped the contents of my purse onto the gold bedspread. Besides my wad of hundreds held together by a rubber band, I noted a frayed linen handkerchief, a few pennies, a lipstick, a dainty powder compact, and a silver fountain pen. It offered no identification, nothing to prove I was who I claimed to be. And where did all that money come from?

I closed my eyes and massaged my temples. Where was I before I left the subway? Grainy images flitted behind clouds, but I couldn't make them out.

I scraped everything into my purse and hurried to the lobby, boots grasped in one hand. I hopped across cold marble, pausing at the front desk long enough to pay my bill. Whatever my Hudson Valley assignment, I wouldn't be returning. I couldn't risk another heart-pumping interaction with a certain cadet. If I saw those eyes again, I might abandon everything. I didn't know what would happen if I disregarded an assignment altogether. Nowhere probably didn't allow me to forge my own path through a numbered in-between life.

I zipped up my boots and sashayed through glass doors. A wall of frozen air smacked my face and took my breath, but I leaned into it and plowed toward the bus stop. I had five minutes to spare before the bus arrived.

I followed twin headlights as they levitated between river and sky, the road a rocky pathway to West Point's gate. Ahead of the bus, a lone figure ran along the center of the road. Darkness obscured his features, but his posture mimicked the only cadet I shouldn't want to see.

Richard.

I inched toward the drive, to run my fingers through the disappearing aura of an almost-friend. When was the last time I called someone *friend*, or trusted myself to another human being? But I conjured no one since I lost my son.

The runner kept his eyes on slippery pavement, an obstacle course of patchy ice. The cold should've rendered his lungs two solid chunks, but adrenaline worked miracles with strength and endurance, not to mention concentration.

And attraction.

I squinted through another exhale. Mist reminded me I was alive. A Nowhere life, yes, but what was living in any guise if one was always cautious? I cupped my mouth and shouted, "Richard!"

He sprinted beyond the hotel entrance and skidded to a halt. His breathing was slower than my own by the time I reached his side, but I didn't miss how he cocked his head to the right and watched my approach. I matched his stare, because I wanted to relish my last fleeting opportunity with him. Maybe he'd make an impression, and I'd beat the rules of

Nowhere and recall him someday.

Richard's lopsided smile met mine. "Theo?"

"Yes," I huffed.

"Lucky me, running into you."

"I'm glad I can thank you again for your help."

"They don't require you to keep cadet hours, you know."

"I'm sorry?"

"Guests don't have to rise to revelry. You can claim your beauty sleep, though if I'm honest, you really don't need it."

"Oh, I need it. I didn't sleep at all last night."

"Another thing we have in common, but we cadets like to think we're superior to regular folks. Don't tell anybody."

I grinned. "I'm far from regular."

"Right you are."

Richard's eyes never left mine. When I bit my lip and looked away, he nodded toward West Point's entrance. The bus's red taillights receded into town.

"Guess you missed the bus. I got a few minutes. Let me buy you a coffee."

I studied his uniform, the whole production leftover from the previous night, right down to stale tobacco smoke. I allowed myself to touch his sleeve. "No offense, but did you stay out all night, Richard?"

He closed the gap between us and cupped my elbow with one hand. "I'll tell you all about it over coffee."

I nodded and let him lead me through the Thayer's double doors. Another hour wouldn't matter, would it? I ignored the image of my Conductor wagging his finger and daydreamed instead. Maybe Richard was my Nowhere assignment. Wouldn't that be convenient, given how I got woozy whenever I thought of him?

We squeaked past stark modern chairs and displays of weaponry. People usually succumbed to the need to fill silence with sound, especially when their thoughts were loud. I settled onto a leather chair opposite Richard and appreciated his measured silence.

And other things.

He waved toward a tuxedo-clad waiter. "Can we get some coffee? And maybe a plate of pastries? You know, the one with the strawberry and apple hand pies."

I unbuttoned my coat and slipped it from my shoulders. "Sounds like you've done this before."

"Yeah. I'm surprised the guy didn't offer to bring me my usual."

"I thought cadets were supposed to be in their rooms all night."

"Well, technically we are, but I'm a pro at skirting the system. You know how it is, the need to grab some time alone, right?"

The waiter returned, filling our cups and setting down our plate of baked goods. Pockets of dough steamed with promises of gooey fruit. I picked up my mug and breathed the aroma. "I've been alone for a while now."

"Yeah, I figured we had that in common."

When he bit into a pie, crust flecked his lips. I burned to reach across the space. Would he be annoyed if I brushed the crumbs away?

God, what was Richard saying? I gulped coffee. It scalded my throat, but at least I was present.

"I'm sorry?"

"I said, where're you headed? Is the city your final destination?"

"Everybody has to go through the city to get anywhere."

"If you're gonna be there a while, I can get a day pass."

"A day pass?"

"You know, come down there and take you someplace for a proper meal. No strings, Theo. I'd just like to see you again."

I almost spat coffee. Was he nibbling breakfast and reading my mind? As much as I enjoyed flirting with the idea of him, I only did it because I couldn't imagine him reciprocating. Men who looked like Richard never wanted for companionship. Yet, there he was, saying he wanted to spend more time with me.

I bumped the table and rattled the dishes, but I hurried with my coat buttons. "I'm sorry, Richard. I have to go."

Across the lobby, the clock read 5:50. Ten minutes in subzero winds might give me a chance to witness the sunrise, to forget our conversation, to consider my unrelenting desire to take him up on his offer.

Richard's boots thwacked behind me. "Theo! Wait up."

He ran around me and blocked the entrance, his exquisite face more amused than hurt. I folded my arms, hoping they would hide my mortification. One innocent question gave me no cause to flee.

"Look, Richard. I'm sorry. It's just—"

"I'm a baboon. I get it."

"No. You're lovely, but the city isn't my final destination."

"What is?"

"Doesn't matter. I won't be in Manhattan long enough to see you again."

I offered him my gloved hand and knew I'd miss his warmth. But warmth wasn't fire. No matter how much accelerant Richard offered, I was afraid I'd never flame, not like I did when I was fully alive.

Dammit, why did looking at him make me feel like I was fully alive?

I swallowed. "Thank you for helping me find this place, for keeping me company, even for feeding me. But I really have to go."

Before he could argue, I strode toward the exit and let the cold pierce my soul. Nowhere demanded one entanglement with my assignment, not a bunch of extracurriculars. Yet, I stood at the bus stop and acknowledged one fact: I was shunning what could be a fun diversion to go into the city and place myself in the path of someone who probably wasn't my assignment, because how could chasing the General lead to helping someone at a crossroads make their best choice?

I watched Richard leap snowdrifts and disappear into the labyrinth of West Point architecture, and I ached with longing for connection, for companionship. I blushed. Even for something more. "If you're my assignment, we'll meet again," I muttered as I boarded the bus.

When I finally entered the canyons of New York City, it was around noon. A wall of snow collapsed on the track and delayed the train for precious hours. I exited Grand Central and wobbled through a sea of yellow vehicles, the word *taxi* blaring from tops and sides. My heel caught in a grate, and as I struggled to free myself, a truck buzzed my backside and parked up the block. I yanked my foot free and stormed along the frozen sidewalk, determined to tell the truck's driver a thing or two about watching for pedestrians.

The truck's door opened and unleashed the General into the street. He threw the keys under the mat and closed the door.

I swallowed my rant and hid behind a light pole until I heard his footsteps decrescendo along snow-packed pavement. I didn't question how convenient his appearance was, because I believed Nowhere would continue to draw him to me. He wouldn't ever let me exist in a world with him. If I wanted to find my assignment in this life, I had to finish him. Like a mechanical beast, I fell in line behind him.

The General strutted a block ahead of me, and I let him set the pace. Smoke wafted around his head as he turned another corner and slipped between two buildings. He was oblivious to my presence.

I hoped.

I sidled up to the alley where I last saw the General and grazed one eyeball around the stone edge.

A foot from my face, a dumpster overflowed garbage. I scanned a man-made chasm littered with trash receptacles, a broken bicycle, and a bum.

But there was no Wilkinson.

Before I talked myself in another direction, I ducked behind the dumpster and crept into the narrow space. My shoes recoiled with every step, even on tiptoe, but I kept my eyes trained on a t-intersection crisscrossed with shaded windows and steel ladders. The tramp camped next to the dumpster and begged for a penny. I dropped three dollars in his soot-blackened hands and continued toward the alley's junction.

Stifled hellos wafted ahead of me along a wave of unexpected city heat. I flattened myself against beige stone and scooted toward the ledge, my heart hammering. The bum's rasp accompanied my peek around the corner, but I never processed what he said.

Wilkinson was halfway down another corridor, his profile obscured by the angle of his hat. Of course, I couldn't overtake him at the back end of a squalid alley. What was I thinking when I followed him there?

Part of me wanted to flee, but I was bolted in place by morbid fascination. I'd never erase what I witnessed. As I fled past the beggar and staggered into the street, the scene replayed again and again. Wilkinson bear-hugged another man like a long-lost friend, and they struck up the relaxed conversation of two people who were comfortable with one another. They were laughing at a private joke I didn't catch when Wilkinson whipped out a leather belt and strangled the life from the man. He never had time to struggle. Right before I registered the sickening snap of his neck, I heard the General sneer, "That's what you get for betraying your country to an enemy spy. Every time I kill a schmuck like you, I become more powerful."

EIGHT: THEO

Heartbreak breeds desperation; desperation demands risk. Wilkinson's possible spying didn't surprise me. Rumors of his Spanish allegiance swirled while he was head of the United States Army. The bastard picked up where he left off in life.

Following the General was folly, but I was obsessed. I admit it. He didn't deserve the element of surprise, not when I could claim it. The quickest way to surprise Wilkinson was his truck. If I hid inside, he might lead me to wherever he was staying. Inspired, I ran to his vehicle and found enough open space to wedge myself on the floor between the last seat and the back door. With two bench seats between me and the driver, he wouldn't know I was there unless he decided to stow something in the rear. Wouldn't finding me be a surprise?

I chuckled at my joke and settled into my spot. My father's voice rattled through my head.

"Never seek vengeance, Theo. Nobody is worth your neck."

If anyone was worthy of revenge, it was Wilkinson. His treachery led to my father's exile. Aaron Burr was a patriot, not a villain. He was acquitted of treason, meaning the whole world should've accepted his noble plans. Instead, Thomas Jefferson and his cronies put a price on his head. For four years, he wandered Europe, unwelcome in his own country, while I wrote letters until my hands cramped, begging every powerful, well-connected person I knew to help me bring him home.

When no one heeded my pleas, I left my son in South Carolina and traveled to Washington, to Philadelphia, to Massachusetts, and I made my case in person. If Aaron Burr came back to America, my son and I would keep him occupied. He wouldn't be any trouble. But one by one, doors closed in my face. Some people relished telling strong women no.

Defeated, I returned home and found some solace with my boy. We savored two weeks before he started ailing. In the end, I lost everything because of the General's lies.

The winners write history. But I know what really happened.

I had every reason to settle the score, but I replayed my Conductor's instructions. Revenge wasn't a noble cause. It didn't lead anyone to an honorable life. I examined my heart and concluded I couldn't kill anyone for the sake of killing. No, I was protecting my own Nowhere life.

I was still a woman navigating a world controlled by men. Nothing about being female was different in 1950, as far as I could tell.

Footsteps pattered through a crevasse of buildings and snow. I curled into a fetal position and held my breath against the stench of engine oil and stale tobacco. The vehicle rocked sideways and took the General's weight. He fired the engine and dropped his belt onto the floor behind him. I watched it uncoil inches from my grasp. A fast-paced orchestra blasted my eardrums, wind instruments set to an unfamiliar beat. I tried to work my fingers to my ears in the tight space, but I needed my hands to keep from rolling as we screeched along the street. When the General trumpeted a fart into his seat, I didn't draw breath until sparklers fired through my sight lines.

Pain needled a warning along my bottom leg, its circulation fading. I shifted a few inches and willed Wilkinson to halt, to reach his destination. I would crawl under the seats and use my unexpected appearance to grab his murderous belt. Before he fully registered my presence, I would strangle him and witness what happened when a Nowhere man died. Maybe I'd linger long enough to watch him be sucked into eternal damnation.

Murder was nothing to Wilkinson, but life mattered to me. In weighing the balance between my chance and his, I valued my life more. If I tried to kill him while he was driving, I would probably die, too. I wasn't sure how cars worked, but I understood physics. A body wouldn't survive a crash above a certain speed.

Traffic buzzed through my metal cocoon, and the front door squawked on its hinge. How long had we been traveling? Did I fall asleep?

Outside, it was dark. Gelid air whipped at my coat when the General slammed the door. His staccato footfalls receded along a hard surface. I eased my aching body from its hiding place in time to glimpse his back vanishing into murk. A dashboard clock glowed the time: 6:35 p.m.

I wasn't in New York City anymore.

Curiosity overcame fear. I scooted under the rear seat and into the leg space between the front and middle seats. When I was sure he was gone, I sat on my knees and pressed my face against the glass. Streetlights illuminated snow piles on either side of a sweeping roadway, its edges ringed by one-and-two-story buildings. Overhead, a dusty arm of the Milky Way bisected a slice of sky. We were far beyond the limits of the city.

The back end of Nowhere was the perfect place for Wilkinson to die.

With shaking hands, I groped under the seats for the belt. Killing a subhuman villain wouldn't change me. I had to take charge of the situation to find my assignment and earn the chance to see my son again. No mother would squander such an opportunity.

When I touched the cold clasp, I dragged it toward me and wrapped its ends around my trembling hands, leaving enough space to wring Wilkinson's neck. Before I scrambled back to my hiding place, a side door ripped open. The General stood there, leering.

He dragged me into the street by my hair. My scalp burned when he flung me onto ice-strewn pavement. "I can't wait to be finished with you," he sneered and stood over me.

"I knew you'd never let me exist in the same world as you." When he reached for me, I used my boot heels to kick away from him. Gravity rescued me with an epic roll downhill. Ice shards ground into my shoulders and knees as the world spun and spun and spun. I crashed into a snowbank and stumbled to my feet, drunk from my unplanned tear down an incline. Hands on knees, I gulped air and willed the world to stop moving.

I stood upright to find the General a foot from me. His breath stung my eyes, and his grip on my elbow sent me to my knees. Pain radiated up my arm and shrieked through my jaw. His taunt hurt more. "You think I didn't see you, cowering in the back of my truck?"

"I wasn't cowering."

The stars blurred together when he drilled his fingers into the nerve at my elbow, but I wouldn't cry.

"I knew you were there."

Another twist of agony.

"The whole—"

And another. Oh, God! The pain!

"Time." He released my elbow and tossed me to the ground. "It's the reason I drove straight to this backwater. My old stomping grounds. There's a place around the corner. I'm going to walk you there right now, all right? Nod once if you understand me."

I bundled tears in the back of my throat and hacked them into his face. A better use of grief, spewing it on the person who inflicted it. But he didn't flinch. He wiped his face with his coat sleeve and never stopped leering, his Nowhere eyes locked on mine. It was the same expression he used on the witness stand, when he wove lies about my father.

When he wove lies about me.

The General dragged me through a snowbank and reached the sidewalk. He kept a vice grip on my arm and nudged my ribs through his coat. "Feel that? It's a gun. You show any sign of struggle, and I'll shoot you. Got it?"

What choice did I have? If I didn't fight, I might be able to exploit a misstep. Anyone would've believed us a couple out for a romantic stroll. We trudged past darkened hair salons and pawn shops, under the chasing bulbs of a theater's sign. I scanned the street and wondered where all the people were.

I waded after Wilkinson with misgivings, and my hesitation gave him the upper hand. I knew he wouldn't flinch over finishing me.

But I still had a chance to eliminate him. Wherever we were headed, he considered it an acceptable place to murder me. Which meant I could outwit him, maybe get to him first.

His voice slithered through the gloom. "I know what you're thinking, dear Theo."

"You don't know anything about me."

"Oh, but I do. You blame me for your son's death. We need to discuss him"

"Don't you even utter his name. You lied about my father and testified against him in that farce of a trial. You ruined his life, and because of it, my son died. Dammit, I died, too."

"I never lied, Theodosia. I'm sorry you won't let me prove it."

We tripped around a corner. A solitary streetlight illuminated a patch of snow further up the block, a bow-tied gift of a chance.

I wrenched free and grabbed his arm. Wilkinson's blood filled my mouth when I bit his wrist. In his surprise, he fired a wide shot, giving me a moment to kick his gun into a snowbank and reel away from him. I was free to right the scale, to rid the world of the General's menace. I spat chunks of flesh into day-old snow and charged toward him, aiming for the one area that always felled every man. I didn't mean to be predictable, but lacking a weapon, I figured I'd use his groin against him.

I barreled toward his privates, certain of my mastery, but the bastard sidestepped me. I rammed face-first into another snowbank, shocked anew by the unlimited bounds of cold. Stars whirled overhead as he dragged me to my feet and cocked cold steel next to my temple. I locked onto Wilkinson's eyes and prepared to wake up on another Nowhere train.

Before he pulled the trigger, a new voice shouted. "Hey! You in trouble, ma'am?"

NINE: RICHARD

I didn't let Theo's rejection put a damper on my day, because let me tell you, plenty of girls wanted cadets. Hell, I figured I'd visit a couple in Newburgh later. You know, let them repair my dented ego. I blasted through drills and Russian classes and inspection, like I wasn't living in the shadow of some spook's ultimatum, because I wasn't. I'd find a way to get rid of George and stay at West Point. It was the way to a decent, upstanding life.

But that was the problem with George, see? Always gumming up my intentions. As I rushed between morning classes, he stepped into an outdoor archway and blocked my access to Grant Hall.

"Why'd you burn my picture and throw it in the river, Dickie?"

That was George. Bastard didn't believe in pleasantries. I kept my expression neutral and tried to step around him, but he stuck a beefy leg in the way and got up in my face, nose-to-nose with me.

"I've a good mind to force your decision right now. Destroying classified documents. It's an actionable offense."

"What action, George? I mean, yeah. I destroyed your bloody

photograph, because you didn't really want evidence like that out there."

"You need to calm the fuck down."

He pushed me into a corner and blocked my escape. While I willed my breathing to return to normal, he chopped one end of a cigar. "Nobody could trace that picture to me. But it doesn't matter. I've got more copies, and I can spread them around."

"Why would you implicate yourself in a killing?"

Smoke streamed between his lips when he leaned into me and whispered, "I won't be implicating anyone but you, Dickie-boy."

Understanding thwacked me like a couple of high-caliber bullets. "You'll tie me to her death with bullshit evidence, right? Some concocted web of circumstantial hogwash won't prove anything, but somehow, in our world, it'll prove everything."

"I didn't pick you from a pack of bland recruits for nothing. Thanks for affirming my choice."

"Damn you to hell, George."

He clicked the top of an engraved brass lighter and blew smoke in my face. "No, that's where you'll deserve to be. You're letting the American people down. Don't you see that? You ought to want to protect your country from the Soviet threat."

"Never."

"Think about it, Dickie. The Commies may detonate an a-bomb on our shores, maybe even blow up your selfish-ass life. How will it feel to see the carnage and know you could've saved countless lives, yet you chose to stay here?"

"You're bluffing."

"Am I? I can give you a couple of things to prove I'm not."

"How will I know those things are real?"

He spread his arms wide. "When have I ever lied to you?"

What a joke. I ducked under his right arm and stepped away from him. "I already told you, George. Find somebody else. You know better agents, people who'd actually cream themselves to be given Moscow."

"But everybody's set on you, Dickie. And here's a little something to help make up your mind."

He closed the gap and slipped a wadded paper ball into my coat pocket. I worked off a fur-lined glove and fished for it. When I finally brought it out and smoothed its haphazard folds, my stomach threatened to turn itself inside out. I stared into Alice's dead eyes. Her decapitated head floated in a pool of blood.

Here's the thing I never told anyone about Alice.

She came to see me, after she delivered me to George at the wrecked cathedral. She didn't want me to think she betrayed me by letting George yank me around. George gave her a different story about our meeting, some garbage about congratulating me on getting into West Point, but I knew better. The bastard wanted to let me know he could call me back to spying at any time.

I observed her from my chair across the room. Maybe she was lying, and maybe she wasn't, but I didn't care once she unbuttoned her winter coat and slipped it from her shoulders.

She was naked under that thing.

Before it hit the floor, she was on me. We only did it the one time, but once was enough. I'd spend the rest of my life dreaming of the day Alice knocked on my door and said, "I'm done with spying. Want to celebrate?" Because that was our fantasy. Once I graduated, she'd find a way to leave the agency and join me in America.

I was realistic enough to know we'd probably never be together. Maybe that's why I allowed myself to care for her more than I should've.

I lunged for George, ready to pummel the bastard to a pulp in front of my fellow corpsmen and everything, but he wrenched my wrist between his fingers and reminded me where we were.

"You've got a few more days to make the right choice, Dick Cox. Think long and hard about the lives you're saving. Take this posting, or end up deader than your friend."

Before I told him to fuck himself, he let go of my arm and walked away, his tobacco stink the only reminder he'd been there.

As I passed the entrance to Grant Hall, he shouted, "See you in a few days."

My cadet commitments be damned. I couldn't stay locked up at West Point with everything at stake. So many people never lived life because they were too scared to go for the life of their dreams. Not me, especially not when I could dust off the best of my training and head off campus in a flash.

I made it through afternoon mess and went back to the barracks. It took me a few minutes, but I forged a convincing evening pass, left a copy in my S.O.'s inbox, and hauled ass for the three o'clock shuttle. One pit stop would tell me where to start digging for intel to deflect George and reclaim my life. Plus, a jaunt through the valley to my favorite Newburgh watering hole was just what I needed, you know? One drink and space to think, with plenty of time to make it back before curfew.

Even my S.O. wouldn't argue with my logic. He let loose sometimes, too.

Once I made the bus, I settled into my seat and studied the play of sunset on my surroundings. Fiery ice dammed the river as we chugged along its western shore. Its surface looked like some kind of arctic snakeskin along the channel. The river never really froze all the way across. Man was it something. I could almost hear its secrets bounce along the gorge's granite walls. If I asked nice, it might even tell me where George was holed up. He had to be close by.

I averted my eyes from the water as we rounded the cliff at Storm King Mountain, because what bastards designed a road with no shoulder, nothing but a sheer drop to the river? Place always brought on vertigo, my head a damn yo-yo on a string, a shame since the mountain yielded one of the valley's orgasmic views. I used my camera and snapped a picture to distract me.

Upriver and down, I took in otherworldly peaks and sunlit river ice, and I almost believed that Lenape story, the one about the woman of the river. For thousands of years, natives made pilgrimages to the river's shore, searching the water's surface for a glimpse of dead loved ones. They believed the Hudson was a portal to the underworld, a watery place where their dead and our reality knocked against another. And sometimes, if they came when those realities merged, the Lenape woman brought spirits dripping to the surface. She levitated with them above the water and encouraged them to wave. In those greetings, she allowed the grieving to see their dead one last time.

In George's world, I got one final wave to the future I wanted before I disappeared. Wouldn't be any Lenape woman of the river to reveal my spirit to anyone.

If I defied George, he might let me stay at West Point for a while, might even let me graduate. But I'd live the rest of my life waiting for a bullet or an anonymous mugging or an unexplained gas fire where no gas line existed. Explosions were big time in George's world, because they killed the target and annihilated evidence in one blow.

Who was I kidding? Either way, George was taking my life.

But my nagging inner cynic needed the answer to one question, one tiny detail George might've forgotten to secure. Was his behavior authorized from on high? And if so, was he given a range of candidates to choose for this purpose? Or had George ignored the choices, zeroing in on me? Was George forcing me into duty as a kind of punishment for leaving Europe? Because it'd be just like George to stalk me to West Point and hammer me into a life I detested, when all the time his superiors gave him several possible recruits.

One person might know which scenario was true. My former radio guy. When Alice and I went underground, he beamed instructions into a hidden earpiece, giving us intel about building layouts, enemy informants, and unguarded exits. Stuff like that. Before I left West Germany, he gave me a portable telegraph device and told me to reach out if I ever landed in a patch of trouble. I couldn't make the initial contact over a secure wire, you know? Once he got my signal over a public line, he'd know to set up his device and wait for my transmission.

I jumped off the bus and popped into Western Union. When I slipped the clerk a wad of cash, he let me into the back office to transmit my own message. A single ping to my contact's regular post on a telegraph machine.

If he was still assigned to his regular post. Dammit, eighteen months was a long time to be away or to sit in the same agency assignment. But I had hope. Before I left Europe, we agreed he'd get a message to me if he moved.

I sent my ping and waited. Sweat broke out on my upper lip after one unanswered minute, but when I didn't hear anything after five? I scrubbed the space of all evidence and was about to bolt through a side door when the machine rocked to life. One solitary ping in answer to mine.

We were square. I wanted to jump up and down on the desk in celebration, but spies keep their cool. I'd set up my gadget after midnight and tap out the agreed upon code to verify my identity.

If all went well, I might have enough information to devise a plan to get rid of George, or at least break his hold on me.

I hoped.

It was dark by the time I hung a right and jogged down a snow packed alley to the back entrance of Hotel Newburgh. One drink in the Green Room, my favorite basement bar, and I'd head back to campus to prepare for a long night. I put a bare hand on the frozen door pull and paused to look up. Stars glowed low enough to touch, like crushed glass on black velvet, a billion twinkling blessings on my plan. I liked to stop and look around every chance I got. Because Alice's death underscored one truth about my life. I never enjoyed the scenery when I was in the Army, you know? Never stopped to experience the world around me in my hurry to penetrate a target and get the hell out. I left that life to build the one I wanted, and damn if I wasn't going to succeed. Too many people listened to George and his fear.

I swept one last glance over the wintry landscape and prepared to go inside, but the peace was obliterated by a scuffle at the end of the alley. A woman and a big guy argued, and by the looks of her crumpled posture, he was winning.

Without thinking, I kicked up my step toward the commotion. "Hey! You in trouble, ma'am?"

That big asshole dropped her quick-like and ran. By the time I got there, she was on her feet, glowering at the far corner. Her forehead was mottled with dirt, but I still recognized her.

"Theo? You okay?"

She grabbed my arm. "Don't worry about me, Richard. Go after the General! Now!"

TEN: THEO

Richard left me on the frozen sidewalk and pounded after my nemesis, his footfalls light as he ghosted through a pool of streetlight. I wiped my mouth and examined scratched fingers, my blood already solidifying in the frigid air. Were Nowhere souls alive or dead? I breathed and I bled.

But I couldn't be fully alive. Nowhere men and women had to be walking corpses animated by purpose. It wasn't until I looked into the General's eyes that I realized how true it was for him. His eyes were dead. No light or life or mercy or humanity burned within them.

One thing carried over from life. I was thinking too much. I couldn't let Richard pursue my nemesis alone. He didn't know what the General could do. I tripped after them, my mind whirling with more questions. What Nowhere life was Wilkinson on? If it wasn't number thirteen, killing him would only send him back to his version of my train. Maybe I wasn't thinking big enough. I longed to eradicate him from history's timeline and make it as though he never lived.

I turned and broke into a downhill sprint. Moonlight glowed on the ice-sheathed river at the base of a steep incline, and a train whistle mourned further up the valley.

I had to cross the river. My existence was a cinematic reel of steam trains and subways, coal smoke and trolleys, always with a common theme: My Conductor. He would know how to get rid of Wilkinson for good.

It was my last thought before I blacked out, probably a delayed reaction to the trauma Wilkinson put me through. I came to in another snowbank, whiplashed by insistent shaking. Richard's mouth moved close to my face, but I couldn't make out what he said. I struggled against the wet hem of my coat and croaked, "General."

Richard held a handful of snow against my hairline. "Shush. Don't try to speak."

"He's vicious."

"I didn't catch the guy who assaulted you, Theo, and I feel bad. I really tried. By the time I got around the corner, he was gone. But he dropped this."

He held the General's cougar skin scarf in his other hand.

My voice burbled through melting snow. "Please, Richard. Get rid of that thing."

He ignored me and stuffed the scarf inside his coat pocket. "Might be able to use it to ID him, you know? It's a pretty memorable piece."

"It makes me sick."

"You think you could describe him? File a police report or something?"

I pushed his hand away and willed myself to stand. As I knocked thawing snow from my coat, I screamed and kicked at the snowbank and sobbed until tears froze on my cheeks.

Because I died an unresolved death at twenty-nine, I was trapped in Nowhere with a maniac. Scores of people got tidy deaths, but not Theodosia Burr Alston. My father groomed me to be exceptional in life, educated me like a man, and introduced me to well-connected people. I was queued up to be a noted woman who would have a place in history, a forward-thinker girls wanted to emulate. Death squandered those gifts. My disappearance didn't make me a winner, able to write my own story for others to study and believe. But I could still testify before any jury. I would swear to my story if anyone would believe a living, dead woman. I drowned at the hands of Spanish pirates after our ship survived a storm.

My testimony didn't matter in Nowhere, and no living person would ever figure it out. My death would remain unresolved, meaning I had to carry out my assignment.

I had to help a living soul find a better life. I wiped my eyes on my coat sleeve. My Conductor was my only hope.

When my voice croaked and I was spent, Richard took one tentative step toward me. "I'm no expert here, Theo. Hell, I don't know much about life or grief or pretty much anything. But I'm a good listener, and I'm available right now. We can pop into a bar nearby and decide what to say to the police."

"I can't go to the police."

"Why not?"

"I just can't."

I opened my purse and fumbled for a handkerchief to wipe my face, avoiding the temptation to pull out my compact and study myself. "What a sight I must be."

"Other than a vague scratch along your hairline, you're perfect."

His warm fingertips hovered next to my temple. For a few seconds, I considered what life might be like with him, a few exquisite moments before I stepped beyond range of his touch.

"I can't do this."

"What? All I want is to help you figure out what to do about that guy." He offered me his arm.

After a beat, I slipped my hand through his elbow and let him steer me toward the center of town. The words *Hotel Newburgh* clung to a building's side, etched in lit tubes of red and blue.

"There's a bar called the Green Room in the hotel basement. Quiet spot when nothing's happening at the Ritz Theater. I was headed there when I, ah, when I rescued you."

"Thanks. For the rescue, I mean."

He held open a glass-and-brass door and followed me into the lobby, his hand a light pulse in the small of my back. Golden damask wallpaper lined the walls of a carpeted entryway. Richard nudged me past the check-in desk and directed me to a discreet door at the end of the hall. A dingy stair spiraled downward into darkness. I gripped the railing to keep my footing, distracted by Richard's breath on my neck.

What would happen if I turned and fell into his embrace? Would he resist the urge to kiss me?

I stumbled two steps from the end, and Richard grabbed my arm and guided me to the bottom. I stepped away from his heat and patted my face. "I'm sorry. That whole thing left me a little out of sorts."

"Understandable. It unsettled me." He offered me his arm again, and I wedged my hand next to his ribs. Did his heart beat a little faster? Or was it mine? He glanced sideways and smiled. "A drink might settle your nerves a bit. I'll buy."

We crept along another hallway awash in soft light. Mellow music thrummed and scratched. I understood why Richard liked the place. It was the perfect atmosphere for him and his fellow cadets to shrug off the rigors of West Point.

We came through swinging doors into a rectangular room, every wall obscured by drapes of burgundy velvet and gold braid. A solid block of mahogany defined the bar.

I waited for my eyes to adjust. Vacant seats and tables were scattered around the room. Richard took my hand and led me to a circular booth in the back corner. Did his fingers brush my neck when he took my coat? Or did I wish they had?

Either way, Richard helped me into the booth and tucked our jackets over one arm. "Be right back with a couple of drinks. What's your pleasure?"

"Madeira if they have it."

He was back before I had time to get out my compact and inspect my face. In one hand, he held a cordial glass, full to the rim. It never made it to the table. I took it from him and downed it in one long draught. Sugar balanced the drink's heat.

"Guess I was right. You needed a drink."

When he took the glass, his hand touched mine. Energy surged up both arms and bounced around my brain. I shook through an exhale and locked onto his eyes. "You didn't give me time to fix my face or anything."

"You don't need to."

"Now I know you're a flatterer."

"If you want to freshen up, the ladies is through those curtains across the room. I'll have another drink for you when you get back."

"Thanks."

He nodded and clicked his heels toward the bar, and for a few fleeting moments, I wondered what it would be like to press my lips to the back of his neck, to lose myself in him.

Wet and reddening from the fantasy, I popped to my feet and headed toward the restroom. At the sink, I patted my cheeks with freezing water to douse my ludicrous longing.

But was it ludicrous?

Every time I entered the Hudson Valley, Richard was there. My Conductor told me I'd find my assignment after I left the Garrison train. Richard bumped into me two minutes later. He was at the bus stop this morning and almost kept me from my ridiculous search for the General. And when Wilkinson was ready to end my Nowhere life, Richard saved me.

Revelation struck me in the gut. I sank onto a padded stool and muffled sobs with my handkerchief. Richard was my assignment. My good deed was ripped from one of my son's fantasy books, where one person must make the other fall in love with her to break some spell. Only I was afraid I'd disappear as soon as Richard uttered the words.

My charge was to help him. I couldn't get involved with him.

I couldn't.

Hard to Die

ELEVEN: THEO

"You okay?"

Richard set another cordial glass in front of me and slid into the other side of the booth. Heat burned my throat when I downed the contents in one shot. I couldn't help it. Richard as my assignment was too much.

I rubbed a crescent of lipstick on the glass and avoided contact with his blue eyes. "Can I have one more?"

"I got you a water, too. And some peanuts. Why don't you tackle them first?"

Peanuts were sawdust in my mouth, but I washed them down with ice water and dragged my eyes to his face. I couldn't avoid looking at him all night. Instead, I attempted to smile. "I'm sorry I got you mixed up in my problems."

"No big deal. I'm glad I came along when I did. Can you describe that guy for the cops?"

"He was, he was a . . . a colleague of my father's."

"You know him?"

"Unfortunately. Things didn't end well between them. He accused my father of things he didn't do and forced a trial."

"A court martial?"

"Something like that."

"Oh yeah? What's your dad do now?"

"He was a lawyer who dabbled in politics."

"Was?"

"He's dead."

His hand shot across the table and took mine. I liked the way his callouses scratched my skin. I wanted to pull him to me and let his rough palms caress my neck and—

I jerked my hands free and trapped them under my thighs. The leather seat squished when I sat on them.

Richard withdrew his hand and gave his attention to his beer. "Theo, I'm sorry. I didn't mean to startle you."

"No, please. I'm sorry, Richard. I'm not myself tonight."

"Let me get us a final round."

He waved to another man behind the bar. I only glimpsed his slicked white hair. He stood and approached the table. I noted his three-piece suit and handlebar mustache. In my world, men like him either owned things or pretended to. Which type of man was he?

Richard stood and saluted. "Hiya, Frank."

"Dick Cox. Billy didn't tell me you were with us."

"It's not an official visit."

"I see."

Frank unbuttoned his houndstooth jacket and flashed a gold watch chain before turning his attention to me. "And you are?"

"Theodosia. Theo."

"Well, Theo, I'm Frank Banner, and I own this lowly establishment."

Richard sat and rapped his knuckles on the table. "Think we could get another beer and a madeira? And maybe some more peanuts?"

The right side of Frank's mouth wrinkled in a half-smile. "Certainly."

As he padded toward the bar, Richard stood again. "Excuse me, Theo. I'm the one who needs to freshen up now. Be back in a few."

I watched him move across the space, lithe and easy and confident. He was muscular without bulk. But I wouldn't ever know for sure, because I knew Richard was my assignment. Stripping him couldn't be part of any Nowhere mission. The place was too perverse to allow me any real fun.

"Your drinks." Frank hovered next to the table, balancing a small tray. He set the beer in Richard's place. "Boy's too young to be drinking."

"Really? How old is he?"

"Twenty-one. Only a sophomore at the Point. Drafted into almost two years of Army service ahead of admission."

"That's why he seems so mature."

Frank motioned to the empty bench. "May I?"

"It's your bar."

I scooted toward the center to give him space. He was probably a good six-five, but he folded his height into the booth beside me.

"What brings you to the Hudson Valley, Theo? Family in the area? Skiing, perhaps?"

"The valley's home. I mean, I was born in Albany. Grew up in New York City. We vacationed here a lot when I was a girl."

"Really? Who would holiday in Newburgh?"

"I meant the area. A friend of my dad's had a cabin on the backside of Storm King Mountain."

"I didn't know there were cabins up there these days. Last one burned to the ground forty, fifty years ago."

"And sometimes, I stayed at an inn in Poughkeepsie."

"Several fine ones over there."

"But I can't remember the name."

"Ah."

He tapped manicured fingers on the back of the seat and studied me, almost like he knew my secret. I wasn't part of his world.

"Thanks for taking care of her, Frank."

Richard sat closer and threw his arm around my shoulders. I leaned into him, too relieved to be aroused by his touch. Something about Frank unsettled me.

I never got to explore that thread, because Richard downed most of his beer and placed the bottle on the table. He winked at Frank. "Think you could give us a ride back to West Point?"

Before I could protest, Frank whipped out his watch and clicked the cover. A family crest glowed in the engraving, but I couldn't make out the letters. "It's dead tonight. Nobody'll miss me. Finish up and meet me out back in ten." He sprang to his feet. "Oh, and everything's on me."

"Thanks, man."

Richard left his arm around my shoulders.

"Why'd you think I'm going back to campus?"

"You're not holing up at the Thayer?"

"I don't know what I'm doing. I checked out this morning, because I meant to be in the city tonight, maybe start for home tomorrow."

I stopped and bit my lip. I didn't have a home. I wandered from life to life to life. No common thread tied everything together.

Except my Conductor. His final words sizzled through my subconscious. "Finish your assignment and find out what comes after Nowhere."

Why did Richard need a better life? What was his struggle? Getting closer to him was the only way to find out, but as I took in his profile, I knew where it would lead.

I twisted my handkerchief in my lap. If I spent another night at the Thayer, I could pop across the river and search every train until I found my Conductor. Maybe if he answered with enough questions, I'd work things out for myself.

My day settled, I turned toward Richard to tell him I was ready when his lips brushed mine. Delicate, like he knew more pressure would startle me. When I didn't flinch, he let his lips linger on mine, a sweet pressure that built until our mouths dropped open. I pulled him to me and drove my tongue into his willing mouth. His buzzed hair set my fingertips alight, and I writhed to get closer to him, my brain a wanton hum of desire. His callouses tickled my neck, but when I willed his hands to wander further, I realized what I was doing.

"I can't, Richard."

I fled the booth and left him there, breathless and hot, and I longed to die all over again. In the bathroom, I splashed more water on my face and straightened my curls. I wasn't a prude. My father described his carnal conquests in detailed letters, information I used to master a string of lovers. I knew the difference between sex and love, and I relished many good romps before my father married me to a southern planter's money.

But in the lonesome bathroom of a basement bar, I didn't want to think about my past. I didn't even care about the General. Richard made me crave the white light of passion, the seething heat of two bodies merging from sheer need.

Hard to Die

TWELVE: RICHARD

Another rule of espionage: It's better to get lost in the part you play.

When she returned from the ladies room, I took Theo to Frank's Jeep, gentleman-like. No hands on her anyplace. I settled her in the front seat beside Frank, and I took the space in back. I mean, I had my own secrets to keep. The whole George thing and Frank's selling me a weapon.

Oh wait, I skipped that part. See, Frank didn't want it to be known around the valley, but he was an arms dealer. Smuggled weapons all over the world using the mafia and whatnot. I didn't want to know details.

I hit him up when I got to West Point. Another intelligence type told me what he was up to. Hell, we even bought shit from time to time, and his bar was the perfect cover. Anytime I wanted to get off campus and practice target shooting with serious firepower, he loaned me a better gun than I could get my hands on at West Point. When he showed me his watch fob, I knew I'd find a piece in the men's room. Never the same thing twice.

And Theo thought I had to take a piss.

This time I wasn't looking to hit targets. I requested firepower from

Frank, because I needed a means to snuff George. A backup plan, in case I couldn't roust up a legitimate reason to make him go away.

Between the clerk at Western Union and Frank, damn George cost me two wads of bills in one night. I left Frank a coded note and some cash at the Western Union, his designated spot. A little while later, I picked up my handgun in the Green Room's john. Frank left it taped above the water line underneath the top of the toilet tank. This was one sweet pistol, small enough to fit in a holster attached to my calf. When I strapped it on and lowered my pant leg, nobody could tell it was there.

Which made me kind of happy Theo broke up our make-out session. If she got handsy or clothes started flying, I didn't know how I'd explain the gun.

But it was early. I didn't have to report to the barracks for another two hours. I was pondering where to hide my gun in Theo's hotel room because I was determined to see the inside of it that night. We had plenty of time to finish what started at Frank's bar.

Frank's brake squeaked, and he glanced in the rearview mirror. "Wait there. I'll walk the lady inside and drive you to your barracks."

Theo pulled the door handle and hurried from the Jeep. She didn't even look back when she said, "Goodnight, Richard."

"Wait. Whoa whoa whoa."

I stormed from the Jeep and managed to grab her coat sleeve, but Frank's voice pulled me in his direction.

"A word, Dick."

Fuck. What did he want? More money? I turned to Theo and tried to keep my voice innocent and unthreatening. "Please. I don't have time for anything more than a final drink, because I've gotta be back at the barracks soon."

"Richard, I can't."

"If you're determined to leave tomorrow, it's my last chance to spend time with you."

She bit her pillowy lip and I knew I almost had her.

"One drink. You on one side of the table. Me on the other. Thirty minutes. No more."

"Deal. Lemme have a quick chat with Frank, and I'll meet you inside."

"I'll arrange a room for myself and wait inside the entrance to the hotel."

She walked toward the Thayer. I dragged my eyes away from her ass and stuck my head inside the Jeep, my horny frustration leveled at Frank. "What? Can't you see I'm about to get lucky here?"

Frank stared straight ahead and kept his wrinkled hands on the wheel. "Don't get involved with her, Dick. I've got a bad feeling about her."

"Huh? She's gorgeous, and she's leaving tomorrow, so what's the big deal?"

"I don't know, Dick. You leave me a message insisting you need your own weapon, which is absolutely fine. It's what I do."

"Then what's the problem?"

"Some guy came into the bar about fifteen minutes before you. Said he needed a handgun, no preamble. Well, since I didn't know the man, I feigned ignorance, but he was wearing the same scarf I glimpsed inside your coat pocket."

"Frank, that's great! You can describe the guy who tried to rough Theo up."

"But I don't want to, Dick. The guy was dirty. Claimed to be military, but he was no branch I've ever seen."

"Write down every detail you remember about him, okay? I'll pop off campus sometime tomorrow, and we'll go over it together. May not make a difference, since Theo's determined to leave and all."

"Just be careful around her. It's awfully suspicious, her arriving in town around the same time as your, ah, your friend." Frank put the Jeep in gear. "See you tomorrow."

I slammed the passenger door and jogged toward Theo. I found her where she promised she'd be. Her skin glowed. I gave her my arm and walked through the lobby, but my mind churned with Frank's warning. I mean, the guy was right. Spies couldn't trust anybody, but lack of trust didn't stop us from a fling. Keep your enemies closer, right?

And as I pulled out a wooden stool at the bar and watched her coat slide from her shoulders, I knew how to make her trust me, and I'd get as close as I wanted. I ordered as if we hadn't left Frank's, another beer and madeira, and settled in beside her, close as I dared. I could feel heat radiating from her arm to mine, even though we weren't touching, yet.

I sipped my beer. "You and me, we've got something in common. This General guy's your problem, and I get it, because I've got a ball-and-chain of my own."

"Someone's harassing you? Why?"

"I met this guy in Germany. He was a ranger. I was constabulary . . . civvies called us military police. We were thrown together once in a while. Patrolling the zone between us and the Soviets."

"Soviets?"

"Yeah, you know. Russian bastards. Anyway, he's riding me about some made-up infraction. Threatening to take it to my superior officers here."

"What'll happen if he does?"

"I don't know. Demerits, probably. Or a military review. But I've got a few days to figure out what to do. Don't worry about me."

"But I do."

Electricity popped between us when I covered her milky hand with mine. "Theo, I didn't come in here to burden you with my problems. I only told you that story so you'd know I understand. Now I've got a good hour. Why don't you go up to your room and wait for me? Because you and I both know that's what we want."

She yanked her hand away, but she didn't leave. "Richard, I . . ."

Her voice trailed off as she lost herself in my gaze, a look that telegraphed everything I wanted to do to her. Damn, I was ready to hoist her up on the bar and take her right there.

She slipped from the stool, and let me tell you, Dick's cock stood sentry when she whispered in my ear. "Give me five minutes. Room 223."

Soon as she disappeared, I paid the check and bolted through the lobby to the back stair. I unstrapped my gun and buried it inside my coat. I wrapped it in the cougar skin scarf, because she wouldn't touch that thing.

I took the stairs three at a time and made it to her floor with one minute to spare.

Radio static flittered behind closed doors as I walked to the other end of the hall and found 223 next to a table spangled with a spray of gladiolas. The door was ajar. When I pushed it open and stepped inside, Theo's voice purred from someplace in the darkness.

"Close the door, Richard, and come to me."

Hard to Die

THIRTEEN: THEO

When he shut the door, I only saw his outline in the dimness. He threw his coat over a chair and moved to stand in front of me. Worries fled as his mouth devoured mine, and I responded, pushing my chest against his and letting my hands wander to his muscular bottom. I couldn't wait for him to tear into my clothing, but he took his time, turning me around and tangling his fingers in my hair. Chills scattered along my skin as he feathered hot kisses on my neck, and his expert hands worked through the buttons of my dress.

I moaned and arched my back when his callouses grazed my hard nipples, and he responded by relieving me of my dress and slip and bra. He flung them into darkness, and I turned to face him in my garters and panties, my hands tearing at shirt buttons and belt buckles, needing to feel the sizzle of his taut skin on mine. When my breasts touched the planes of his bare chest, my head fell back, and I almost shouted with desire.

I'd waited so long.

He held the small of my back as he lowered me onto the bed and covered one nipple with his mouth. His masterful fingers caressed my other breast, and I arched my back again and ground into him, separated from his hardness by two flimsy strips of fabric. He licked his way down my stomach, and I moaned when he removed my panties.

"Please, Richard. Take me now." I craved the white space of ecstasy.

His eyes didn't leave mine as he kicked aside his briefs and stood there, bulging and oh so ready. I was too lost in his erection to stop him from burying his face between my legs. He swirled his tongue until I was in free fall, bucking against his face and tearing the bedspread, blinded by orgasmic pleasure.

"God, you taste so good, Theo. So, so good."

In one move, he was inside me, drilling in and out. I braced my legs against the bed and squeezed every time he tried to pull away, my eyes on his shaft disappearing inside my womanhood.

The image sent me over the edge. Another orgasm tore through me, and I shrieked in time with Richard's frenzied thrusts. With a shout, he vibrated through his own climax and fell on top of me, his muscular chest slick with sweat. We lay there, tangled together and spent, and Richard caressed my cheek.

When my breathing returned to normal, he kissed my nose. "I kept waiting for the phone to ring, you know. Or for somebody to knock on the door and tell us we were too loud."

"I made sure the rooms around us were empty when I checked in."

"Oh really? You knew you were gonna invite me up here when you got out of the Jeep, didn't you?"

"I knew I shouldn't, but I wanted to."

He took my mouth with deep hunger, and my loins fired to life again. I wanted to forget the Conductor, the General, who I was, all of it, and claim this as my best life.

"You sure you have to leave tomorrow?"

"Yes, Richard. I've got to stop the General before he—"

"Before he what?"

"I meant before I run out of time."

"Let me help you. I mean, I'm pretty good at research. Give me some details. I might be able to find a way to nail this guy."

His nostrils flared, inches from mine, and I drank in his high cheekbones, his satisfied blue eyes. Anything to remember him. Once I divined how to help him, I would be cast into whatever came next. I touched his brow, and my throat caught when I whispered, "I need to do this on my own."

He kissed my forehead and stood, his hard-planed nakedness accented by moonlight from the window. I burned anew watching him walk across the room.

"How'd my pants get over here?" He laughed from behind the chair and dragged his uniform over athletic legs and a still-glistening chest. As he buttoned his shirt and slipped into socks and boots, I was bereft. Time waned faster when we knew it mattered.

He grabbed a pad of paper and a pen from my night table. "Here's the number for my barracks. If you change your mind, you call me, okay? Tell whoever answers the phone to come get me, or leave a message with the best time to call you. If you won't let me help, at least tell me what happens with this General guy."

"You'll hear from me. I promise."

I wrapped myself in the bedspread and followed him to the door. He shrugged into his overcoat, but not before he pulled me to him and kissed me until my covering pooled on the floor and his hands roamed my breasts.

He broke away and opened the door to a crack. "Gotta report to my barracks in ten minutes, Theo. Call me, will you? I really hope to see you again."

I listened to his footsteps fade, my thoughts a churning mess of desire and duty. Because when I figured out how to help Richard—if that was even my assignment—what would become of me? My Conductor didn't tell me what happens once I accomplished whatever mission equaled the nebulous *better life*.

My head throbbed from the uncertainty. I dove onto the rumpled bed and massaged my temples. Answers were elusive beasts, teasing beyond the reaches of my reality, but I needed something, anything to guide me to the right path.

My Conductor.

I would force him to give me answers. Finding his train was the key to everything.

Resolved, I stumbled to the bathroom and flicked on the light. I started to run the bath. Steam swirled toward the ceiling, and I sat on the edge and watched the bathtub fill. At least, I would encounter him clean.

While water crashed into porcelain, I padded to the main room and fingered Richard's compact, masculine handwriting on paper he left next to the telephone. My soul screamed to dial his number, to tell him I'd see him again and again.

Back in the bathroom, I sank my body into the sauna-like tub, but my mind wouldn't relax.

What was Richard doing? Was he thinking about me? Did he sense a gap since I'd been with a man? Or, like my Conductor said, did my forgotten Nowhere experiences include other encounters? Because if they were anything like the one with Richard, I wanted to relive them all.

Not that I didn't have plenty of life experience to replay. I was always adventurous. After all, I was my father's daughter.

If students studied my father and me in history classes, what did they learn?

Some people called Aaron Burr *the American Don Juan*, and with good reason. When he cast his remarkable eyes on a woman, she believed she was the only person in the universe.

I wasn't biased because I was his daughter. Both before and after my mother, his conquests were as legendary as his appetites were robust. The man relished sex as a necessary component of life, along with eating, sleeping, and learning. To him, sexual desires weren't base or carnal; they were a normal, natural part of being alive.

When I hit puberty, my father gave me license to experiment with sex, taking care to make sure I understood various contraception methods. From the time I was twelve or thirteen, he escorted me to parties and pointed out both the best and worst traits of the assembled women. "See that one, Theo? She doesn't know her profile is captivating and therefore doesn't use it to its best advantage. And over there? She arranges her skirts to flash a hint of ankle now and then. Not too much. Just enough for any man to imagine where it leads. And that's your power: Never forget women are stronger than men. Embrace the woman you are meant to be."

He was always right. I practiced my wiles and lost my virginity a few days before I turned fourteen. By the time I was betrothed to the man my father chose, I couldn't count my sexual partners, men old and young and round and muscular, but I knew what lit me from within. Pleasure and knowledge were the rewards of being a progressive woman in a repressive time. I navigated the world of men and convinced most of them I belonged. When I couldn't convince them, I took charge: although they seldom acknowledged it, most doubters eventually worked behind the scenes to open more doors to me.

Did people look at oil paintings from my era and think we were all stuffy and proper, with limited lives to match the borders of the frame? In my day, I studied historical figures, and I sometimes stared into their painted eyes and relegated them to a one-dimensional life.

I knew it wasn't fair. We didn't always wear our best portrait clothing, because we were lucky to bathe once a week. When I wanted to relieve myself, I almost always used an outhouse. Nothing elevated wintry candlelight like a companion in my bed. As long as I never fell in love, I was safe.

Of course, by the time I realized I was in love, it was too late. It happened. Once. I sobbed when he remained loyal to the only person my father wouldn't countenance. I told him his decision would end us and it did. The bastard never knew the wreckage he inflicted upon my heart.

I swished hot water over my stomach, my breasts, my neck. It sizzled in the places Richard touched, and I wanted to be with him again, craved him in a way I hadn't wanted a man since another one ruined me. I wasn't fool enough to love another man again.

Besides, I was supposed to help Richard and move on to whatever came after Nowhere. I couldn't allow myself to love him.

FOURTEEN: RICHARD

My George project could wait a couple of hours, because let me tell you, I air-walked across campus that night. Hell, I expected Theo to have some experience given she was a few years older than me, but not so much I'd be walking on clouds. I owed her for clearing my head, you know, handing me the extra focus.

And once I got rid of George, my first order of business would be spending more quality time with Theo. All part of the life I sought when I left George and his damn spy operation. If I resented my life near its end, I wanted it to be because *I* messed up.

That settled, I pushed through the door and charged along the back stair of my barracks. George's ultimatum ran out in a few days. It was time to contact the person who could tell me whether his game was legit. After lights out, I'd wait until my roommate fell asleep to grab my contraption from a hidden compartment in my desk, and I'd slip through our window. If I gave Joe a little sleepy time help, who'd blame me? I didn't need him waking up and seeing me access my secret spot. Plus, it took time to assemble everything.

Maybe I'd get what I needed quick enough to sneak into Theo's hotel room and convince her to go another round before sunup. Temptation made me stiff. Damn, I liked being with her, but I couldn't afford the distraction. Once I got my life sorted, I'd see her again.

Unless she called me. If I heard from her, George and his cronies couldn't stop me from getting more of what I wanted.

In my room, I found my roommate holed up at his desk, his head haloed by a desk lamp. Joe didn't notice me come in. He jumped when I sneaked into the room and thwacked my cupboard too hard, but he was always jittery. I figured a scare would put him where I needed him: Out of sorts.

He rubbed his eyes and peered at me through thick glasses, study-drunk. "Dammit, Cox. You made me bite the inside of my cheek."

"Sorry about that."

"What're you sneaking around for?"

"I wasn't. You were just wrapped up in your work. What are you studying?"

"Biology. Got an exam tomorrow morning."

I went to our grimed-up sink and ran some water in an amber glass. Before I handed it to him, I used my finger to stir in a sleeve of sleeping powders. Hey, I wasn't a bad guy. I gave him something to put him out without leaving him hungover the next day. I didn't want his grade to suffer because of my dilemma.

"Here. Swallow some cold water. It'll help you concentrate."

While he chugged my offering, I changed into a set of sweatpants and a West Point sweatshirt. I'd barely warmed my mattress when he wiped his pimply face and looked at me.

"S.O. wants to see you. Soon as you got in, he said."

I threw my legs over the side of the bed. "What does he want?"

"Something about that mess pass from the other day. Claims you never signed in for dinner over at Hotel Thayer."

"Yeah. I didn't. Not a big deal."

I opened our door and hurried to the other end of the hall. My S.O.'s domain. I rapped on his door, but it was already open halfway.

He looked up from his desk, his skivvies spotlit by a swinging metal lamp screwed into one corner. "Cox. Come on in."

"I need to close the door, sir?"

"Nah. I'm sure this won't take long. You know I've got to follow the formalities, right?"

"May I sit, sir?"

He waved toward a folding chair, and I sat. Stories spun out better when the target was on my level. Eye-to-eye, you know?

When I was settled, he fanned through his clipboard and pulled out a paper. "Here. This is the other night's log from the Thayer."

"Sir?"

"Didn't I issue you a mess pass to eat in the dining room with a visitor?"

"Yes sir, but when we met up Grant Hall, he decided he wasn't hungry for more than conversation. You know, a catch-up."

"What do you mean?"

I cleared my throat and started yapping, earnest-like. No heavy-handed bullshit. Without shifting an eye or squirming, I told my S.O. my visitor was one of my superior officers from Germany, a ranger. Morbid fella. I didn't like him and couldn't understand why he looked me up, but I went out with him for old time's sake, because people could change, right?

He nodded, his red pen already willing to sign off on my tale. Because guess what? Most people never wanted the whole story. Oh, they asked superficial questions, but they weren't interested in details.

"So where were you if you didn't go to the Thayer? Because you didn't stay at Grant Hall for your little confab."

Damn. S.O. wasn't usually a details man.

"I sat in his car, sir. Visitor parking lot next to Grant Hall."

"Anybody see you?"

"No sir, but you can check the gatehouse log book. I never left campus."

"All right. So tell me. How'd your little reunion go?"

"George hasn't changed, sir. Not one bit. Drinks more, and wouldn't stop until I joined him. Toasting our reunion, he said."

His eyes flicked to his paperwork, another sign of waning interest, but I piled on a little more for good measure. "You know stiffs like that, sir? Rolled out more tales about his exploits after I left Germany. I drank more booze to dull the agony of listening to him drone on and on and on." I shuddered. "Hope he's gone for good, because I sure don't want to see him again."

I knew he bought my story when he started to lose interest, but his signature on my official excuse was gold. No more questions about George—case closed. I thanked him for understanding and strutted toward my room, confident I'd have the same success with George if I applied my training and stayed alert.

No surprise, I stalked into my room to find Joe already snoring on his bunk. What I fed him wouldn't cause a headache. I snapped off his lamp and crawled in bed, my knees to my chest, boiling in my winter gear and waiting for lights out.

Soon as they flickered off in the hallway, I fished along the back of my desk and stuck my fingers in the groove to spring my hiding place. A secret compartment, one foot by one foot by one foot. What I kept in my room was nothing compared to my cache of goodies hidden elsewhere on campus. Don't ask me how I got any of my spy stuff there, because it's classified.

I dragged out my wireless telegraph contraption and wadded the General's cougar skin scarf together with my gun and some bullets. A shove and click, and they were safe until I was ready to make a move on George.

I tied the box in my own wool scarf and hung it around my neck to keep my hands free. Once I was sure the noise wouldn't disturb Joe, I crawled through the window and climbed down three levels in twenty seconds flat. I stuck behind the snow-covered shrubbery until I reached the corner of my barracks. From there, I waited for the sentry to march past, but when I saw him, I didn't need to worry. The guy didn't even look my way.

After his footfalls faded, I darted across a parking lot, keeping low and using cars to shield me. My thighs burned by the time I crouched behind the fin of a red Chevy sedan at the other end of the lot. Daily drilling kept me in shape, but spy moves abused muscles in different ways. It took a body a while to get used to all the crouching and waiting.

I adjusted my load and marked my destination. Fort ruins zig-zagged on a rise ahead, one of the highest points on campus. West Point was a Revolutionary War fort before it was a military academy. Those old guys needed a sweeping view of the river to monitor enemy threats and keep the British out.

Trees formed my cover. I broke for the stone walls, rebuilt from the original plans. One spot along the top of the wall would serve my purpose. I cased the place when I first arrived at West Point and made sure it had a power source. With all the tourists tromping through it, the administration electrified the ruins years before. Lucky me.

My box needed one outlet to fuel the wire. I pulled my lock picker from the side of my box and made short work of the closest gate. Wind whipped snow into ghostly shapes as I hurried up metal stairs to my spot. At its pinnacle, it was open to the sky on the river-facing wall.

I scraped away several inches of snow and settled in, my box fired up and ready for action. With a penlight, I sent my ping and waited for one response to give me every answer I needed. Answers about Alice, about George, about me.

When the thing started whirring, it didn't stop with one ping. I got out my pencil and scribbled a quick translation of the code spooling along the tape. But what I read sent me zooming to my barracks, through an obstacle course of cars and sentries and snow piles, tape streaming from the contraption cradled under my arm.

Dickie-boy! STOP.
George here. STOP.
Your only rat is dead. STOP.
Be ready to join me. STOP.
Or die. STOP.

FIFTEEN: THEO

Thinking about Richard was maddening. My Nowhere life unfolded, while I wasted precious time. I needed to find my Conductor and force him to answer my questions. He had to tell me what to do.

Because the shuttles stopped running after curfew, I called a taxi. My destination: Garrison, New York, the last place I saw my Conductor. Nowhere trains ran all night, so I didn't need a ticket. I shivered on the same train platform that launched me into Richard's path.

Richard.

I sighed and twisted a curl around a gloved finger. How could I get close enough to convince him to let me help him? Sex wasn't intimacy, regardless of quality.

To distract myself from useless longing, I counted snowflakes and cataloged things I'd learned since I first landed in this Nowhere life: I was in Nowhere because of my unresolved death; to break free, I had to do a specific good deed, something I had to identify and execute myself; and if I failed, I wasted another Nowhere life. I figured we got thirteen chances to complete an assignment, because one or two tries wasn't fair when an afterlife was at stake. It wasn't my fault I disappeared at sea, my death unresolved. I was being punished for something I didn't cause, unless I wasn't supposed to board the ship and meet my father.

I rubbed my throbbing temple. I was running out of time. I didn't want to experience the consequences of squandering thirteen Nowhere lives. Before I got that far, I had to know.

Trains were a way to run from the truth. Or to find it.

I spent the night riding train after train after train. When they stopped, I made a crude bed in Poughkeepsie station. At first light, I rode from Poughkeepsie to Grand Central, and I checked every Hudson Valley station in between. I searched compartments, questioned scattered passengers, and even cornered conductor after conductor.

By the time the train rumbled across the East River into the Bronx, I collapsed on a hard bench, too shattered to continue my search. Imagination wove monsters along the northern tip of Manhattan, trench-coated men who lurked beyond the window, waiting to squeeze my neck with a belt. I wasted the whole night. The sun would rise soon, and I was no closer to figuring out what to do. The General still lurked in the shadows of my twisted afterlife.

I didn't realize I was crying until fingers worked a handkerchief into my hand. When I glanced sideways, my Conductor was there, straight-backed and attentive on the bench beside me. "Forgive me for being overly familiar, but you looked like you could use a friend."

"I've been looking for you all night." I murmured into crisp linen, its tea-stained surface smeared with the remnants of foundation and mascara. "I must look frightful."

"We all have days."

I pivoted toward him, drank him in. His freckled countenance emanated quiet strength. I flailed toward his energy, worn down by the swift passage of water over my own granite veneer. "Yes. Well, this Nowhere life is one long slog through the same day."

"It feels that way sometimes, doesn't it?"

"Why do you always speak in questions? I'm being stalked by my father's arch enemy, and I'm falling in love with a West Point cadet. Oh, and get this: I'm sure he's my assignment. Can I even love someone here, someone who happens to be my assignment?"

"Did I ever say you were soulless?"

"Please, please answer me."

He took off his glasses and rubbed each lens with a cloth. "Nowhere inhabitants are human beings trapped between life and the hereafter. You experience the same emotions anyone does, because you're a human soul."

"How am I supposed to convince Richard Cox to open up to me when I just want to dive into him?"

"Don't you think it's natural to feel a strong attraction, a magnetic pull, to your assignment?"

"Is it?"

"Did passion ever make your life better?"

Yes, passion improved my life for a season. He challenged my intellect and made me ecstatic with pleasure, until he abandoned me for his career. Every person I ever loved left me: My father, when he was forced into exile; my lover, by leaving me for a job; and my precious son, when death claimed him. "I can't live through another heartache, Conductor. I just can't."

"How do you know you'll be required to live through it?"

"I don't. That's what's so frustrating. I really don't know anything."

I slumped against the bench and watched the valley's snow-covered mountains undulate on the opposite side of the river. I turned to my Conductor and touched his arm. "You're supposed to have all the answers. I thought Nowhere Conductors saw everyone's destiny."

Laughter burbled through his lips. "Me? How can I see your destiny when I can't even remember my own life?"

"Your life? You were alive?"

"I don't know who I was, but yes. I lived a life nobody can outline, because I failed my thirteenth attempt to get out of this place. I never completed an assignment."

"What happened?"

"As you know, I can't remember any of it. I woke up here. Another Conductor greeted me and handed me this uniform. 'Put this on,' she ordered."

I studied the plastic name badge on his right pocket. "It's blank."

"Because I'm nameless. Listen to me, and listen well. You don't want to reach the end of your thirteenth Nowhere life. You'll fall from history's timeline as if you never existed, doomed to be a nameless Nowhere Conductor or similar menial task for all eternity. If hell exists, it's knowing I used to be someone, and now I'm no one. Forgotten forever."

I pressed the handkerchief into his cracked palm and held it there. "Can I do anything to help you?"

"Yes, you can go back out there and succeed. Complete your assignment and get out of Nowhere, because I'm punished every time you fail."

"Punished? How?"

"It doesn't matter. Like I said, my situation is the most hellish form of eternal torment. Don't end up like me."

My eyes roamed his freckled face. If I killed the General and wasted one of his thirteen Nowhere lives I would be defending myself. His death would improve my existence. Fear wouldn't govern my actions. I was never a person to avoid an adventure. Accidents might happen, or enemies may rise, but so what? I wouldn't risk missing more of what life offered by avoiding, by hiding, by giving in to fear.

I tore my eyes away from the arctic valley and concentrated on my Conductor's words. "Garrison's coming up. That's your stop."

Before I asked another question, he pushed me through an open door and onto the lonesome platform. Snow drifted around the fringes of a thousand footprints. I leaned into the wind and counted headlights on the far side of the river. Two. By two. By two. Did one pair mark the General, already primed for our showdown?

SIXTEEN: THEO

"Looks like you need a ride."

The General emerged from the shadows at the far end of the platform, his face lit by weak moonlight. I scanned the station windows to see whether anyone else was inside, awaiting a city-bound train where it was warm. I glimpsed a lone commuter, maybe two. Would they see me try to overpower the General and push him to the tracks?

"I see what you're thinking, dear Theo."

"You don't know anything about me."

"Oh, but I do. I'm your godfather, remember? The man who loved weaving stories for one of his favorites? You've always been one of my favorite people, Theodosia."

"Do you always betray your favorites?"

His step echoed on the platform. "I never betrayed you. I tried to teach you to watch people, to keep an eye out for their true motives, but you always wanted to see good. I knew how much you'd suffer when you were grown, because most people aren't good. They care about using you and advancing themselves."

"Like you did with my father and me."

"Your stupid father failed, and his failure exposed the rest of us, including you. Somebody had to take the fall for the mess we made, and since he failed to organize an army to invade Mexico, he deserved what he got. Why can't you see that? I turned him in for you, because I loved you like a daughter and wanted you to live a full life."

"You're nothing but a twisted, self-serving liar."

The day he reported my father for treason, he lost all right to call me his goddaughter. He knew how much I worshipped Aaron Burr. Was he jealous? Of course, I loved my father more than my godfather. My mind backtracked over those last few words: Loved my godfather. I loved him once, before he destroyed my life.

He stood a yard from me. "We've been approaching our reunion all wrong. We made a good team, Theo. We could work together again. Here. In Nowhere."

"I already told you, Wilkinson. I'll never work with you. What good could possibly come of partnering with a devil?"

"You could help me find my wife. Remember her?"

I gaped at him. If the General loved anyone in life, he loved his wife. Ann came from old Philadelphia money, but she followed him through every backwater Army assignment he took. I could still smell her hair powder and feel the weight of her arms around me. She was the first person to step in when my mother died. My father was destroyed by grief, locked in his study for days, when Ann Wilkinson knocked on our door at Richmond Hill. "Jimmy sent me. I'm here to help you take over this household."

When I fell into her arms, she stroked my hair and whispered, "I'll never replace your mother, Theo, but Jimmy and I love you almost as much."

The General ground his cigar under his heel. "I lost everything when Ann died, including my mind. Surely you understand, because you knew her."

"She was the best thing about you."

"She was. That's true. I live every empty day in this place searching for her soul."

Her soul? Is that what happened to people whose deaths were resolved?

Their souls lingered somewhere within reach for us Nowhere victims to find? Was my father close by, waiting for me to recognize him? Was there a way I could see my son, maybe hold him again? I'd do almost anything to reunite with the two dearest people from my life.

I took a step toward him. "How can you find her soul?"

"You don't know what happens when most people die, do you? People like my wife and your boy, their bodies release their souls to merge with another life."

"That's not possible."

"Think about it. How many times did you change your mind when you were alive? Maybe you decided a lover wasn't interesting, or you asked your father about a new course of study, or you decided to become a mother. Do you think you made those decisions alone? Now, imagine you were being acted upon by souls merging with yours. When they died, they lived on by becoming part of you. They molded you into the woman you became. Doesn't it give you hope to think of your son that way?"

A tear escaped my eye and froze halfway down my cheek, because I envisioned my son, alive and whole and breathing through another life. I longed to know what adventures he sparked in others. Some part of him might reach through the void and know me.

"I can help you find him, Theodosia. He's out there, waiting. If we join forces, we can work together to recover the souls we loved most in life."

"But how? They won't be the same people we loved."

"Your son's in there, though, just waiting to hear your voice and take over the body he inhabits. You can hold your son again, if you join me."

His hand trembled inches from mine, and I longed to take it. Nothing would make me happier than knowing my son lived on in others. I wanted to watch him doing positive things through another life. It was the closest I might ever get to seeing him again. How could I refuse Wilkinson's offer? Only a depraved mother would say *no*.

No. The man who pushed me in front of a train couldn't give me a reunion with my own flesh and blood. I'd be foolish to believe him.

"I can't trust you, Wilkinson. I need more proof."

"Proof I'm not the liar you think me to be? All right." He reached inside the front of his coat and produced a stained envelope. "Here. It's all the proof you need."

When I slid my nails under the flap, two squares of paper fell into my hands. One was covered in looping scrawl.

A note from your father to me.
Circa 1801.
General J. Wilkinson

I tore away Wilkinson's handwriting to skim the older words, written by a hand I knew. My heart hammered in my ears when I fled. I clambered onto the morning shuttle and fanned my face, leaving the General alone on the platform. It wasn't often a girl was forced to read her father's treasonous admission.

Wilkie: Let's proceed with conquest of New Orleans.
Jefferson and his cronies be damned.
Long live our New America!
A. Burr

Did my father lie to me? Was he the reason I watched my son perish? I reread the words until they blurred together. My father told me everything. He shared his ambitions, his disappointments, even details of his sexual conquests with me. If he planned something treasonous, I would've been the first person to hear the details. He penned passionate missives about his project with Wilkinson, enlightened details about how my plantation-owning husband could free his slaves and how I would vote and hold office. I rubbed my thumb against Aaron Burr's supposed words, and I couldn't believe he wrote them.

The General forged them somehow. I was sure of it.

SEVENTEEN: RICHARD

Two nights with no sleep sucked for the average West Point cadet, but they kept me awake for five days during my spy training. I hated that kind of torture the most, but it taught me to milk the sleep I got. Besides, shut-eye was for people who didn't have to get shit done under pressure.

And George just threw me into a pressure cooker. I was running out of time, and he was turning up the heat.

I grabbed a nap and got up before revelry. If I fell in line for morning inspection, I was in bed all night, right? An hour before sunup, I rappelled down the side of my barracks and hiked to the river, my incriminating translation tape wadded in my coat pocket. Once I memorized it, I didn't need it anymore.

As the sun streaked across the horizon and set fire to my frozen wonderland, I flicked a lighter and burned George's message. Ash floated from my fingertips and scattered across the icy water, while I stood on a wooden dock above it all. I exhaled fog into light snowfall and stomped to kick-start blood flow to my brain.

Spies were improvisational geniuses. We made shit up as our circumstances demanded. My situation called for some intel on George, a little dossier chronicling who he was and where he came from. Sources at the West Point library would lead me to contacts, connections, people who might spill his secrets, given the right incentive.

I knew how to apply incentive.

I stayed long enough to make sure the last of George's taunt got swallowed by the sludgy channel before turning toward the stairs. With half an hour before revelry, I could take my time. But as I reached the top of the stairs, someone approached me.

"Theo?"

I almost didn't recognize her from a few hours earlier. Her feral eyes darted past mine, and she muttered something about completing an assignment.

What assignment? Was she a student someplace? Did she have a job to get back to? I searched her face, torn between wanting to kiss her and realizing I knew nothing about her. Hell, spies were given assignments.

Was she a spy?

Her flushed cheeks were peppered with flecks of mascara. My tongue burned to lick her skin, but I kept control of myself and waited for her unseeing eyes to focus. "Richard? I'm not sure what I'm doing here." Her eyes clouded with fresh tears. "I'm not sure about anything. Not anymore."

I knew when to ravish a woman and when to listen, you know? I pressed my body to hers, let my arms encircle her in a temporary home. I expected her to sob into the front of my winter coat, but she just let me hold her, quiet-like. We stayed like that for several minutes, our bodies and snow flurries and the sweet light of sunrise.

Finally, she whispered, "Have you ever been forced to choose between several options, only you didn't know which one was right?"

I rested my cheek on her hair and held her closer, but I didn't say anything. Sometimes people told us what we wanted to know when we gave them space to talk. She shuddered through a breath and continued. "And if you made the wrong choice, your life would be ruined?"

George sprung to mind, but I couldn't tell Theo about him. Instead, I kissed the scratch along her hairline and stroked her cheek. "Yeah. I've been there."

"What happened? What'd you do?"

"I came here. To West Point. I knew it'd lead me to a better life than the one I was living."

"But you couldn't have been on a wrong path. I mean, you were overseas, protecting our country from an enemy."

I sighed. How could I explain what I did without lying, because I wanted to be honest with her. Our connection was baseless if it sprung from a lie. "Sometimes, people do wrong-headed things in the name of protecting freedom. It's easy to write off the death of a bomber, for instance, if one kills him before he blows up a bunch of people."

"I see that."

"But sometimes, choices aren't so clear. You stare into the eyes of another human being at the end of your gun, and you know he probably loves someone back home. Maybe he left a sweet note in her lingerie drawer for her to find after he's gone. He made little people who look like him, and he loves them more than anything. And you think, 'he's probably just like the me I want to be.' He didn't do anything to you, but you have to shoot him before he pulls his trigger, because only one of you can go home and claim the prize."

"You killed people? Like that?"

"I followed orders. It's what good soldiers do . . . but we don't always like what we do."

Her bruised lips found mine, and I lost myself in her taste, her tongue, her magic, like I'd never find it again. I feathered kisses along her neck and groaned, "I wish—"

"What?"

I cupped her chin with one hand, and I memorized the light behind her eyes. "I wish I'd met you some other time. You know, when we could figure out what this is."

A train whistle bounced along the icy valley, and Theo extricated herself from my embrace. She ran one finger along my cheek and sighed. "I wish I'd met you some other time, too, where I could explore a bit of life with you and see how it turned out."

I stepped toward her. "Then why can't we? You want it. I want it. Let's hold hands and leap, Theo, and damn the rest of it."

"I can't."

"Why not? Your life can't be any messier than mine is right now."

She bit her lip, her face flushed with longing. I saw it there, flickering behind her eyes. I know I didn't imagine it. But when she spoke, her voice was steely with resolve. "I have something else to take care of first. It's why I am here."

"Maybe I can help."

"I'm not sure you'd understand."

"What's so awful that you can't let me in?"

"Please, please give me a few hours, a little space to decide how to frame things for you."

"I'll give you space if that's what you want, but I can't promise not to keep trying." Before she could argue, I took her elbow and helped her along the slick walk, grateful for the shitty errand that led to finding her. She cared for me. I could see it. I wasn't just some overnight romp she'd repeat with a different guy in a week, and as I felt her heat pulsing into my hand, I knew she was more than meaningless sex to me. The possibility of her made me even more determined to beat George for control of my life, because I wanted it to include her somehow. The chance to really know her was all I needed.

Yeah, I probably sounded hokey, but I knew the signs. Alice was the last woman who tied my heart in knots. We made all kinds of promises, but we knew we'd never be together. Two spies wouldn't work, even if she found a way out. I used my love of Alice to evaluate every girl I met, because I knew what I was supposed to feel when it was right.

Theo was right. She just was.

When we got to the end of the path, I turned her to me, her mouth close enough to claim. I ran my finger over her bottom lip and muttered,

"How can I check on you? I promised to give you space, and I will, but I want to make sure you're okay."

"I'll reach out to you."

"What will you do in the meantime, besides think about me?"

She stifled a smile. "I don't know. It's like I'm trapped in that story, the one by Washington Irving. Did you ever read *Rip Van Winkle?*"

"Sometime in junior high. It was set here, right?"

"Up the valley. But Irving based it on an old Dutch fable, a story about how Henry Hudson and his team of explorers returned as dwarves."

"Really? Who told you that?"

"Does it matter? I probably read it somewhere, and I remember being fascinated. Every twenty years, they lured another soul to the highest peak in the Catskills, lulled her to sleep, and caused her to disappear."

Her breath warmed my face when she moved closer. "Promise me, Richard. If I walk away from this place and vanish, don't look for me."

"But that story's a fairy tale. You'd better believe I'll find you again."

"Or I'll find you."

When she was gone a few minutes and the warmth of her skin faded, I wondered whether she was ever there.

Hard to Die

EIGHTEEN: RICHARD

I wandered from morning mess to class, my brain a damn fog of impatience and disappointment. Theo needed space, my contact was probably knocked off, and I had a few days to come up with enough evidence to salvage the rest of my life. I needed some sorry detail George missed, and let me tell you, the bastard didn't miss much. He was the kind of agent who'd agree to a casual poke with the devil to kill his intended target. Nothing was unethical or illegal when performed in the name of the USA, because we had to keep the American people safe from a Soviet super bomb and Communists bent on destroying our freedom. No matter how many times George recited his story, I still had a hard time with it. He was too driven. What was in the whole super bomb story for him?

But in spite of my deadline, Theo was all I could think about. I longed to track her down and tell her everything about me. If we pooled our resources, maybe we could figure out how to get her through whatever problems she faced, and at the end, she'd let me be part of her life.

I passed inspection and skipped my midday meal in favor of swimming laps. Water was where I landed to work through a conundrum and come away clean. It was calming, if that makes sense.

Fuzzy sunlight streaked through cracked windows, but my backstroke didn't quiet my internal chatter. I needed information quick-like. To move against a target, an operative required as much recon as possible, but I couldn't make a quick trip to Europe. Nope. Not possible.

Could I reach out to someone else, though, someone I worked with on a mission or two? Not everybody was in George's pocket. Hell, a couple of my colleagues professed to hate him, but spies were trained to voice opinions other people wanted to hear. Strong views got people talking. Some saps yapped like a listener was rain after a long drought, and I congratulated myself for doing them a favor. At least they got shit off their chests before I killed them.

I windmilled my arms and matched names with faces and places, but no helpful party jumped to mind. I flipped onto my stomach and butterflied through the water, a different perspective for the same problem. Sometimes, working backward got me to a solution better than tackling a thing head-on.

Chlorine burned inside my nose, and I gulped more with every breath, but I stuck to my lane. Stuff never got resolved when a person took the comfortable path. A badass willing to get results didn't shun discomfort. I gave it the finger and dug deep, and I usually found my answer.

In my gut, I knew George was telling the truth. He killed Alice, and he probably had some trumped-up evidence to nail me with the crime. In my former world, nobody was innocent until proven guilty.

Nah, that was bullshit.

Guilt was decided by the bastard gunning for you, either to protect his reputation or secure a higher-up's. The organization really worked like the mafia, only, because we were fighting the Soviets, everybody thought we were the good guys. People never understood how much freedom they gave up to call themselves free.

I splashed from the pool and dripped a wet trail to my locker. Lacking an inside contact, who could I call?

George handed me lots of gruesome clues, but I still wasn't convinced. Hell, I learned to falsify pictures. We used them all the time to bully targets. I wouldn't put it past George to use my best skills against me.

With the military brass at West Point, the campus library was stocked with all sorts of information: Washington's notes from the Revolutionary War, a letter written by Hitler himself, menus from the swankiest restaurants in the city, and military records for everyone who served.

Maybe the campus library would have a complete military record on George. It'd be sanitized, sure, because he's a spy, but I still might be able to learn more about him. Weakness never lurked in obvious places. I might unearth some minor detail I could use against him.

My undershirt froze to my damp skin as soon as I stepped into January air. With two hours until evening mess, I buttoned my wool coat and jumped snowdrifts, making my own path to the library. My plan was kind of ballsy, but my situation moved beyond safe and comfortable when George gave me the snap of Alice's head. Plus, I had little doubt he killed my contact.

I'd try anything if I could face George with the power to tell him to get the hell out of my life.

I clattered up the steps of the library and pushed through the heavy wood door. Stacks were arranged like city blocks, with nooks and benches for study. I blew through them to the reference desk, a wood-paneled fortress in the middle of everything. Mr. Henry ruled it.

He didn't bother to stand, though I doubted he saw me coming. He was always doodling tall ships, and his salt-and-pepper beard was discussed and dissected by the cadets in a place where everyone sported a clean face and a white-walled buzz. Weird guy, Mr. Henry.

When I made my request, he fingered his mustache and regarded me over rounded specs. "Biographies on Army leadership, you say? Can you even decipher such greatness, Cadet Cox? Because I don't want to waste my time."

I squirmed behind the walnut counter and played my role. "I wouldn't dream of wasting your time, Mr. Henry. Just point me in a direction and

I'm good."

"I doubt you can find them by yourself."

Mr. Henry heaved himself to his feet and stuffed himself into a patched tweed jacket. The seams groaned when he tried to match button and hole. He gave up and marched into the stacks, his jacket flapping around him. "Too much chair time on my latest masterpiece produces too much me."

"You mean those ship drawings?"

"Do you honestly think I spend all my time doodling, Cadet Cox? I design my own ships-in-a-bottle, and I build them myself. You have no idea how much time it takes to produce one creation. I've won several awards."

Seriously? For a few seconds, I would've given my right eye to have Mr. Henry's life. As boring as it probably was, at least he was living on his terms.

"Can I see them sometime?"

"Don't patronize me, Cadet Cox."

"I'm not. I think it's a nifty hobby."

"Nifty? Don't be daft."

For all my cadet drilling, I had to jog to keep up with him. He wove in and out of shelves, pulled up at a heavy steel door, and pushed it open to a crack. "The basement. I hope you aren't easily frightened, Cadet Cox."

"I can hold my own."

"Well, just so you know, Hudson Valley lore lurks in every crevice of our library. Do you know how long this site has been occupied by humans?"

I opened my mouth, but he didn't wait for my guess. "Almost 12,000 years. Since the last ice age. When melting glaciers dammed the upstate route to the sea, everything burst through here and shaped the very rock upon which we stand."

He groped through his vest pockets and handed over a pointed flint. When I took it, visions surged through my brain. I saw rituals, fires, and faces I didn't recognize from my lifetime. I dropped the scary relic, but Mr. Henry caught it before it hit the floor.

"Happened to you, too, did it? I always wonder about the stories of the people who came before us. What were they really like?" He rubbed the flint between his fingers before returning it to his pocket. "History is full of ghosts."

Huh? History was a bunch of dead people. We remembered the ones who actually did shit, right? It was what I thought before I touched Mr. Henry's flint. I often studied the Hudson Valley landscape and even tried to capture its beauty on film, but other than the Lenape woman, I never thought much about who came before me. How many souls touched this place since it formed? I hoped no remnant lurked in the damn basement.

Mr. Henry flipped a switch and herded us down steel stairs into a dusty, windowless cave. Binders and stacks of loose paper covered every surface. I couldn't imagine how much dust was trapped down there.

"Recent United States Army rosters and biographies are over there." He pointed a crooked finger toward a murky corner and turned toward the stairs. "You'll find them broken down by unit and year. If you come across anything you don't understand, bring it to me. I might be able to help you. Oh, and don't fold, crease, or cut anything."

When he shut the door, I shivered. The quiet hurt my ears, like a stone rolled across a tomb's entrance. As I picked my way through thousands of names, I wondered how I'd ever find the right one. I coughed through a haze of paper mites and lugged my first set of listings to the research table near the stairwell.

After scanning names for almost three hours, I hadn't come up with a single match. Hell, it was almost like George didn't exist. I shuddered and kept scanning names, convinced I'd find a match.

I didn't find a name until the last book, but hey, it was something. I scribbled scant details on a scrap of paper and got out of there. Inside the lobby, I took out an unused mess pass and jotted instructions to myself, impressed with the ways I varied my handwriting. When I dropped it with my S.O., I'd buy myself another night to sneak into Newburgh and make a phone call. George didn't scrub one detail from his past. If I was lucky, I could use it to rid myself of him for good.

Hard to Die

NINETEEN: THEO

By the time I walked through the hotel entrance later that afternoon, I welcomed the heat billowing through the lobby doors. Maybe it could weld together the pieces of my heart, because after reading my father's scribbled admission of possible treason, I'd never be sure again. How did the General forge my father's handwriting?

I sagged into the counter and awaited the clerk. While he checked in another guest, I rubbed my pounding forehead and cataloged every paper I had once kept. Aaron Burr's letters had mingled with mine in a steamer trunk. I hid it in my berth, determined to go through everything together when I reached him in New York. I didn't have a hidden vault of correspondence as backup. Whatever I might use to refute the General's manufactured evidence perished with me.

When the clerk turned to me, I leaned across the desk and shook his hand. "I'd like to extend my stay a third night."

"And you are?"

"Theo Alston."

"Ah, yes." He rifled through a stack of cards and dangled a buff-colored envelope between two fingers. "A message arrived for you. The night clerk didn't want to wake you when it arrived."

I clung to the envelope and waited until I was locked in my room to slide one fingernail under the seal. "Please be from Richard," I whispered as I tore a single card free.

> *Meet me at the restaurant.*
> *Top of Mount Beacon.*
> *Tonight.*
> *9:00 p.m.*

Regardless of my conundrum with the General, I was supposed to help Richard navigate a crossroads and make his best life choice. I couldn't avoid him and help him at the same time. Wilkinson was my distraction, a diversion that would cause me to fail. I tossed aside the General's forgery. He didn't matter. Richard did.

I went to the desk and pressed my nose into Richard's lingering essence. How I yearned for his supportive embrace. A Nowhere life was untenable without the touch of another, and Richard cared for me as much as I wanted him. I knew he did.

Wherever I went after I completed my assignment, I refused to spend this chance slogging through darkness alone. Richard couldn't help me decide what to do about the General's offer, but he might let me get close enough to help him with his struggle. He mentioned a messy life on the path earlier, and I missed it in my muddle. My Conductor was right. I needed to stop making things too hard. I'd meet Richard at the top of Mount Beacon, and I'd embrace what we both wanted.

* * * * * *

When the shuttle dropped me at Peekskill station a few hours later, I spent an hour prowling the beach. I intended to grasp what was in front of me, but history kept getting in the way.

My son loved to stop our carriage rides from the city to Albany. The Peekskill beach was one of his favorite spots to wade. Usually, I let him frolic long enough to force us to spend a night.

Sleet obscured the granite cliffs across the river. I was warmed by the memory of my boy's echoing laughter. His cadence pinged through a century-plus-long tunnel and dribbled into my senses. Rocks and trees, mountains and water bellowed four parts of his torturous symphony.

Sobbing, I fell to my knees. "I still miss you. So much. What if Wilkinson isn't lying and I really can see you again?"

A train whistle blasted in the distance, and I sprinted to catch the train to Beacon. I nabbed a window seat in the last car and watched scenery flash through frozen marshland, icicles, and granite-rimmed tunnels. Smoke belched from riverfront factories. My father never could've imagined the valley as I witnessed it, pristine and yet corrupted by man.

The train stopped, the door slid open, and I stepped onto another windy platform in Beacon, New York. On my way through the station, I stopped at the ticket counter and talked through a hole in glass. "Can I walk to the base of Mount Beacon from here?"

A baggy-eyed woman shot one look my way and nodded. "Awfully cold night for a hike, but if you follow Main Street, you should get there in about thirty minutes or so."

"How do I get to the top?"

"There's an inclined train."

"An inclined train?"

"Yeah. You know, a funicular?"

"What's that?"

"It's this contraption you ride up the side of the mountain. Gravity pulls a set of cars up the mountain with the momentum of the cars coming down."

The physics of her explanation matched what I learned about gravity. I couldn't wait to ride it. "Can I get a ticket here?"

"Nah, get your ticket at the base of the mountain."

I left the station near the river's edge and started climbing. A main thoroughfare lined with dark shop fronts and factories paved the way to Mount Beacon. I rushed past signs touting bricks and fancy hats and electric blankets, though I couldn't imagine sleeping under a cloth heated by a current. How did it fail to burn the bed's inhabitants? I preferred several inches of hand-sewn quilts.

My boots clinked over a bridge. The frozen falls at Fishkill Creek trickled through ice, and I stopped for a few seconds to consider how it mimicked my situation. Under the layers of grief and forgotten experience, I was still me. Nowhere didn't change my love for my son. It didn't rob me of my craving for romantic love and connection. I watched the inclined train creep up the side of the mountain, and I realized I still relished learning. Maybe Nowhere was my chance to reclaim my life, one I lost when I disappeared at twenty-nine, and reconnect with my boy by teasing his soul to the forefront of whoever he currently occupied. After the way I died, I deserved both.

I stopped at the bottom of the mountain and stood in line at the ticket office, a whitewashed structure with a window marked *Tickets for Inclined Railway! See the Hudson Valley from the restaurant at the top!* As I paid my fare, Richard's face flashed through my consciousness. I couldn't wait to see him again.

A few yards ahead, five or six people blew into their hands and jumped from foot to foot on a wooden platform. While I joined the line, cars groaned up the hill and met another set coming down. One grouping balanced the weight of the other.

"Remarkable," I breathed.

As soon as the arriving cars were empty, I beat snow from my boots and shuffled into a compartment. Two benches faced each other across a narrow box. I sat on the uphill side, determined to witness the sparkling valley on the climb. Breathless, I grasped a cable. The car jolted from the shelter and inched up the mountainside. My ears popped with the whooshing past of downhill cars. I swallowed and surveyed Newburgh's twinkle lights reflecting between floes of ice.

The car teetered to a halt near Mount Beacon's crest, and I stepped onto another platform, intoxicated by new experience. I pushed to the exit, uninhibited and eager to seize Richard, flushed with momentum. I regretted pushing him away and telling him to forget me, but I didn't know how else to put some distance between us and gain some perspective on him as my assignment. Stubbornness always clogged my ability to see things clearly. It was why I boarded a ship when the weather wasn't promising all those years ago. I needed to grieve with my father more than I cared for my safety.

But the only way to help Richard was to spend time with him. I couldn't tell him everything about my life, but I hoped he'd understand how much I could help him once he got to know me.

A shoveled path led to another building, its walls formed from rough-hewn logs and its entrance spangled with *Restaurant* in green neon. I picked my way along the well-worn path and scanned my surroundings for Richard's familiar dirty-blonde head. My boot hit a hard corner, and I tumbled into a snowdrift. Damn my constant need to focus on my feet. Laughing, I crawled to stand and knocked snow from my sleeves. Impatience made most people clumsy.

I stepped over the ragged stone and found another sign. *George Washington Camped Here During the American Revolution.*

"What an ironic spot to stumble upon you, dear Theo."

I whirled toward the General's voice. It emanated through evergreens lining the path.

"How did you know I was here?"

Tobacco smoke preceded him into the light. When he materialized, he stood on the opposite side of the snow pile and sneered. "I'm supposed to meet someone up here. Didn't expect to run into you."

I glanced around for someone to witness our interchange. Diners lingered at the restaurant's windows, and a few more straggled along the path. I stepped toward the restaurant. "I need to get inside, General. I'm meeting someone, too."

"Really? Maybe we can share a table."

"I don't think so."

When I moved to step past him, he squeezed my arm and yanked me toward him. His breath was an ashtray, inches from my face. "I've got my handy gun again, Theo. Smile at anyone who passes, like we're having a friendly conversation."

I nodded, and he released his grip on my arm. "Have you considered my proposal?"

"How do I know it's valid? I mean, you've always been less than truthful."

"I think I proved what they said about your father."

"Did you?"

"That note from him to me—"

"Proves nothing. You might not be talented enough to mimic my father's handwriting, but you know people who are."

"Believe what you want. I already know where your son is."

A couple moved past us on the path, or I would've slapped him. My son would never show himself to Wilkinson. It couldn't be true, not in any lifetime. "You're bluffing."

"Am I?"

I lunged for him, but he stopped me with an unseen click. Another man wandered past, and I couldn't tell him I was one gunshot away from another failed Nowhere life. Since I expected a bullet any second, I muttered, "You're a bastard."

"And you're meeting—what do you call him—Richard? Aren't you?"

"Who I'm meeting isn't your concern."

"He doesn't care about you. Haven't you been around long enough to learn most men fuck without feeling?"

"You know nothing about me."

"I know you miss your son, and I know you blame me for his death. Let me take you to him, Theodosia. I know where he is. He wants to see you in this life."

I spat a wad of saliva into his right eye. "My son wouldn't have anything to do with you."

He wiped his eye with the back of one hand and chuckled, "I guess you'll never know."

Another visitor darted up the path. When I realized it was Richard, I thundered toward him. "Richard, he's got a gun."

TWENTY: THEO

The General blocked the path, and Richard took me in his arms and pushed me behind him. "Are you all right?" Before I answered, he turned to Wilkinson. "Pretty cheap, George, scaring innocent women to pass the time because I was late."

George? Who was George? I glanced between the General and Richard, confused by their mutual familiarity.

The General blew smoke into frigid air. "I wouldn't be sure she's so innocent."

Richard turned to me. "And he doesn't really have a gun. The bastard likes to pretend he's a heavy, but believe me, he's the biggest blowhard you'll ever meet."

My mouth worked to form words, but no sound escaped. I studied the two of them, so relaxed in each other's company, and I couldn't fathom how Richard knew Wilkinson.

"How do you know each other?" I whispered.

"Army." They both said it at the same time, clipped and businesslike.

The General flicked ash into the snow. "Maybe you ought to ask her how she knows me."

Richard stepped off the path and turned to me. "You know George?"

I'd never seen Wilkinson with a more satisfied expression. "We've worked together."

I couldn't deny it. I helped him and my father with their plans, because I hoped it would make a better world for my son.

Richard didn't interpret my silence the same way. "Who are you working for? Which agency?"

"Agency?"

"That's why you're here, Theo, right? I mean, I don't really expect you to level with me. Spies never tell the truth."

"Richard, I'm not a spy. I swear it."

"How can I believe you, when I just caught you with one of the most notorious spies in the United States Army?"

I believed Wilkinson was a spy. Everyone whispered about his Spanish duplicity when he was head of the United States Army. My father swore he could prove Wilkinson was on the Spanish Crown's payroll, but no one ever pressed it. At least, not in my lifetime. When I vanished, the General was somewhere in New York state, preparing forces to charge Montreal and expand our nation's northern boundary.

But how did Richard know the General? I disregarded Wilkinson's laughter and reached a hand toward Richard. "Please, Richard. Believe me."

"I don't know what to believe. Not anymore."

A tree branch cracked in the quiet forest. Richard diverted his eyes to locate the sound, giving me precious seconds to scamper between the trees.

"Theodosia! Wait!"

I never looked back. I followed a narrow trail downward, propelled by gravity, confusion, and fear. At a switchback, I fell face first into a snowbank and crashed into a tree, but I couldn't rest. The General might still be on the mountain, and Richard was probably looking for me. I ignored fresh agony and stumbled onward. My legs broke the snow's surface and sank to the hip, but I couldn't stop. I waded through waist-deep sludge.

Branches switched my cheeks and chewed into my hands. How, how, how could Richard know Wilkinson?

Sweat trickled into my eye, and my heart raced until my nose went numb. I leaned into the crusted bark of an elm tree and almost vomited my lungs into snow. I wished a Nowhere soul could be invincible, impervious to the limitations of a living body. I remembered reading fantastical stories about ghosts who felt no pain, and I heaved again.

I was no phantasm, no shade, but I was determined. It counted for something.

I swiped my face with my sleeve and continued my trek downhill, but where was I headed? I couldn't go to the train. Richard would expect me to ride it to the nearest shuttle stop. The General already caught me at train stations, and he could probably stalk me to my Conductor. Either way, trains exposed me.

Bare branches wove uncanny shapes overhead. I unbuttoned my coat to let steam escape and reeled toward a wooden structure near the mountain's base. Wilkinson was too unfit to pursue me down a mountain trail. He always enjoyed food, tobacco, and liquor, and his paunch revealed little change in his afterlife habits. If Richard followed me onto the path, he would've already overtaken me.

But either man could have hopped the incline to the bottom in a bid to cut me off. Wilkinson also had his truck. He could use it to block my access to the river.

The river! Why didn't I consider it before?

Because of the historic lack of bridges, ferries were part of the Hudson Valley's history. With bridges spaced up to forty miles apart, it wasn't easy for a person on one side to work in a town across the river. Ferries connected communities until bridges were built. At the hotel, they told me one ran between Beacon and Newburgh in all but the coldest weather. The channel almost never froze.

Nobody would suspect the ferry. If I could find it, I could ride across the Hudson, walk to Newburgh bus station, hop a public bus, and go somewhere to regroup.

I picked my way toward the road. How could I convince Richard I wasn't a spy? I kneaded my aching forehead and reconsidered his behavior.

He was my assignment. That was why I would try, and try, and try.

But given his entanglement with the General, he didn't have to hold sway over my heart. I tried to blot out emotion as I hurried past the mill house on Fishkill Creek. Main Street storefronts blurred in my periphery. Undetected, I stomped across railroad tracks and down the embankment. The Hudson's ragged surface glittered in the moonlight.

I tramped onto a dock flanked by river ice and was relieved to find it empty. The ferry idled alongside, the gangway cleared to offer admission. When I peered through windows coated with icy spray, I saw no other passengers.

A woman waited on deck, her shapeless body sheathed in odd rubber pants with boots attached. She watched me. "Going to Newburgh?" She shouted over the engine.

"Yes."

She met me at the top of the bridge, her hand outstretched to take my fare. I unsnapped my purse to count it into her palm. A nickel and two pennies were the price of my escape. She closed her fingers around the coins and gestured below deck. "I'm Captain McCrea. Sit anyplace."

Before I moved in the direction she indicated, she unhitched the gangway and shoved it inside the boat. When it was stowed, she squinted my way. "What happened to you?"

I appraised my disheveled appearance. My coat hung wide. My shredded gloves and bloodied hands were no match for the gnarly mass of hair slicked to my face and neck. She probably thought I was a thief fleeing a crime scene, implications I opened my mouth to deny.

But she waved me away. "Take a seat. Any seat. I don't care where, though it'll be mighty cold on the topside."

"I'll stay below deck where it's warm, thanks."

Captain McCrea cleared her throat. "Ice stands to make things interesting. Hope you've got the constitution for the ride."

TWENTY-ONE: RICHARD

Well, fuck me. I never thought I'd wind up on a snow-swept mountaintop on a frosty January night.

Theo was crazy, maybe too crazy to be a spy. I mean, hell, I tried to follow her through the dark forest. With sheer drop-offs lurking everywhere, I gave up quick-like. When I came back to the path, George was gone.

But what was she doing with George? Her reactions were too honest, too raw, to be on his level, but she could be smaller time. Was she his stooge on the ground, the person who fed him information about me?

Damn Theo. Before I swung into the library, I popped into the Thayer and left her a note. It couldn't hurt, right? Women liked to be pursued, to know they were desired, and I wasn't being anything but honest. I wanted to spend more time with her. When I got to the top of Mount Beacon, I was a cocktail of horny and hopeful, because she responded to my message and agreed to meet me.

I was an idiot. Now, she feared me, and why wouldn't she? I saw her with George, and for a few seconds, he made me assume the worst.

I stalked past loved-up couples, sucking face and groping each other under the stars. Exactly how I thought my night with Theo would rev up, you know? I plunked down change for the ride down the mountain, cursing myself over how messed up I was. I mean, damn, Theo was messing with my head.

Seeing her with George didn't change that. In a weird way, the sight of them together made me want to protect her even more. If she worked for him, I could knock him off and talk her to my side, right? I'd convince her she didn't need to delve any deeper into the spy life, maybe even tell her about Alice's fate. I hoped George might slither from the shadows of Mount Beacon, because I'd shoot his ass dead. I'd be done at West Point, but not incapable of carving out a new life someplace else. I could live somewhere beyond the government's clutches. It wasn't the life I envisioned, but I'd still live on my terms.

The night pressed on me, menacing and ruined. I cracked the window of the incline car and let the frigid wind blow, but it didn't alter my mood. Revelers rumbled uphill in the opposite car, and I wanted to blow a few holes in their carriage and let them know life wasn't one giant party where everything works out. People tried to screw up good plans every minute of the day.

People like George.

He was gone. Sure, maybe he lurked around the mountain's base, but I doubted it. George followed me to meet Theo. Beating me up the mountain in his truck was easy. And damn if I didn't show him how much I cared for Theo, how fucking much I cared. He used every weapon he had to force me to his will. Hell, he'd give me a day to stew, and he'd show up on campus to gloat. I'd deal with him later.

Theo, on the other hand, well . . . she was snowballing downhill. If she made it to the bottom unscathed, she had four options: A taxi, a train, a bus, or a boat.

Or she could walk, but with overnight temperatures plunging below zero, she wouldn't choose that option. Theo was classy. She came from money, I could tell. She might not go back to the Thayer, but if she was

George's lackey, she might lead me to his valley hideout.

Damn, I didn't want to be right about her.

I stepped onto the platform at the foot of Mount Beacon and cased the sleepy-town landscape. Should I head back to campus or try to find Theo?

"Need a ride?" George's truck idled a few feet from me. He leered from the driver's side, and I wanted to smash his face. Instead, I plodded around the truck and climbed in the passenger seat.

"Is Theo working for you?"

He ignored me and downshifted through the parking area. When the truck skidded onto the road, I gripped the dash and glared at him. The damn clock face even mocked me. "She is, isn't she?"

"Why don't you join me to find out?"

"And who would I be joining exactly?"

He glanced sideways. "What does that mean? You know the organization, Dickie."

"Yeah. You're right. But I don't know who you are."

"Oh, come on. Does anybody really know who anybody is in this business? I'm as straightforward as the next spy."

We idled at a junction. Through the trees, I glimpsed a strip of frozen river and the lights of Newburgh. George surprised me when he hung a right instead of taking a left toward the Peekskill Bridge and West Point. "Why'd you turn right?"

"Thought we'd take the scenic route. Give us some time to come to an understanding."

"But the next bridge is Poughkeepsie. That's almost an hour further upriver."

"So what? I got time."

"Well, I don't have time for a scenic tour of the Hudson Valley. Besides, the bridge may not even be open when we get there."

"I'll take my chances." He gripped the wheel and kept the truck in the lane. Pale light made ghost-like shadows on his face. I blinked to get rid of the otherworldly picture, because damn, in those few moments, the guy was more than a shyster. It was like he inhabited another plane, you know?

"Who are you, George? I mean, really? How can you expect me to rejoin your team when I can't even find a shred of your existence in the official Army rosters."

"Why are you miffed about that? Plenty of spy types aren't listed anywhere. It's common practice. Once you join me, your Army days will evaporate, along with your whole damn life." He snapped his fingers. "Like you were never born."

Was that true? Because I wanted to make my mark on this world. If I followed George or whoever he was, I might bag a few bad guys, but beyond the bounds of the agency, nobody would ever know. I'd walk away from everyone I knew. Hell, I wouldn't even be able to tell my mother I was alive someplace. She'd eventually believe I was dead, and I was afraid it would kill her. I didn't want my mother to accept her son's death without kissing his cold hand goodbye or giving him a decent burial.

I still had one option: The phone number I found in the roster. If I called the commander of George's supposed Army unit during the war, he might confirm my suspicions. I got to know the guy in West Germany. He liked me, meaning maybe he'd spill a few secrets to reveal George never served during the war, at least, not with the unit he claimed. Hell, I wasn't sure George served anywhere, but I didn't want to accuse him of lying about his military service.

Not yet. I needed something to use against him later.

We bumped along the road upriver. Whenever I saw the Hudson, I wondered if Theo was out there. Did she make it down the mountain? Would she speak to me again? I voiced my last question aloud. "Is Theo a spy? I mean, if you want me to join your team, I need to know something about its members."

"Theodosia has her talents, but I wouldn't say discretion is one of them. Too much like her damn father."

"You really knew her father?"

"Yes."

I swiveled in my seat, lit by firing connections. "Were you the guy I caught roughing her up the other night outside the Green Room? The one

I chased?"

"You've got the facts wrong. I don't know what she told you, but the bitch crawled in the back of this truck sometime when I was in the city. She thought she was hiding all the way to Newburgh, but I knew she was there. When I stopped, she sprang from behind the seat and attacked me, all wild and trying to strangle me with an old belt. Like she thought she could overpower me. I turned things around on her pretty quick, but she's a shrew, Dickie. She was still going at me when you saw us."

"Why'd you run then?"

"She was rehashing ancient history to do with her father. The girl has some delusional daddy worship going on. I mean, she's a nutter, but she's clever. If I stayed in that scene, I wouldn't win, would I? She'd accuse me of trying to rape her or some other nonsense, and I'd be clogged up in a legal drama." He looked my way. "I don't have time for legal dramas, Dickie. Do you know what's getting ready to happen?"

"What?"

"Remember I told you about a guy named Fuchs?"

"You said he was helping the Soviets build a super bomb."

"Yeah, but he was on our payroll. He worked on our super bomb first."

"So he's a traitor?"

"He's being tried for treason in a couple of weeks. The story's gonna break, and the country will lap it up. Everybody's damn afraid of the Soviets right now, and this news will add gasoline to the fire. The American people love to work themselves into a frenzy over some fear, don't they? I think it'll help push the Washington politicians over the edge. The bastards will have to vote to fund our super bomb program, but we've got to know what the Commies have. Senators are pressing us for answers, and you're the one who'll get them. You're giving us the advantage, Dickie. Saving the whole world from a nuclear holocaust. You're the only spy who can do it."

"Bullshit, George. Ask me to trick a target into believing I'm Russian so I can get close enough to blow his Commie brains out? I'm your man. But the science side of things was never my domain. I don't even know how to talk to those oddball professor types."

"We already have your first list of targets. You don't have to worm your way into anyone's graces. You're just in, kill, take intel, and out."

"And what happens after that, huh? When does it end?"

George's truck clunked across the Poughkeepsie bridge, but he took his eyes off the roadbed long enough to wink my way. "Didn't I already explain the agency to you, Dickie? It's a family you can never really leave. Get used to it. You're one of us now. You always will be."

TWENTY-TWO: THEO

"Want a splash of hot coffee before I pull out?" The Captain waved a steaming pot in my direction.

I nodded. She trooped over to me and handed me a mug. Liquid caffeine warmed my fingers and thawed my nostrils. I cupped my hands so nothing spilled on our lurch from the dock. The engine hummed through the quiet water, but my thoughts were elsewhere.

Richard knew the General. When I ran into that bastard at Mount Beacon, Richard was the person he awaited.

"Dear God," I whispered. "He thinks I'm in league with Wilkinson."

Why did he call Wilkinson *George*?

I rose to return my mug to the galley, and I realized the engines were stopped. The boat rocked in the channel, a slight left-right-left-right. My feet clanged on the metal floor, and the noise hurt my ears. I opened a door to the outer deck. "Captain McCrea?" I called. "Is everything all right?"

Blinding light robbed me of sight. Before I lost consciousness, brutal pain tore through the side of my head. Blackness engulfed me and cold turned my bones brittle. My body was entombed in ice, the inside of my skull a teeth-chattering clamor. No matter how I punched or kicked, I couldn't break free of my rimy coffin.

My great-grandfather's face floated before me. Jonathan Edwards was the fire-breathing preacher who wrote *Sinners in the Hands of an Angry God*, a fitting condemnation of his great-granddaughter. In my current situation, I wished for the flames of hell, but I couldn't imagine dangling over its abyss.

My dying brain turned to another doomed woman, Lot's wife. When she looked over her shoulder, pining for her old life in Sodom, she became a pillar of salt.

I'd never see my son again, but I couldn't join him, either. I looked over my shoulder and scoured my life for clues to alter my plight, but everything I grasped ran through my fingers like salt.

Drool fused my cheek to steel. Sleep was failure's featherbed. Would my face rip if I tried to break free?

"Won't do any good to struggle, Theodosia. You're making those knots tighter and tighter."

Where was I? I forced my eyelids to form two slits. Captain McCrea stood, arms crossed, at the far end of the outer deck. I ratcheted my head sideways and winced as my flesh cracked. I was tied to the hull. No wonder I was freezing. My layers couldn't protect me from the cold, especially when parts of my clothing were already wet. But when I opened my mouth to scream, for blankets, for heat, for salvation, for anything, my jaws were plugged with cloth, two hinges stifled by a gag. Rough edges chafed the sides of my mouth.

I drowned the first time I died. I knew how to accept the rush of water, understood the pointlessness of a fight.

Besides, hypothermia would rock me to sleep before my lungs filled. Water washed my memory clean. I could already hear the train whistle in the distance, its shriek of steel-on-steel. Another Nowhere life wasted. I failed again.

Tears froze along my cheeks. I couldn't apologize to my Conductor, because as soon as he uttered my name, I wouldn't recall this experience. When the Captain threw me into the depths, would anyone from this life remember me? My heart fluttered. Would Richard remember me?

Captain McCrea teased me back to Nowhere. The boat stopped in an iceberg field. Crenelated edges ricocheted off the metal hull. She dumped spent coffee grounds into the river and crouched next to me. "I suppose you're wondering what my story is. I guess it won't hurt to tell you, since it'll die with you."

I pushed along my left side and propped my head at a neck-wrenching angle to stoke the flames of pain. I might not remember McCrea's story when I opened my eyes in my fifth Nowhere world, but I wanted to hear it anyway.

"You were born up in Albany, right? Wait, why am I asking you questions? You can't answer me."

I craned my neck to see the lights of either shore. Something, anything to tell me whether I might survive the swim to land. If the Captain untied me before she threw me overboard, I might last a few minutes.

Her eyes followed mine. "Nobody'll hear you drop into the water. We're in the middle of the Hudson, too far from any town for anyone to see you fall. Now, let's get back to Albany. General told me that's where you were born."

She was in league with Wilkinson. Of course, she was a Nowhere soul, too. She rested her chin in her hand and propped her elbow on one knee.

"Didn't spend much time in Albany though, did you? Aw, there I go again. Asking questions you can't answer."

I forced paralyzed fingers against the knot securing my hands. If I could loosen it, I might have a chance.

"Your daddy trained you to be a snob early, didn't he? Taking you into New York City and educating you like a boy." She spat.

My father taught me being female had nothing to do with station in life. He never wanted me to settle for a lesser role.

"I don't reckon I was much remembered when you were coming up. I told you my last name was McCrea, but I didn't give you my first name, did I? It's Jane."

She snickered when I almost choked on my gag. "Yep, you recognize the name. The General told me you were smart. Took a while to build the legend of Jane McCrea. But you and me, we're in the same boat, if you'll pardon the cliché. I'm some sort of Hudson Valley martyr these days, but that wasn't the case when you were alive. I was just another forgotten woman. A victim of the frontier. Probably murdered by natives."

Her knees popped when she stood and walked over to a metal cupboard. She opened a door and produced a fur rug. The boat seesawed as she threw it over me. "You're gonna be gone in a few minutes, but watching you seize from cold is giving me the shakes."

She covered me in bear skin and tucked the edges through arms and legs that were hog tied behind me. I used the cover to work my wrists against the ropes.

The boat scraped another clod of ice, but she ignored it and resumed her crouch. "What was I saying? Oh, who I was, before I wound up in this hell. Because I think we can both agree that hell'd be better than this place. Going from life to life to life without remembering what came before. I couldn't do it anymore. Figured if I holed up in some out-of-the-way place and didn't call attention to myself, nobody'd much care whether I ever completed my assignment. Most everybody forgot my life anyway. Why should my Nowhere be any different?"

I nodded, desperate to deflect her attention. My fingers worked through another loop of rope. It loosened a bit, and I blessed my dainty wrists. Almost there.

"I don't know how many times I've cycled through this place since that pack of natives killed me. Five of them. Ambushed our homestead outside Saratoga. I was alone, see. Prime opportunity to strike. Dragged me into the yard and stripped me naked. One of 'em scalped me while another peeled ribbons of skin from my left leg."

My hand popped from its fetters. If I could locate the root of the knot, both hands would be untied.

"You getting sick yet? You vomit with that gag in your mouth and you might choke yourself." She creaked to her feet and looked over the side of the boat. "I predict you'll be a human ice cube in three minutes, tops."

My feet were dead to my knees. Cold froze its way from my extremities to my core. I drummed my head against the hull to help me concentrate, to stay awake long enough to free my hands and mount a surprise attack.

As she swayed in my vision, I wondered. How long had it been since she met a woman from near her time? Jane McCrea perished before I was born, but I remembered her story. Everyone repeated it to me when I bushwhacked through aboriginal territory to view the falls of Niagara. While I fantasized about being the first white woman to witness the thundering water, my friends cast fear everywhere. "You don't want to end up butchered like Jane McCrea."

Everyone but Dad wagged fingers and pursed lips and called me too fearless, too masculine, for my own good. I always admired Jane for defending herself and her family. She was a feminist, like me.

My other hand snapped free. I worked both hands into my lap and rubbed them together under the blanket, desperate to restore circulation before Jane pounced. We neared the end of her story. I couldn't have more than a minute, maybe two.

Her voice croaked. "Who knows? Maybe the General's right, and you'll see your boy somewhere in this hell." She grasped the edge of my fur covering and moved to straddle me.

My hands sprung to life and encircled her neck. I couldn't feel my fingers, but I locked eyes with her and squeezed her flesh. She thrashed against me. Her fingernails dragged meaty tracks into my hands, but I was beyond pain. Bloody spittle landed on my cheek.

She choked three words. "You die. Now."

With superhuman strength, Jane flipped me onto my back. One arm held me in a stranglehold while the other hand yanked my hair. Her hot breath flamed against my ear.

"You won't remember this when you wake up in your next round of Nowhere, but I want you to know you could've saved that boy. What's his name? Richard Cox?"

My ribs crunched into the boat's rim, and I winced. The world spun as Jane tightened her grip on my neck. "The General wants your Richard to be a spy again. Want to know how I got that information? I run dirty messages for him. That's right. Our General's on the Soviet payroll, selling American secrets from his perch high up the chain of command. And he's keen to force your Richard back into service, or he'll kill him."

On Mount Beacon, Richard kept asking me which organization I worked for, but he was giving me a path to accomplish my assignment. He needed my help to avoid Wilkinson and build his best life, one that didn't involve spying, assassinations, and double-dealing. Those were stalwarts of the General's world. I misread the signs.

Jane McCrea propped my head over the boat's edge. Ultimatums and missed signals swirled with an arctic chill a few yards from my face. What would happen to Richard when I woke up on another Nowhere train? I wouldn't even remember his name.

"I've wasted enough time." Jane McCrea snarled next to my ear and stopped my suppositions. I'd never know who Richard was or what we might've been.

The boat tipped when Jane released me, and I slid over the side. My bound legs sank through slush and water, and my fingers clawed solid ice. In ten or fifteen minutes, my solidifying organs would sink me.

I swished toward watery light, my last conscious thought one plea. "Please let me remember. I can't make a life with Richard, can't tell him I'm sorry, can't fall in love. But I believe I can find my son. I believe he's out there, living a piece of someone else's life. Let me find him again. Please."

TWENTY-THREE: RICHARD

Newburgh was a steep haul from the riverfront, like the ancient glacier blasted the place with a tantrum, but I couldn't spend another second with George. I made him drop me near the Green Room, figuring I'd get a shuttle back to campus. My head throbbed from the stink of George's truck and his stories. The best liars always sprinkle their yarns with truths the listener can validate.

I didn't doubt George's super bomb story. Hell, it made sense. The Soviets were working to catch up with us in the arms race. They already exploded an atomic bomb, but if what George was saying was true, they were getting some help to leapfrog ahead of us. He wasn't just blowing a bunch of fear-mongering hot air. Americans would live under threat of Soviet nuclear attack from now on.

But what about Theo? Where did she fit in? I managed to take a picture of her and George together before I revealed myself. Sure, I could go back and study their postures, but something about the whole thing didn't sit well. Theo was too rigid, too forced. Her claims of legitimacy rang true.

Damn, I was going to have to gather intel on her somehow. At least, I had a picture from my Petal camera to pass around.

My footsteps echoed in the empty streets, but I didn't stop until I pulled up at my destination. I rammed my fist into the steel door and jumped back and forth in the alley, drunk on energy and adrenaline. Frank had to be in his office at the Green Room. He could help me. I mean, the man was legendary in spy circles, and not just for his assortment of weaponry.

I learned all about his Nazi kill rate during the big war, how he posed as a German and penetrated Hitler's inner circle. Some guys even whispered about his role in Hitler's death, because nobody in the military world believed he shot himself. When I got to West Point, I looked Frank up first thing, to rub shoulders with Hitler's rumored assassin. I worked through problems with him, and I always came away knowing how to tackle them.

I raised my hand to bang on his door again, but I didn't have to waste the effort. The door swung wide, and Frank beckoned me inside. I followed him into his plush office. Music and a cadet fraternity party pulsed on the other side of his plaster walls. He assumed his usual spot, reclining on his blasted leather-and-chrome chaise. Ugliest piece of furniture I ever saw, designed by some fellow named Le Corbusier. He glanced at his pocket watch and cut his black eyes my way, but he didn't stop me when I plopped onto one of his Danish modern torture machines masquerading as a chair.

"Dick Cox. Wasn't expecting you this evening, friend."

"I've got a major problem, Frank."

"Major?" He leaned toward me. "You mean, bigger than the problem for which you needed a special weapon?"

"It's all the same thing now."

He rested his white head on the round neck pillow and stared at water rings on the ceiling. Damn Frank never got rattled. He sipped his drink and let his mind whirl through a soundtrack he didn't share. My chest was about to explode by the time he glanced my way.

"What were you doing in Beacon, Cox?"

"Beacon?"

"You went to Mount Beacon tonight. Why were you there?"

"Dammit, Frank! Help me!"

His bony fingers squeezed my neck before I comprehended movement. Buzzers ripped through my ears, a warning my brain was being robbed of oxygen, but he didn't let up the pressure, even when my face started to turn blue and my eyes bulged from my sockets. Instead, he breathed next to my ear, hot air I needed to survive.

"You've always been impatient, Cox. It's your fatal flaw, the reason I'm glad you left the agency and joined your class at West Point. Right decision, if you ask me. Now, I understand you're upset, but I'm going to release you, and you're going to sit in this chair and work through your situation as you were trained. Do you understand?"

White lights skated across my eyeballs, and I nodded. He released me, and I fell to the floor in a fit of coughs, writhing like a sissy while he poured himself another drink and stretched out on his damn recliner.

The parquet floor left a herringbone pattern in my cheek, but I didn't care. Frank had to help me, even if it meant following his rules. When I gulped enough air to talk, I rasped my story.

How I was on my way to place my phone call, you know, to find out whether George ever served our country where he claimed. But when I stopped at the Thayer on my way to the shuttle, I found a message. Theo agreed to meet me on top of Mount Beacon.

Perfect, I thought. Two birds and all that shit. I'd swing by Mount Beacon and pop into someplace on Main Street to make my call. Easy and untraceable.

"Only George blew everything."

"You told me about George's visit and his ultimatum, but what does he have to do with Mount Beacon?"

"He was there. With Theo."

Frank held his glass to his temple and stared at spider cracks in his plaster walls. "I told you not to get involved with her."

"I didn't get involved with her, all right? I mean, I nailed her, and it was stellar. She was delicious, man. I wanted to see her again."

"And that's not getting involved? Dammit, Cox. Some women are meaningless lays, but I knew Theo was trouble from the second you dragged her in here."

"How?"

"Call it listening to my gut. I bet she's working with this George character."

I couldn't fault him for it. Surface evidence led me to the same suspicions myself.

I thumbed through my interactions with Theo and cursed myself. I mean, she was at the train station the night George dragged me off in his truck and started this whole saga. Because I bowled into her, I never sized her up as a suitable partner for George, when she was probably waiting to report my every horny move to him. They probably mocked me the whole damn time.

Frank lounged across the room, sipping his beloved vermouth and extolling the value of his gut. God, sometimes I wanted to smash the man's skull. I sucked that thought into my subconscious quick-like, because I believed Frank could read my mind.

And as the cadet party heated up on the other side of the curtain, I acknowledged my truth: People gave advice, and the same tips could be right and wrong at one time. Winners figured out how to move forward with conflicting advice, and I wanted to be a winner.

My gut told me Theo wasn't hooked up with George. I wasn't just thinking with my dick. Something about her reactions rang true, but I didn't have to take her word for it.

I scooted my chair across the wood floor and sat eye-to-eye with him. "Look, Frank. I know George has tentacles everyplace, but I don't think she's hooked up with him."

"You're just a horny bastard."

"Let me finish, dammit. She kept calling him the General, and she mentioned he used to work with her father when we were in here the other night. George isn't who he says he is. I'm sure of it."

Frank held his empty glass to his chest and closed his eyes. "When you first told me about him, I did a little digging. I have skills as well, remember? I didn't find much, but I'm still convinced your George is a double agent. My gut again. I might still get the goods to prove it."

"Here's the thing. If I can prove George is dirty, I'm off the hook. I don't have to go back to spying. I turn his threats on him, and nobody cares when I blow him away. Hell, the higher-ups would probably thank me."

Frank stood and stalked to his desk, his skinny fingers a whirl on the spotless surface. No clutter for old Frank. "I've got a couple of people I can shake down, fellas on the other side."

"Soviets?"

"Doesn't matter. You're more valuable to me here, even if it means burning some capital and calling in a few favors."

"Wait? What does that mean? Valuable to you here?"

"Come on, Dick. How do you think you got into the Academy?"

"My credentials? I mean, I worked my ass off."

"And your work was noted. By me."

"You?"

I crabbed backwards along the floor. Realization was its own twisted horror. Nothing made more noise than the splat of a hero falling from his pedestal.

"Nobody ever retires from the spy business, Dick. Not even me. And I thought your skills were more suited to your home turf. I wanted you here."

"You got me into West Point, only to force me into the life I fled?"

"You're making it sound worse than it is, but yes."

"Fuck you."

Cold air slammed my face when I pushed into the alley and ran past George Washington's old Revolutionary War headquarters. I hammered down the hillside and followed the riverfront path. Ice groaned and cracked, nature's eerie soundtrack to my impromptu sprint. I pulled up at a bench and scraped ten inches of snow aside to sit, because I needed to think, you know?

Fog hung low in the valley and almost became one with the ice. I couldn't even see Beacon. The whole miserable place was a landscape painting of my life. No matter what I did, I was screwed. Go back to

Germany and serve George or stay at the Academy and be Frank's stooge.
Shitty options, both of them.

TWENTY-FOUR: RICHARD

Our worst options animate our nightmares. I stood at groggy attention and watched my S.O. work through the same first inspection drill. He always roughed a few of us up, like the brass handed him some kind of intimidation quota. I never could predict when his eye would fall on an imaginary wrinkle or a missed spot on my boot, and he'd order me to drop and give him a hundred, and I'd do push-ups until my arms were two numb stumps.

After inspection, I staggered, snow-blind, sunshine reflecting off the white landscape. I was ready to throw myself into my pile of challenges. Frank wanted me on his dirty team. George was pressing hard. Could I even find Theo, if she wanted to be found? Maybe she could tell me how to go poof into the mountainside like she did, and we could clasp hands and flee into a new life together, free of George and Frank.

What the hell was I supposed to do about them?

If I went with George, Frank would probably haunt me for years. If I stayed at West Point and appeased Frank, George would kill me and dump my dead body where nobody would find it.

I was messed up. Couldn't concentrate through breakfast mess, you know? I coded my concerns into notebook margins through every interminable class, words that morphed from Russian to algebraic equations to philosophical rhetoric. Whatever the topic, I couldn't stop writing, questioning, worrying, calculating my options.

Who decided I should be a spy?

Is it immoral for me to be a spy?

What's the point of living if I can't determine the roadmap of my own life?

My feet tap-danced around my desk, the only sign I gave of my compulsion to run to the bus stop, or the train station, or some anonymous outpost in some desolate corner of the globe. The only person I could salvage in the whole miserable mess was myself.

I scribbled in my textbook. *I refuse to live the cipher life of a spy.*

I blotted out my words, a frenzy of pen tearing into paper. My philosophy wouldn't matter when I stared up the ass end of a gun. To have the life I wanted, I had to fight dirty enough to outwit two seasoned operatives who had decades of experience, and once I was done, I'd solve the mystery of Theo. Hell, maybe the key to getting rid of George was buried in his convoluted connection to her father. Back at the Green Room, she mentioned a court martial or some kind of trial, and the details of those proceedings were recorded. West Point was a repository of the military's dirty deeds. If Mr. Henry worked his library magic, maybe I'd use their connection to waste George and find Theo.

If she was alive.

Hell, she had to be alive. I was being a melodramatic candy ass. My hand still shook as I scrawled my next question.

What is death? Deadlines held me in a chokehold, but I knew one thing: Death was accepting a life I didn't want.

My professor called time on my unanswerable questions and stopped my philosophizing. I snapped shut my scribbled ramblings and checked my pocket watch. A classmate nudged past me. "You headed to mess, Cox?"

"Right behind you."

I joined the current of uniformed bodies and streamed into bone-crushing cold. After lunch, my presence was required at afternoon fitness drills. Hell, I'd never get a break.

Make or break, soldier.

A phrase I always mumbled before I kicked in a door or muzzled a target. In the spy game, every action was make or break, but they didn't tell us how much the spy game was like life. We did stuff all the time, never knowing which actions were turning points.

I bypassed the gothic arch of the mess hall and trooped toward my barracks. I had fifteen minutes to weave a story, a quarter-hour to escape my obligations for the afternoon. My feet tapped time through an empty stairwell, seconds I'd never recover on the path to meaning. I marched onto my floor and used my elbow to knock on my S.O.'s door.

"Enter, soldier!"

I saluted my superior officer while he polished his shoes. He was surrounded with stained rags, cans, brushes, and unguents to clean, condition, and shine. His desk groaned with the burden of shoe care products, but he ignored them and snorted into the back of his throat. Snot-ridden spit blotched the toe of one boot. He picked up a rag and rubbed it into black leather. "A loogie's the secret to getting that West Point shine." He cut his eyes sideways. "At ease, Cox. You're late for mess in fourteen minutes, forty-nine seconds. What're you doing here?"

"I need a waiver from afternoon mess and drills, sir."

"For what purpose? You know I like you, but I don't give waivers, even when your momma's dead. Fourteen minutes, thirty-nine seconds, and you're late."

"One of my German friends died, sir. Knew 'em when I was in the Army over there. I'd like to send the family a telegram."

"Denied, Cadet Cox." He hacked another wad and hurled it toward his remaining boot. "You can mail them a letter."

"But this person was special."

"I said denied, Cox. And you have fourteen minutes to report to mess. Don't think I won't check the log to make sure you signed in. Dismissed!"

"Yes, sir!"

I bit off the useless claptrap I was going to utter and retreated. Off I went down four flights of stairs and past the doorway to the basement showers. Next was a sprint across campus. Activity fueled the motor of my mind. If I couldn't find a direct route, my toolkit held plenty of other ways to achieve an end. I pulled up at mess with thirty seconds to spare.

"Cadet Cox, signing in!"

I took the pen and scribbled numbers and a colon next to my name, because the undecipherable was easier to tamper with, you know? The *out* box awaited my official departure time. A lie was an honor code violation. The penalty was expulsion.

But a spy never lied. We were too resourceful to need the crutch. Besides, believable stories came from a well in the soul, the place we cling to as truth. If we convinced ourselves it was true, who could judge it a lie?

Still, lies or no lies, my S.O. would drag his loogie-hacking ass on a tour of every campus log to make sure I reported to mess and afternoon drills. I could lie or use a penmanship trick and go AWOL. If anyone caught me, I'd get a bunch of demerits, and enough demerits also led to expulsion. But until that week in January, I was a good soldier with no demerits to my name.

Not for lack of infractions, you understand. Sometimes, being a decent spy trumped being a good soldier.

I slathered mayo on a slice of white bread and piled ham on top. The soggy mess squished between my cheeks as I jotted my *out* time, a mere ten minutes after I arrived. The sentry studied me but didn't say anything. He was used to cadets who wanted to nap a few minutes during lunch. Lots of us used the time to cram for tests or to nap.

I bought myself fifty minutes.

I hightailed it across campus and slammed up salted steps to Grant Hall. People merged and parted like amoebas in science lab petri dishes. Afternoon mess was a popular time to have visitors, another reason cadets who signed out early weren't examined by their S.O.

I pivoted through a human obstacle course and stopped at the sentry's desk. "I'd like to make a phone call, sir."

"Lucky you. There's no line. Sign the manifest for phone three. You know how it's done."

I recorded my cadet ID and name, the number and person I was calling, and the purpose of the call. Nothing was private at West Point. Every activity, from phone calls to dining privileges to inspections, was logged. Time in. Time out. I smudged the person's name and number with my pinky finger and handed the clipboard to the sentry. "Phone three, you said?"

"Yeah."

I scooted around the desk and walked to the corner. Five telephones occupied a wooden ledge, each separated by a glass divider. Nothing private, remember?

I pulled up a chair to the middle phone and dialed my intended. Damn, *intended* made it sound like a date, and believe me, I never intended to date the person on the other end of the line.

If she even answered.

The ringing drilled into my eardrum. Once. Twice. Three times. "Yes?"

I leaned into the phone and threw my voice like a ventriloquist, because I didn't need any guy taking notes. My voice sounded like it was pouring from the mouth of a stupid sock puppet. "I need to see you."

"Not possible. Care to leave a message?"

No hesitation before she cut off my dick.

"Are you still pregnant?"

Static buzzed on the line and stretched into a void. I counted every second in my head. Finally, her voice broke through the infernal hum. "Yes."

I clinched my fist and counted more pops of interference on the line. I couldn't stay on the phone much longer. Another minute, maybe.

"I'll send flowers. Do you know if you need pink or blue?"

"I'm hoping for pink, but blue's a possibility."

I gripped the receiver hard enough to snap it in two. "Okay."

Her voice was lost when I banged the phone into its cradle, but the sentry's bark stopped my bolt for the exit. "Cadet Cox! You forgot to log your end time!"

Lead tore into paper as I scratched the time: 12:22, thirty-eight minutes until I was due to report for fitness drills.

Outside, I squinted to readjust my eyes. Sunlight caught on valley walls and mountaintops, rock crystals lit by ice. Snow clouds didn't weight the horizon, though Hudson Valley weather could change at any time.

Fancy thinking about time when I was running short, you know?

Rather than steer toward the gym, I hauled ass to my barracks and wound down the metal stair to the basement, past lockers and showers and rows of white towels and into the depths of the place. I stopped at my last barrier.

"No going back, Dick," I whispered.

I worked my fingers underneath a drainage grate's metal edge and waited for the blast of cold air to freeze my nails, wind from outside hurled through spongy holes in West Point rock. When the metal popped, I threw it aside and studied familiar territory. Ice stalactites dribbled down the sides of the metal tube, its landscape blocked by darkness.

With one breath, I shrugged off reservations about demerits and lowered myself into West Point's version of Mammoth Cave. AWOL was my intended destination and my only choice, you know?

TWENTY-FIVE: THEO

I snagged on a hook, something solid. It bore me up and up. And up and up and up. It fished me from the depths.

Would my skull crack? When it rammed the under-surface of solid ice, would its circumference burst like a melon?

Drowning was my death replayed, but the freezing water teased another lost memory. Before the Spanish pirate threw me into the sea, he and his cohorts scoured my berth. "The papers," they demanded. "Our leader wants them."

Why did Spanish pirates want Aaron Burr's papers? I thrashed through the water, determined to stay alive, but they weren't finished with me. One of them spat into the water and sneered, "General Wilkinson, he will be pleased."

The General? Wilkinson ordered my death?

I writhed on a platform. Fur scratched patches of my naked skin, and a voice whispered beyond the world I could see. Everything was bent and distorted, or maybe that was me. My teeth rattled, uncontrollable, and I couldn't feel my hands, my feet, my legs.

I was someone's captive.

Wilkinson! He was there.

Must move.

I croaked his name through split lips. One word grew a face.

His face.

Not Wilkinson.

How did he find me?

What was he doing here?

The world swam as I regained consciousness. I waited for its knife-like edges to chew into me. I tried to sit up, but my body was burdensome. I gasped into layers of fur and blinked, a pathetic attempt to adjust to gathering light.

A form shifted on the periphery. "I should've let you drown."

I thrashed against my animal-hide prison and tried to shriek, but only a croak escaped my lips. The man floated over the landscape, his face close to mine. Blue eyes spouted venom. I tried to bite his foul fingers when he clamped one hand over my mouth.

"Theodosia Burr," he spat. "Should've left you in the river. Best place for bad fish."

His sturdy jaw clenched, tanned skin beneath stubble. Cinders flamed in my core, but they didn't yield enough spark to light my voice. It sputtered, a rasp I didn't recognize. "I wish you had, you . . . you—"

"What am I? Courageous? A hero? Savior of your miserable afterlife?" He ran stained fingers over his face. "Call me whatever you want. I'll wait."

"Crazy. Drunk. Everyone knows you killed yourself, Meriwether Lewis. That's how you're sure to be remembered by anyone who bothers to note you. How are you even here?"

"Maybe I didn't commit suicide after all."

"Someone killed you then. Good for them."

"Hate me all you want. You've got your reasons."

"Do you think I gave you a second thought after you pledged allegiance to that bastard Thomas Jefferson?"

"Forgive me for thinking you'd have enough passion to hate me."

I rocked myself to sitting, but my world merry-go-rounded and knocked me backward. I writhed in a puddle of cold sweat, unable to raise my voice, let alone give him a tongue-lashing. My weakness didn't stop him, though.

"At least, I never married," he murmured.

"I heard how many women you slept with on the expedition. I'm surprised your penis didn't fall off from the diseases you caught."

"Spare me. You were no virgin yourself, as we both know."

Maybe I allowed myself to love Lewis because we were doomed. His godfather, Thomas Jefferson, hated my father, and if that wasn't enough of an impediment, Lewis had no family money. I lost my heart before I realized we could never be.

Like I did with Richard.

Richard.

I still wanted him, even though he probably believed me to be a double agent hooked up with the General.

"James Wilkinson. He's here, Lewis."

"You think I don't know all about Wilkinson? Come on. Give me a little credit. Hated the bastard when I was alive, remember? Oh, wait. You and your dear daddy loved up to him, as I recall."

"Don't you disparage my father."

"You made your filthy deals with Wilkinson while I was trying to hold a whole territory together. He made my position impossible when he held the Upper Louisiana governor's job ahead of me."

"No. Dad had nothing to do with that."

"Guess dear daddy had nothing to do with shooting Hamilton. Or with undermining Jefferson's presidency."

"They hated Dad."

"Can't argue there. Your dad was despicable."

"Go to hell."

"Been close to hell for ages. As have you."

He moved behind a pile of bricks and returned with more skins. I coughed when another few inches of fur released a cloud of dandruff. "You were only in the water a few minutes, but we need to warm you up. Can't light a fire right now."

I withdrew into the blankets and refused to look at him. Heroic explorer. What nonsense. He probably forgot how to light a fire. He made his men do everything for him and took credit.

"My father hated you, you pompous cretin." But as I convulsed in another fit of coughing, Lewis lifted the covering and pulled a metal cup from near my feet. It froze to my lips, but he wouldn't remove it until I drank. "Melted some river ice using your body heat. You need to drink some water."

The cold beverage burbled through my lips and tore through my core. I tried to swallow my own rejects, but Lewis's hand cradled my head. "Don't get worked up, Mrs. Alston. You've been unconscious a few hours. When I fished you from the river, your skin was already slicked with a thin film of ice. You think I'm a bastard, but I'm decent enough to save your worthless excuse for a Nowhere life."

Lewis would never stop reminding him how much I owed him. I forgot how his face changed when he smiled. Angry planes gave way to a hard-edged grittiness lesser women found handsome. Fur prickled my face, but covering up was the best way to stop looking at Lewis.

"You know how this place works. Next time you see me, we won't remember any of this."

"Is that how it is for you, too?"

He stowed the cup near my feet and stood there. Our eyes locked, but he never blinked, and I lacked the stamina for a staring contest. What was the point of looking at Meriwether Lewis? It only broke my heart.

I wanted to forget that part of my life. I rolled into a fetal position and tightened the skins around me.

Lewis rubbed his hands over his leathery face. "Do you recall how you died?"

"I drowned."

"Well, you've got more memory than I do."

"What do you mean?"

"I was on the Natchez Trace. Stopped for the night. One of those frontier stands. Woman innkeeper."

"I remember reading about it in the papers. Jefferson said you always suffered from melancholy."

"He would say that, wouldn't he? With me dead, he could make sure he was remembered for the Louisiana Purchase. My men and me were a footnote."

"So what's your version, Lewis? Did you kill yourself? Or were you murdered?"

"Don't know. I came to in a New Orleans bar, and I return to it every time I take a run through this place. Been stranded in Nowhere a while."

"So that's why you're here. Your death's a mystery. Like mine."

Lewis reached under the furs and retrieved the mug. His fingers brushed mine when he handed it to me. I recoiled against his heat and tried not to spill liquid everywhere. His mouth turned up at the corners as he stepped backward and took a seat on a rock. "Drink that. I've got jerky when you're ready for something solid."

My hands trembled, but I poured most of the water down my gullet without drooling and held it toward him. "More?"

He kept his fingers on the other side of the mug when he took it from me. Once, I craved his warmth, but I told myself Nowhere would never be that cold. He rested the mug on the pallet beside my head and sat on the brick-strewn ground nearby. "How'd you die, Mrs. Alston?"

"Lewis, I may loathe you, but you may as well call me Theo. Takes less energy from the mission at hand."

"Which is?"

"I've got to finish my assignment."

"Well, my assignment is to kill James Wilkinson, and you're going to help me."

"As much as I'd like to make him suffer, why do you think I'd ever align myself with you?"

"You used to love aligning yourself with all kinds of men. Did you prefer the bottom or the top?"

"Shut up, Lewis. Why do you think Wilkinson is your assignment? I thought we were supposed to lead a living person through a crossroads to their best life. Wilkinson's not alive."

"That's beside the point. If it weren't for my assignment to snuff Wilkinson, I wouldn't have been there to save you."

"How?"

"What do you think I was doing on the Hudson in the middle of the night? That McCrea woman is working with him, and I wanted to see what she was up to. Thought maybe she'd lead me to him, but I found you instead."

I rolled onto my back and studied the canvas of sunrise and clouds. A granite cathedral parted the sky. "Where are we?"

"We're on that island in the middle of the Hudson."

"The one with the ruined castle?"

"Yeah. Natives claimed it was haunted. Heard General Washington mostly avoided it during the Revolution. This was supposed to be some millionaire's summer house, but he died before it was finished. Place like this is full of ghosts."

"I guess we fit right in."

"We're not ghosts, but I'd like to make Wilkinson something worse. I want to make him fail in Nowhere and erase him from history, erase his connection to my life."

"You don't even know which life he's on."

"Twelve. He's on twelve."

"How do you know?"

"Doesn't matter."

Lewis's smugness always drove me mad. I lurched to my feet and tried to charge him, but when I stepped on my wrap's hem, it dropped to my waist. My nipples hardened in subzero air. Lewis's eyes pinpricked my exposed skin, and I yanked the covering to my chin. "Who undressed me? Was I like this when you found me?"

"Your clothes are hanging over there." He pointed behind the wall. "But somebody had to get them off you to keep you from freezing to death."

"You violated me!"

Warmth surged through my fingers. I faltered toward him, determined to slap the disgusting leer from his face. His words knocked me on my backside instead.

"I'd stick my manhood in a rattlesnake's mouth fifty times before I'd touch you." Lewis wrapped another pelt around himself and dismissed my self-righteous rage. "Your clothes are dry. I mended a couple of holes and made everything like new. Probably still need these capes out here, but I'll leave you some privacy to get dressed. Shout when you're decent."

My eyes lingered on the place where he disappeared. A fissure in an unfinished wall led to another roofless room. I yo-yoed on unstable feet, my muscles still sluggish from my impromptu swim. Almost freezing to death was like recovering from a hangover.

I couldn't believe it. Meriwether Lewis. The object of my enmity. I didn't want to owe him anything; yet, I owed him everything.

I tugged my dress over my head, but my nylons and garters were ruined. "I'm presentable."

Lewis strolled through the doorway, his lithe body sheathed in leather pants and a double-breasted wool coat. He walked toward me, and I awaited another verbal jousting. Instead, he whispered, "Do you know how your boy grew up without you?"

Galaxies collided as my tangled emotions unraveled. "How dare you. He died before I did. I watched my only son die."

"Theodosia, I'm sorry."

"You caused your own dear mother that torment, only she didn't have to weight your eyes with pennies in a piteous attempt to unsee what death did to them. She wasn't forced to wash your cold corpse or make small talk with the neighbors while your body was on display in her dining room. She didn't collapse behind the wagon that rolled you to your grave or watch the earth consume the best thing she ever made. Maybe she suffered the regrets I carried since my son's death, but I'm sure if we could resurrect your mother, she'd still tell you being sorry doesn't help."

I bit my hand to stop the volley of words, shot from the pistol of my soul. Before teeth broke skin, Lewis pulled me to him in a one-armed, awkward embrace. I beat his chest with my fists and sobbed while he whispered, "I didn't know. I didn't know. I didn't know your son died before you. I didn't know." Over and over again, until I cried myself dry for the ten thousandth time, because no mother ever stopped aching when her one superlative accomplishment died.

Lewis handed me a tattered square of cloth, a red *ML* stitched into one corner. "It's clean." He turned his back while I honked my nose into frayed linen.

"When I said I was sorry about the boy, I meant sorry *for* him. I lost my dad when I wasn't much older than he would've been when you died. I can't fathom what losing my mother would've done to me. Can't think about it, even now."

"Well, I had the privilege of watching him die, so save your misplaced empathy. When I looked at my son, I was watching my legacy."

When his azure eyes locked onto mine, I couldn't believe Meriwether Lewis was dead like me. He gulped air and rubbed lean-fingered hands over his angular face. "Forgive me. We men try to say the right thing, even if our words miss the mark. I wonder if I've ever stood in front of my dear mother in some Nowhere life. Talked to her from this side of the divide. Do you think she heard me? Sensed I was there? When she missed me most, was it because I was right there with her, holding her hand?"

"Lewis."

"Merry. Everybody calls me Merry here."

"Merry. I'm sure she knew you loved her."

He turned and hiked toward a window, all business once again. "We don't have time to play catch up. Not right now. Wilkinson's out there. He thinks you're gone, and he doesn't know I'm here. Now's the time to join forces. Hunt the bastard down and get rid of him."

TWENTY-SIX: THEO

"I'm not partnering with you." The blasted man swerved from enticing to ordering me around in seconds. It was little wonder he couldn't find a woman to put up with him. I tried to clinch Merry's elbow, but he slipped beyond my grasp.

"Don't think you have much choice, Theodosia."

"Theo." I spat it through gritted teeth. "I told you I go by Theo."

His mouth curled into a dazed half-smile. "You mean, I get to call you what your friends call you?"

"I never said I considered you my friend."

Merry stepped onto my turf. His warm breath blazed against my cheeks and cut off my rant. "Hate me, Theo. As much as you want. Pour it on. I don't care. But you're going to work with me to rout Wilkinson."

"You can't force me to do anything with you. Besides, what if it's my job to get rid of him, and accepting your help isn't part of my Nowhere plan? I'm not wasting another life here because of your misplaced expectations."

"How about a sign then? Would that convince you?"

"A sign? I'm not superstitious."

"Neither was I, until I stepped from my New Orleans bar this time around. Guess where I found myself?"

"A brothel in the arms of another man?"

"You're so funny, Theo. No, I stood in a train station, mere feet from you."

"You were at Grand Central?"

He nodded, close enough for me to count flecks of ink swimming in his eyes. God, how I once stared into those eyes. I looked away, while Merry cleared his throat. "Saw the whole thing between you and Wilkinson, but you boarded the train before I could intervene. I followed him instead."

My face flushed anew, and I stumbled backward. "Where'd he go?"

"You don't know? You've been spending a lot of time with the fellow he met."

"Richard?"

"You sweet on that cadet?"

I couldn't stop my telltale blush. "Just tell me about Wilkinson. How'd you track him from the station?"

He spread his sturdy arms wide and laughed. "I got myself and my men across thousands of miles of unexplored country. Found them when we got separated. You think I couldn't manage a simple shadowing exercise? Especially with Wilkinson?"

Again with the bragging about his prowess and resourcefulness and smarts. How I hated his Great High Explorer routine. I leaned toward him and issued my challenge. "So? How'd you do it?"

"Stashed myself in the back of his truck."

"I tried that, too."

"Fascinating contraptions, motor cars. Wish I had time to learn to drive one."

"Yes, 1950 is a drug to the scientifically minded."

"So you're saying I'm smart?"

I pretended not to hear his question. "What happened in the truck? When you were in the back, could you follow anything?"

"Heard their whole conversation. He's in a quandary, that kid. I can understand why he wouldn't want to go back to spying."

"Richard never said anything about espionage."

"I heard the whole business. Your Richard was a spy."

"He's not my Richard."

Merry waved his hand and shooed my protest like it was a southern no-see-um. "Richard's got two choices: He goes back to Europe and resumes the life of a spy, forsaking West Point and the path he's carving for himself. Or he dies. He's got maybe a couple of days to make up his mind."

Richard misled me.

Or did he?

Merry sat beside me and worked a dinged coffee mug between my fingers. He removed the stopper from another leather flask and sniffed before pouring brown water into my cup. When I had enough, he lifted his mug in a mock toast and studied me over the rim. "Whiskey. My bartender tells me not to drink here, but I slip in a little when I can."

"That's an odd rule. I can drink whatever I want."

"I don't know what your Nowhere guide is like, but mine's a selfish cretin. He's mad because he failed in every Nowhere life, and now he's stuck being a forgotten bartender for all eternity. I swear, he wants me to wind up like him."

"He doesn't sound anything like my Conductor."

"Consider yourself lucky."

"If there's such a thing as luck in this place." I sputtered as heat slid down my throat. "Why didn't Richard tell me?"

"Oh, come on, Theo. Your exalted daddy kept government secrets from you, like I took certain sensitive information to my grave. The kid probably can't trust anybody."

"But he kept pushing me to trust him."

"Means he doesn't have to talk about himself, and when he does, it's bullshit."

"He didn't bullshit his way into my—" I bit my lip and stopped.

"What?" Merry's knee brushed mine when he tipped his legs toward me.

Electricity sometimes sizzled sense into its victims. I put aside images of Richard's face as he writhed above me, because I couldn't have him.

Not again. Not ever. Especially since he suspected me of working with Wilkinson.

"If we work together to nab Wilkinson, can we give Richard the life he wants?"

Merry pinched my arm. "You really do have a thing for that kid."

"No, I don't. Maybe he's my assignment. Or maybe I'm just trying to find a way to justify vengeance, because it doesn't fit with the *best life* version of Nowhere my Conductor spelled out."

"What do you mean?"

I held out my mug and accepted two more fingers of whiskey. After I gulped a mouthful, I continued. "Almost every time I see the General, he rolls out one possibility I can't ignore."

Merry mixed water with my whiskey, his eyes on me. "Which is?"

"He says he knows where my son is."

I jumped when Merry's mug clattered on a nearby rock. He loomed over me, his face distorted. "And you believe him? Damn, Theo. The man never uttered a true word in his miserable life."

"Why do you hate Wilkinson? He never did anything to you."

Merry's body vibrated with rage. "Never did anything to me? He told the Spanish army to hunt down my western expedition and kill the whole corps, but they never found us. When I replaced him as governor of Upper Louisiana, he poisoned the position with enough discord to keep me from succeeding. He turned everyone against me."

His face warped with secret realization, and he wrapped his arms around himself. I crept toward him, afraid of frightening a feral animal. Would he strike or flee? I hovered near his elbow and whispered my question. "What?"

"What if he's responsible for my death?" He wheeled on me, his nose almost touching mine. "What if he killed me?"

"But you said you didn't remember how you died."

"I don't. But I believe Nowhere gives us a chance to erase people who never deserved to live. People like James Wilkinson. If we can force him to waste every Nowhere life, he'll be completely forgotten. It'll be like he never existed. Who knows how that might impact your father's story? My story? Maybe we'd reclaim our lives without the interruption he caused."

I swallowed more whiskey, courage to blur the edges of what my soul screamed to accomplish. I never imagined myself as executioner, as someone to decide who deserved a place on life's timeline.

I couldn't believe partnering with Meriwether Lewis was the only way. "I won't do it."

"But it's the only clear path out of Nowhere."

"That's your opinion. I have my own. You don't know what happens after this place any more than I do."

I scrutinized our position, the bank of broken dreams and naive fantasy. Merry threw the last of his things onto a pile and dusted his hands on his rear end. "Fine. You do whatever you want. Just so you know, I'm using this place as our base."

I perused the ragged square of sky through the open roof. A flawless sunrise, but Hudson Valley winter was a fickle thing. "It's not *our* base. I'm not working with you, and I'm definitely not camping, Merry. You're used to living like a savage, because you are one. I'm not."

"I can make this place air tight. On the expedition, the natives taught me to live through winters you can't imagine."

"Well, I have a hotel room. A real bed. Indoor plumbing. I've gotten used to the luxuries of modern times."

"Whether you work with me or not, you can't go back to the hotel."

"You can't tell me what to do."

"Thank about it. Does Wilkinson know you're staying there?"

Did he?

He probably lurked around the West Point campus to intimidate and threaten Richard, but I never saw him. When I was on site, I practically never left my room, but that didn't mean a staff member wasn't bribed for information. Maybe the whole thing with Richard was his excuse to shadow me. But when Jane McCrea threw me in the river, I lost my handbag. The rest of my Nowhere money was in my room. I needed that, at least.

I grasped the other end of the last bearskin and bumped Merry's fingers when I handed it to him. For a few seconds, I relived making a different bed, helping a man crawl through my upstairs window at Richmond Hill before my father caught him with me.

I stepped back, an effort to clear my head. If Richard knew my whereabouts, did he tell the General or somehow lead him to me? I stomped snow from my boots and avoided Merry's accusatory gaze. "I don't know what Wilkinson's figured out about me."

"If you don't know, then you can't go back there alone. We'll get whatever things you need, and we'll camp here."

"But we can't sleep in the same space, Merry."

"Because we're not married?"

"You know I wasn't a virgin when I married. You're a big part of the reason I wasn't."

Merry closed the space between us, his hot breath a flame on my cheeks. "I remember every time we were together, before your dad decided to campaign against Thomas Jefferson in the presidential election. I was never happier than when your path was marrying me."

His head spun sideways when I slapped him, but I held my ground and refused to show him how much he hurt me.

Merry rubbed his jaw and laughed. "Don't worry, Theo. I can't stand to be near you for more than fifteen minutes. Your pontificating about Aaron Burr drives me insane."

"I know you fart in your sleep."

"I'll keep to my own space." He motioned to the opposite end of the rocky island. "Over there. You can dream about the sounds I make when I'm dozing. I'll try to keep any overnight guests from screaming when they come."

"With Wilkinson prowling around, you won't have time for visitors. You can't do more than one thing at a time."

I stormed toward the hidden cove and waited by Merry's canoe. The thought of him bragging about his sexual conquests made me seethe with contempt, especially since I was one of his conquests. I pretended to count icebergs and snaked my eyes uphill. Merry's powerful body worked to disguise his cache of supplies under limbs and scrub, and I followed every bulging muscle.

Damn Meriwether Lewis. I couldn't spend another second with him. When he ran to the beach, I was already halfway to the northern shore. The river was solid on that side of the island. The ice would lead me to the train.

Lewis could pursue the General however he wanted. Because everything was finally clear. I knew how to help Richard. The General and Lewis could fight to the death. I'd use my own wiles to get through Nowhere.

TWENTY-SEVEN: RICHARD

Ice water stuck to my fingers, my only guides through the maze of caverns beneath West Point. Every castle was propped up by a bunch of secret passages, right? At least, they were in Eastern Europe and the Soviet Union, the only ones I ever wormed my way inside. West Point was built like a lot of medieval castles: On a rocky outcrop with a long view of the terrain. All the better to see potential invaders.

Which was why we used tunnels. Every time I crawled into one, I imagined myself as that literary hero. Edmond Dantés. The Count of Monte Cristo. I used his last name as a decoy for my kills sometimes.

If we wanted to escape the rigors of cadet life, we splashed through ancient rock tubes, carved when the last glaciers plowed through the place 12,000 years ago. Most guys used them to sneak out to area bars or down shots while they played poker. We picked dumb ways to blow off steam, but it kept most of us sane.

My boots slipped on the icy floor as I felt my way toward the easiest exit, a hole that hung two hundred feet above the river on the rock's southern side. We usually avoided the route during winter months, but I was willing to risk it.

I had an appointment to keep.

I hacked through a wall of deep freeze and balanced on a rock ledge. The angle of the sun highlighted another ribbon of frost marching to the river. Getting out of this underground hallway was a routine maneuver, but guys still got butterflies before they flung themselves wide. I groped for the first handhold, crude indentions that cadets, or someone, carved into rock long before I showed up. Chunks of frozen water crackled under my feet and cascaded down the mountain's face, and granite filed skin off my fingers. Salty sweat stung my eyes, but I blinked and kept moving, intent on my riverfront destination beyond the Thayer.

Damn Thayer. I didn't have time to think about Theo, you know? Not with George and Frank bearing down on me. Daylight reflected in the windows, and I wondered whether she was up there. Did she make it back last night? Was she sipping tea and watching me pick my way down the cliff? I scolded myself and turned my attention back to the descent. The damn woman was in my head. I needed to find out whatever I could about her.

First things first though. I had more pressing intel to ferret out.

About twenty feet from the end, I fell from the sloped wall and roller-coastered toward a gate ringed with barbed wire. I swiveled feet-first into the slide and tensed to hit the gate's center. My momentum blasted it open, and I bumped a few yards onto river ice, where I sprawled, coughing and planning my next move. The train station closest to a bridge was Peekskill. Almost thirteen miles downriver.

I wiped melting snow from my pocket watch and checked the time: 12:47. Not AWOL.

Yet.

I lugged myself to wobbly feet and shoe-skated toward the abandoned boathouse. On the path above it, Theo wove her story about vanishing like Rip Van Winkle, and I was too goggly-eyed to see the signs. That morning, all I wanted was to kiss her again.

Damn, I still wanted her.

I shook my head and turned my attention to the terrain. The deepest part of the Hudson hugged the rocky curve at West Point. The rock itself was visible for miles. The superintendent told us the granite was so impenetrable, even the mighty Hudson River had to bow down and go around it.

The water's depth kept the current moving regardless of temperature, meaning the West Point channel was usually wide and open. I assumed the AWOL Princess, my boat, wouldn't be checked out. Who'd be idiot enough to go for a joy ride in subzero windchill? Well, besides me?

I was part-owner of the Princess. Me and a few yearlings pitched our funds together and sold our S.O. on a convincing reason for a shared boat: Geology. A bunch of us studied rocks first term, and we needed a boat to go out in groups and collect samples from some of the spots only accessible from the water. You know, watery crags surrounded by sheer cliffs, the face of Storm King Mountain, places like that.

Remember, lies weren't really lies if the liar believed them.

And the S.O. didn't call bullshit, because he was generally a good guy, so we let him use the thing as a love craft. He serenaded his various girlfriends and floated them to some private cove and screwed their brains out every chance he got, meaning he looked the other way with some of our stuff.

The last dock almost touched the Hudson's strongest current. I clambered along it, my sights on a boat cover near the end. More than a foot of snow sagged into every unsupported crevice and crack, making the task of removing the tarp a pain in my ass. Winter was heavy when it happened in bulk. I struggled against the snow's weight, my feet sliding along rickety wood sprayed with wet.

I stopped fighting the cover long enough to hear a train whistle upriver, probably at Beacon. Hell, I needed to be on that train, because I wouldn't see another one for an hour or so. I threw myself into snow-scraping and tarp-pulling, a frenzy of movement. If I tore the tarp away and pushed the boat, I was close enough to open water to hop in with the current.

Long as I didn't crack the boat's hull in the process.

Another train whistle ghosted over West Point's rocky twin on the opposite side of the river. It was lower but still obscured Cold Spring. The train had to be there. "Gotta hurry."

"Where're you going, Dickie-boy?"

George bore down on me from the opposite end of the dock. His heavy stride rocked the wooden structure and caused me to lose my grip on the cover. I slapped into river ice and skidded underneath several vessels. I thought it'd take George a while to find me, but I was wrong. George's hand pushed into my space.

"Let me help you out of there for a little spy-to-spy chat."

I fumbled with my pants leg and cursed myself. Damn stupid timing, leaving my piece in its hiding place, but I couldn't very well take it out in front of my roommate. He was an understanding guy, but not that understanding. I just wanted to get the hell out of there, you know?

Instead, I gave the bastard my hand and let him pull me back to the dock. I knocked icy snow from my overcoat while George lit a cigar and watched me. "I said where're you headed?"

"How'd you get in here?"

"I've got military credentials. The fellas at the gatehouse let me in anytime."

"I'm in a hurry, George. Tell me what you want and let me get out of here."

"They moved up our rendezvous, and I hauled ass over here to tell you."

I folded my arms and waited. Might as well pretend to care, right? When I didn't say anything, he went on.

"Midnight. Meet me at the abandoned castle on the island upriver."

"I thought I had a couple more days."

"Negative. Too much is happening on the Soviet front. You need to go in now and grab whatever information you can about their super bomb. When Fuchs is convicted of treason, all hell's gonna break loose. I need something concrete to give my congressional contacts and press those bastards to fund our program."

"What changed since last night?"

He sucked in smoke and blew rings. They distorted as soon as the wind grabbed them and flung them downriver. "I thought about our encounter on the mountain last night. You may think I missed it, but I saw the way you looked at Theodosia, right before you clocked her with me. You care about her, don't you?"

"I don't really know her."

"Doesn't matter. I know how the heart screws with a guy. I made some contacts and pushed things up, because I don't want you to make the biggest mistake of your damn life."

"Maybe going with you qualifies as my biggest mistake."

He flung his cigar across the ice and grabbed me by the front of my coat. I almost sneezed when his tobacco breath hit my face. "You pass on this mission, Dickie-boy, and you won't be around long enough to stick your cock in her nasty Soviet pussy. She'll turn on you and destroy everything we've built. I won't let that happen. Soon as I'm finished with you, I'll find her and repeat what I did to Alice. Understand?"

I pushed away from him and straightened the front of my coat. He stood there panting and more pissed than I'd ever seen him. Theo couldn't be Soviet. Dirty, maybe, but not Soviet.

"I'm going into the city. I need to get some things settled, especially now. All right?"

He drove his index finger into my chest to underscore his point. "Don't you shit me, Cox. You show up tonight, or you die."

TWENTY-EIGHT: RICHARD

George wasn't one for idle threats, you know? As I negotiated the ice-choked Hudson, I knew two truths: He would kill me if I refused to go with him, or I could kill him. Popping George didn't bother me. I offed plenty of guys in Europe.

But I was desperate to know whether his scheme was endorsed by the agency. His death wouldn't count for much if another goon showed up and ordered me back into service with tales of a Soviet super bomb. With both Frank and George bearing down on me, I needed to know who backed them up, because one person couldn't issue conflicting orders. If I was supposed to work for George, I couldn't be on Frank's team and vice-versa. One of them was making shit up. I played my last remaining card in hopes of discovering which spy was the bigger liar. And because I only had one shot, I'd try to find out about Theo, too.

I left the boat on the Hudson and dashed up the slope. I sidestepped memories of other broken rules and made for the entrance of the arch-windowed train station. Daylight winked on glass as I plonked down cash, pocketed my ticket, and ran across the bridge to the train. I almost steamrolled the conductor to make it before the doors closed, but she didn't give me a hard time. Always liked her train best. She kept it classy. You know, spic-and-span.

"What happened to you?"

As she punched my ticket and stuck it into a slot on the seat ahead of me, I noticed wet patches on my overcoat. Rotten leaves and twigs made interesting rick rack.

"I fell trying to catch the train." I picked leaves from my coat to keep from making eye contact, and I made sure to hold onto them. She'd swat my head if I scraped them onto her pristine wood floor. She moved beyond me and punched the next passenger's ticket.

I stifled a yawn and marked brown cattails whizzing past the window. George probably figured out where I was headed when I got to the city. Was he on other side of the river, following me? A road snaked between the mountains over there. Given the wintry conditions, I'd be gone before he reached my destination, but that didn't stop him from asking questions and finding out who I met.

George and Frank spelled out one imperative. I had to stand up for the life I wanted, not whatever they intended.

When I was discharged from the Army, I was assigned a liaison. You know, a person inside the bureau who could help me transition into the normal world. She was also on hand to troubleshoot if anybody discovered my past or threatened to expose me. But I could only contact her when I considered my situation dire. She might be able give me answers. I needed to know whether George or Frank were rogues with selfish motives or operatives with blessings from on high. I'd take what she said and decide whether to meet George, go with Frank, or strike out on my own.

As the train slowed into the tunnels under Grand Central, I leaned on the window and hoped I didn't misjudge my position. Cars pitched with every bump over connected rails. Hell, I didn't want to join the ranks of former agents who disappeared without a trace. What happened to those guys, really? Did they die an unsung death and pass into whatever punishment came to spies and assassins?

I didn't want to end up in that situation. I had to be smarter, you know?

So I positioned myself in a mess of humanity headed toward Grand Central's planetarium-like central hall. When they gawped at the star-studded ceiling, I mimicked them, just a West Point cadet gearing up for a debauched city night. With one eye, I scanned a stone-lined corridor for what I really needed: An off-the-rack men's shop. Because if I didn't want to look like a West Point bullseye, I needed to dress the part of someone else.

Thirty minutes later, I emerged from the shop decked out like a businessman on holiday. Didn't all those dicks wear a three-button herringbone jacket, contrasting slacks, a pocket square, and a fedora? If I pulled my hat to my eyebrows and changed my posture, I wasn't the same target. I carried my cadet duds in a dinged-up briefcase and hoped nobody noticed my boots. I loped up the main stair toward Forty-Second Street, and let me tell you, I even changed the way I walked. I strutted through Bryant Park, past the lions guarding New York Public Library. Nobody glanced my way.

My destination loomed on the skyline, a sanctuary I could claim if necessary. The Thirty-Fourth Street YMCA was both shelter for cadets and front for spooks, basically the heart of Manhattan's dirty military establishment. Its face of stone and burgundy brick hid America's craziest sources and unlikely people in need of alibis. My liaison would meet me in a windowless room buried within the block.

I trained my gaze on the spinning door and pushed into the Y's shabby lobby. Place offered nowhere to sit and an inadequate bell to summon the attendant. It clanged into emptiness when I struck the brass lever and woke a sleepy student, all pomade and pompadour flourish. He leaned his bony elbows on the desk and talked through a toothpick dangling from his lips.

"Yeah?"

"I need to see Gudrid."

"Gudrid, huh?"

"Yes."

"This is the Y*M*CA. We don't let no women in here."

I leaned across the desk and fisted his shirt. "I think we both know that's not true."

I held him for a beat to make my point and let him go. The toothpick dropped from his lips in his hurry to run a ragged fingernail along a manifest. He stopped on a line and tapped it twice. "I see it. This you?" He held the dingy book under my nose, and I nodded when I saw the name.

"That's me."

"Conference Room two. Down that hallway. Take a left at the end. You'll see it."

He picked up a red pencil and lined through my details, and for a second I almost believed he was blotting me out. I stifled foreboding and walked toward my meeting with Gudrid. When I opened a walnut doorway with a gleaming number *2*, I was relieved to see my liaison already there.

"Dick Cox." I only knew her as Gudrid. Originally from Iceland, she defected from the Danish military when the Nazis occupied Denmark during the war. She sat at one end of a polished table, her hands clutching her distended stomach.

I took the chair nearest the door and marveled at how much tougher women were. I mean, damn. She sat tall and was all business while carrying around a basketball in her gut. I pulled out a chair and sat opposite her. "You've been busy since the last time you saw me. Congratulations."

She fingered a blonde braid and nodded. "What is it you need?"

"They said you'd always tell it to me straight. Is that true?"

Gudrid bit her lower lip and nodded. "It's my job to keep you close to the organization in case we need to reel you back. You know that, Cox."

"You know George, right?"

"I'm not here to answer meaningless questions."

"But what if George is trying to force me back into spying right now? Showing up at West Point and threatening me if I don't do what he wants."

She shifted in her chair and looked over my head. "George. He recruited you as a spy. Of course, I know him. When did this behavior start?"

"He showed up at West Point a few days ago with a story about the Soviets building a super bomb and how we have to get ours done before they do. He's basically forcing me to be the guy who does the intel on the Soviet program. He claims we risk nuclear holocaust if I don't take this mission. Is this true?"

"I can't comment on our Soviet intelligence."

"I don't give a shit about that."

"Then why are you here?"

"I want to know if George is acting on a higher authority, but I'm not finished. There's Frank, the former agent-turned-weapons-dealer. Remember him?"

"This conversation is ranging well beyond the parameters you were given, Cox."

"But I need to know how he's connected to George. Now do you remember him?"

"Yes."

"Well, he claims George is double-dealing with the Soviets, and he wants me to join him to suss out and eradicate Communists from our shores."

She tapped the table with her finger. "Anything else?"

"George claims he killed my former partner, Alice. He gave me some pretty gruesome pictures. Is she dead?"

"You're full of questions, aren't you?"

"I have one more. There's this woman, Theodosia. Theo, for short. Both George and Frank claim she's dirty. Frank says she's working with George, and George insists she's a Soviet operative. Do you know her story?"

She rocked herself to stand. "You clearly don't understand why you're supposed to come here. I'm to give you a safe place if you think a former target is threatening to take you out. You should know better than anyone how we operate. We don't ask questions, and we certainly don't answer them. If I were the enemy, do you have any idea how much intel you just gave me?"

My fist burned when it hit the table. I jumped to my feet. "Dammit! This is my life. My. Life. George is telling me I have to go back to Europe now. Frank wants me to spy for him here. And I just wanna graduate from

West Point and live a normal life."

Gudrid leaned into the table and put her hand on my sleeve. "Sit."

I obeyed, as dogs sometimes do.

She sat back and crossed her hands over her stomach. "Listen to me, Dick, because I won't be able to say this twice. People are fighting over you."

"People?"

"The heads of different units within our organization. Damn McCarthy's making everybody question everything, and our leaders are no exception. People up the chain are fighting for turf. I don't know how it'll end for you. You're a talented spy. We never let anyone go for good, not outside of a body bag."

"But a spy who doesn't want to spy is a liability."

"You're smart, Dick Cox. We let you go to West Point, because they instill training we need in a spy. Your commission was never a path to a normal life. You're going to rejoin us at some point. We need proven men like you to protect our country from the Soviet threat."

I rubbed my eyes to keep from screaming. This again? I was so tired of living in a world governed by fear, but I didn't argue with her. People who see through the cracked lens of fear twist everything to fit their paradigm. I shifted tactics. "Is George a double agent?"

"That's why I tolerated this conversation, Cox. We have enough evidence to believe he is. But Frank's no better, because he's selling weapons to the Soviets. Of that, we're positive, and he defies all entreaties to stop. Dirty money is still money."

"Did George kill Alice? Is she really dead?"

"Enough. Two known dirty agents are vying for you. That's within the bounds of my ability to help you. Everything else is classified."

"But I hoped you'd give me more."

"What's hope in this business? After everything you were taught, you ought to know better."

I rubbed my forehead and stuttered. "I'm supposed to meet George and reenter the agency at midnight."

"Protecting you is part of my job. Go ahead and meet him. Give me the details, and I'll organize a team to intercept him there. But remember our conversation. Nobody leaves this game. You'll owe the agency."

I was afraid she'd say that.

Hard to Die

TWENTY-NINE: RICHARD

Getting to the city and back was too easy, you know? I mean, when nothing went wrong, I knew something was wonky. Juices lurched in my stomach as I steered toward the dock and used a pole to knock ice out of the boat's path. Snow pelted my hands and stuck to my coat, and the air was so cold my body heat didn't melt it. I sneaked a look toward the bend upriver and almost expected to be walloped by the glacier that formed the place. I heard groaning sometimes, a ghost in the landscape. A few more days of snow and nights below zero, and the river just might freeze across.

Snow flew across the dock in a funnel-cloud, a welcome sign. Nobody came to the river while I was gone. I tied up the boat and smoothed the cover. Satisfied, I stuffed my hands in my coat pockets and hustled along the dock, my mind flush with plans.

I needed to get George and Frank together, you know, confront them with their conflicting stories and see who was still standing by the end. I already had an appointment with George. Getting Frank to meet us at the island wouldn't be hard. He loved the place. I'd pay him a sociable call and agree to his terms. Give lip service to working with him. If Gudrid organized a sting to take George down, maybe Frank'd be caught in the crossfire. With both of them gone, I could sneak back to West Point and resume the life I wanted.

I didn't want to think about what I'd do if I ran into Theo. Who was she, really? Besides the wrong person to love?

A faint set of footprints led to the stone stair that climbed back to campus. George didn't mask his tracks when he left.

If he was gone.

I scanned the ridge and started to climb, my eyes ping-ponging between windowed classrooms and windswept athletic fields. George could've been anyplace, you know? I kicked up my step and was almost to the top when Frank blocked my path.

"Think you're a slick one, don't you, Cox?"

"Frank, I can explain."

"Can it. I don't know where you went, but I can guess. I know all about your liaison at the Y."

"Who?"

"We don't have time for games. Now I don't know what the woman told you, but you listen, and you take good mental notes. My orders come direct from the lead man himself. You're to help me vet potential communists before they reach our shores, and if we discover one slipping through bureaucratic roadblocks, it's our duty to intercept them. Hell, you say you want to stay at West Point and graduate. I'm giving you the chance, because I'll help you stay in the corps. When you need to be on assignment, the administration will look the other way."

The edges of his eyes were haunted with something fresh. What was it? Fear? Or the crush of spinning lie after lie after lie?

"What's Theo got to do with this scheme?"

"Theo? Your little girlfriend?"

"She's nothing to me."

"Your choices concern me. I told you not to get involved with her."

"And why's that?"

"Did you ever stop to think she may be with the Soviets? One of those loophole jumpers McCarthy hired me to track?"

"Then why wasn't she onto you when I dragged her into your bar?"

Frank stared into the distance. Snow misted off mountaintops, blown by the wind. "Part of our business is keeping our history a blank slate, right? You don't go around West Point broadcasting what you did in the Army, do you?"

"No. I mean, I'm not stupid."

"All right. So I achieved a lot of success during the last world war. You've heard the rumors about me, I'm sure."

"That Hitler didn't really kill himself? You penetrated his bunker and assassinated him?"

"I can't give credence to rumors, Cox, but this job was a reward of sorts. For my service." He took another step toward me. "Truth is I also negotiated a key surrender. It led to our winning the whole war."

"Which one?"

"Classified. But I ran into your Theo during that time. We never came face-to-face, but I took note of her from a distance. Quite shapely, she was, even though she wore standard issue communist party duds. Those Soviets want everyone to look the same."

I rubbed one hand along my stubbled scalp. I mean, damn. Both Frank and Gudrid said George batted for two teams. Gudrid implied Frank did, too. Theo claimed George framed her father for his own military infractions, whatever they were. George accused everyone else of being dirty. And every damn thing was classified. Of course it was.

Or was it?

"Do I still have time to make up my mind? I mean, spies are most effective when they want to do the work. I need to weigh my options."

Frank considered me through the gloom. "What options? Your country needs you. Communists are infiltrating our shores at an alarming rate. They're working toward high profile positions and top-tier leadership. They've always said we'd topple from the inside, and they're making it happen. You're less safe every day."

"You're just fear-mongering."

"Am I? You spent time over there. You've seen how determined the Soviets are. They exploded an atomic bomb, for fuck's sake. They've got more bombs to drop on every major city in our country. What good is your bland American dream—a picket fence and a family and a boring career— if the Soviets win? You won't have those things, and you'll remember this conversation then. You can make a difference, son. Join me."

Life is just a series of crossroads, isn't it? I picked what I wanted to eat, never thinking my choices could pile up and kill me. I went to class, without playing out the impact of those studies on my life. Hell, I even made friends, without ever considering the people they might become. And I pursued the life I wanted, when lots of badasses wanted nothing more than to take it from me.

I studied his profile. "I'd like to take a little time if you don't mind. Tie up a few loose ends. That sorta thing."

"I'll give you until midnight tonight."

I snaked my eyes upriver, its path muted by a curtain of snow. "Okay, meet me at midnight out on Pollepel, and I'll give you my answer."

"I'll be there. Go fall in with your company. You've still got time to make evening mess."

I didn't stay to find out where Frank went. I mean, I was already AWOL. Might as well make use of the time to tug the only exposed thread of this hellish tale, the one ragged edge that could unravel the whole thing.

I jumped a snowbank and turned in the direction of the library. I was determined to check Theo's story, because it was about damn time I knew who someone really was, you know?

THIRTY: THEO

"Mrs. Alston, correct?"

I whirled toward the voice and stood taller. Height conveyed power, especially when a predator stalked its prey. "Frank. From the bar. I remember you."

Frank Banner didn't stand in Grant Hall's paneled entrance; he commanded it. With his tailored tweeds and groomed mustache, Frank reminded me of my grandfather. Why did I size him up and consider him a threat, even as he offered me a manicured hand?

"What was your given name again?"

"Theodosia."

His smile never wavered.

"Might want to freshen up, dear. You've got a smudge on your cheek. Excuse me." He stepped beyond me and waved to a uniform. "General?"

A walking testament to the variety of ribbon color towered over Frank. Clearly, Frank wasn't preening around Grant Hall to meet Richard. His eyes tracked my trajectory through the room.

I moved behind a column and scanned the uniforms on display. In the profusion of gray caped overcoats, crisp slacks, and fitted jackets, no cadet matched Richard's carriage or build. Still determined, I headed for the door.

"I could heat myself on fumes of rage," I mumbled to myself and scooted outside to scrub my face with a tongue-wetted finger. Out in the open, I'd do my best to convince Richard I was here to help him. I hoped he'd listen, hoped for Nowhere's end, hoped to see my son again. Hope was the only sense in my nonsense.

Richard bolted across a courtyard, his hands buried in his pockets, a man with purpose. I stood on the steps and called his name. At the sound of my voice, he caught my eye and nodded, imperceptible. If he was surprised to see me, his face didn't show it. His eyes didn't leave mine as he altered his path and approached me.

Earning Richard's trust was the beginning of hope. I dragged in breath and prepared to spill my story, his truth for my lie, because I couldn't tell him about Nowhere. It was an unfair bargain for one of us.

Richard's unbuttoned overcoat swung open. He trotted up the steps and stopped a foot from me. I still wanted to fold myself into his arms, but he didn't close the gap between us.

If he was anything, he was direct. "Theo, what the hell happened on Mount Beacon? When I saw you with George, I didn't know what to believe."

"I can explain everything."

"I bet you can."

"Listen, can we go inside to talk?"

He shuffled from foot to foot and studied me. After a few beats, the hard line of his mouth relaxed. I was relieved when he almost smiled. "I don't have time, Theo. I was just headed to the library. All this extracurricular activity's put me a bit behind, you know? If you have something to say, you'll have to walk with me, because I've got things to do that don't include listening to a woman with secrets wag her jaw."

"I'll only take a few minutes."

His nostrils flared. "I don't know who you are or what you're doing here. After seeing you with George, I'm not sure I can believe anything you tell me, but I'll listen."

I clutched the only carrot he offered and fell in step beside him. We followed a plowed path through snow-laden trees. "Remember when we were at the Green Room, and I told you the man who attacked me was once a colleague of my father's?"

"The man who turned out to be George, but you called him the General. I remember."

"Yes, he was a general. My father was a well-connected politician in Washington D.C."

"A senator?"

"He presided over the Senate." I bit my lip and hoped Richard wouldn't compute my meaning. In Aaron Burr's day, the vice president presided over the Senate, though I didn't know how things worked in 1950.

"Ah, so he was elected president pro tempore."

I nodded. "My father met regularly with military leaders. They discussed the size of the force and funding, among other things. Anyway, the General brought my father surveillance that indicated vulnerabilities in another country, weaknesses he believed we might exploit."

"During the last war?"

I ignored his question. "For several years, the General and my father worked in secret to confirm these claims, but when my father decided to act, the General turned on him. He accused my father of treason, and he produced a one-sided trail of correspondence to make the accusation stick."

Richard took my elbow and steered me toward another snow-lined path. "Why didn't we hear anything about this in the news? I mean, it's a pretty sensational story, Theo. If this happened, it would've been on the front page of every newspaper in the country."

"It was all handled in secret."

"I don't believe that, Theo."

"Well, what you believe about the story isn't the point."

"What is?"

"For a long time, the General was a rumored double agent."

"For the Soviets?"

"Not exactly, but if he still used his position to sell our secrets, it wouldn't surprise me." His hand still lingered at my elbow, and I squeezed it. "You mentioned having a lot to deal with, Richard, and I got a sense it was more than the demands of West Point."

"So?"

"I know I haven't really given you enough to trust me, but I believe the General lies at the heart of your dilemma. If he's asking you to do something, learn from my father's story. Do the opposite of whatever he wants. Anything you do for him won't turn out well for you. It'll probably ruin your life."

In my earnestness, I forgot to keep track of where we were. All that mattered was telling my story and having Richard believe me. When I finally surveyed my surroundings, I realized we were at the old fort above campus. Nobody was around.

Richard stopped behind the low stone wall and cleared snow with his boots. When enough was carved away, he gestured toward the indentation. "Sit."

I slid into the cleft while Richard cleared another space a few feet away. When I glanced over the wall, it was the first time I realized we were hidden from view. I cursed myself for getting too caught up in my tale, for forgetting to stay where people could witness Richard's treatment of me. He was so open while we were walking, but his stance was no longer friendly. He folded his arms and regarded me like I was a prisoner to interrogate. Or intimidate.

"I'm waiting."

I jammed my hands in my coat pockets and met his gaze head on. "For what?"

"Your real explanation. Because let me tell you, I've spent the past twenty-four hours gaining all sorts of intel on you."

"Intelligence? About me?"

"Who sent you? Which department? Hell, what country are you working for?"

I blinked. After everything I told him, could Richard still think I was a spy? Without thinking, I laughed at the idea.

Steel cocked against steel, and I stared down the muzzle of a gun. He was cool, professional, an assassin, and I was an idiot for thinking I could reach him. I swallowed and prepared to bargain for my life.

"Richard, what are you doing?"

"I need answers, Theo. Is that even your name? I always thought it was shifty."

"Of course that's my name."

"Where'd you really meet George, huh? After you ran from me on the mountain, where'd you go?"

"I wandered the valley all night. Look at me, Richard. My clothes are rumpled. Don't I look like I spent the night outside?"

He flicked his eyes downward. They burned along my neck and lingered on my chest. He recovered, but not before I saw it. He may not trust me, but something inside him still burned for me. I leaned forward, hoping my earnestness would convince him. "I know my entire tale sounds ridiculous, but I can only tell you what happened and beg you not to do the General's bidding."

He relented and lowered the gun. What could I say to turn him into the man I met at the train station, the one who brought me back to some kind of life? I leaned toward him, hoping he'd see how much I wanted to help him, but when I tried to touch his face, he slapped me aside and stood at attention, the gun aimed at my chest.

"Put your hands in the air. Now."

He kept the gun trained on me while I raised my palms level with my head. Cold gnawed the tips of my fingers. I hoped they didn't tremble, because I couldn't feel a thing.

Richard kept the firearm leveled. "I don't give a shit what you say, because here's what I think. You're working for the wrong people. Could be George or somebody who's crossways with George. Hell, Theo. I'm even trying to figure out if you're Soviet."

"Soviet? I don't understand."

"Who spelled out your mission?" I bit the inside of my cheek to keep from screaming when he cocked the gun and shouted, "Answer me!"

"I don't work with anyone! I'm not Soviet! Please, Richard, believe me!" I spat pleas without taking a breath and hoped it penetrated some remnant of the bond we once shared, but nothing I said got rid of the gun.

"What is your mission?"

Jesus God, how did he know I had a mission?

"You're my mission," I sputtered before he could pull the trigger and end my chances of success. I didn't want to go back to the beginning, to rejoin my Nowhere train, to tell the Conductor I failed.

Again.

"I somehow figured that. But are you here to kill me? To make me pay for my crimes against your country? To recruit me into some other bit of nastiness I want nothing to do with?"

"How can you say those things?"

I reached for his free hand, but he anticipated my move and pinned my arm behind me. The gun's muzzle burned against my temple, and his lips tickled a curl next to my ear.

"Here's a message for your leader. I'm through with everything. All of it. I won't go back for George. I won't go back for world peace. And I sure as hell won't go back for you. I'm reclaiming my life, and they're gonna have to kill me to change that."

With one shaky exhale, he released me. I never saw where he stowed the gun, but it was gone. "Don't forget to give my message to your higher-ups, *Theo*, or whatever your name is."

Before I registered movement, his weight pressed into me, and his mouth devoured mine. I yielded to his tongue and matched his fervor with my own building heat. When he tore himself free and backed toward the path, his voice hacked through my core. "Stay out of my life. If I ever see you again, I'll kill you.

THIRTY-ONE: RICHARD

Spies were schooled to evaluate a target, to question everything, you know? Desire was emotion, a weakness a proper spy couldn't afford.

I never claimed to be a proper spy.

Maybe that's why I wanted out. Paranoia snaked through my armor at the worst times and robbed me of my will to trust anybody. I mean, it was why I held everyone at a distance. A gregarious loner, a living cipher.

As I huffed to the library, my gut roiled with a stew of questions and longing. Did I just alienate the only person who might help me build the life I wanted? I mean, she told me not to join George. Coming from anyone else, it was exactly what I wanted to hear, but from Theo? Part of me wanted to turn around, run up the hill, and tell her I trusted her.

Until the other part of me kicked in.

To spooks, everybody lied until they died. Theo's claims of innocence rang true, but any professional could weave a good line. I snapped my fingers. Those lines usually contained bits of truth. Her whole father story bothered me, and if I asked George, he'd contradict it with even more bullshit. But what if she gave me enough facts to tear through the library and verify something she said?

I detoured through a foothill of fresh snow, determined to suss out the truth. While I didn't know her father's name, his time in the senate would be recent, a few decades' worth of data to scan for possible connection to what she claimed. I'd list every recent president pro tempore of the senate in one column, and I'd look up their family members. If I found Theo's name, at least I'd have confirmation of something. It wouldn't prove the rest of it, but West Point held records of all kinds of stuff. I might find some reference to the drama between George and her father.

In my gut, I figured I'd unearth a link between her and George and the superiors she denied, and if I did? I'd cast aside my damn emotion and pull the trigger next time.

Libraries exuded the passage of time. The musty scent of paper tickled my nostrils as I bolted through swinging doors. I vaulted through the stacks and waved to distract my target from his scribbles on yellow notepaper. "Mr. Henry?"

He stashed his latest bottle-bound masterpiece in a drawer and tweaked his glasses. "Cadet Cox. Are we crawling through the basement today? Or something else even more scintillating?"

"I'd love to see one of your bottle ships sometime."

His face spasmed with . . . what? Amusement? Disdain? He pushed back from the desk and threw his weight into its scratched top. "Shut up, Cox. Now I know you want some ridiculous favor, and I don't have time to grope the seedier corners of this establishment for the likes of you."

"Even if you're the only person who might be able to dig up the information I need?"

"What is it? You're failing your philosophy term paper and need a more sophisticated eye?"

"I already finished it."

"No. Wait. You want me to translate your middling Russian into something intelligent and profound."

If only I could reach across the counter and hit him with my middling

Russian. But I couldn't, and I knew it. I moved closer and lowered my voice. "I need you to help me find the dirt on a suppressed trial. A senator was supposedly involved. You might even know the guy."

Mr. Henry's eyes sparked behind thick glasses. "Unseemly behavior from an acquaintance of mine? How long ago?"

"Years. Maybe decades. Morsels of gossip for everyone you know."

He dropped his voice to a whisper. "Do you have a name for this unsavory character? Or perhaps a timeframe?"

"Negative. I only have two things, and I'm not even sure they're accurate."

"Give me what you have."

"A woman who claims to be his daughter. First name: Theodosia. And the man who accused him of treason. He was a general."

Mr. Henry unbuttoned his vest and fell into his chair, his face a mask of bewildered lines and shadows. He scratched his chin, his concentration centered on a faraway wall. Music trilled from his lips, an otherworldly tongue. "Why is this familiar to me?"

He snapped up a fresh piece of yellowed paper and scrawled with a fountain pen. I tried to follow the lines and circles he etched into the page, but his handwriting was wrecked. Almost manic.

"Mr. Henry?"

His substantial head whiplashed from another dimension. "Cadet Cox? I'm sorry. My memory buzzed with something."

"You know these people?"

"It's not that. The situation sounds vaguely familiar."

I leaned across his desk. "Do you think you can help me?"

"Please, tell me how you came about this information."

I cupped my lips and mouthed, "Not here."

Mr. Henry nodded and creaked from behind his counter. For a portly man, he always led a chase at track speed, bowling through the stacks. He hairpin-turned and scaled a circular stair, personified energy. When we reached the top floor, he motioned me through a low doorway at the end of a gloomy hall. The secretive crown of the building, a place where lots of stuff happened, but nobody knew what went on. All the cadets wondered, you know? What was that space like?

Mr. Henry's head popped around the jamb. "Hurry up, Cox. One would never know you run miles every day."

As soon as I crossed the threshold, he slid three bolts into place and walked around a square table. Open in the middle, it was surrounded by leather chairs. An overhead projector faced a blank screen, and the walls were lined with chalkboards. In one corner, four televisions were stacked on top of each other next to a state-of-the-art communications area. The equipment put my Morse box to shame, a twentieth century homage to the money American taxpayers bled to protect its citizens from the Soviet menace. And the more money we spent, the more our citizens were afraid. Maybe that was the point of it all you know? To fill the coffers of those who stoked the flames of fear.

Mr. Henry picked his chair. Indicating one next to him, he smiled. "Please. Sit. You wanted secure."

I rooted myself in place. "I never said that. I didn't want to have a private conversation at your desk. Too many people down there." I scanned the surfaces of the room. "Where's the recording device?"

Mr. Henry steepled his chunky fingers together. "They told me about you."

"They?"

"'He's not merely a spy,' they said. 'He's an assassin'."

"Who's they? The West Point administration?"

"How many Soviets have you killed, Cox? Ten? Twenty?"

"I don't know what you're talking about." Paranoia roiled through my abdomen, a warning bell. Why didn't I see it before? I stepped backward and positioned myself a few steps closer to the door. "But I'll bet you're more than an eccentric librarian."

"I wouldn't say I'm eccentric, Cox. Librarians are often privy to information about our patrons. We glean it from their interests. The books they request. When they need assistance with research. Even where they choose to spend time within our walls."

"The perfect place to spy."

"When you enrolled here, someone asked me to watch you. Keep a record of what you researched. Books you checked out. That sort of thing."

"Who? Who asked you?"

"You know I can't reveal my benefactor, but I'll answer your other question."

"What other question?"

"The characters you gave me. Theodosia. The General. There's a record of that episode within these walls."

"Where? Where is it?"

"Oh, it doesn't lie where you expect."

I was on him before he finished, my hands around his blubbery throat. His eyes bulged, but I kept my thumbs on his jugular. Rather than looking pained, he twisted his blue lips into a clownish leer. He couldn't die before he revealed his secrets. I relaxed my grip and whispered, "Tell me. Tell me who Theo is. Tell me before I finish you."

He sucked in air and rasped, "I'm just an eccentric librarian who persecutes cadets and builds ships in bottles. Or maybe I can tell you everything about the General. General Wilkinson. I guess you'll never know." Before I could react, his hands closed around my neck, and he thwacked me into the table. I struggled to regain my grip, but he pressed his weight against my air flow. Beads of sweat bubbled along his upper lip. I let my body go limp, a trick I mastered during my spy days. More than one chump thought me dead when I wasn't.

As soon as he released me, I vaulted from the table and wrapped my elbow around his head. I swear, I didn't mean to kill him. My ears filled with the sickening snap of his spine, his face still tattooed with some shred of data to prove Theo's story. Alarms screeched through hidden speakers. Rattled, I released him, and he fell toward the table. His body emitted weird blurbs of light, like someone lit sparklers inside him.

My fingers itched to check his pulse. No time. The sound of boot steps jacked through the corridor. Metal ground in one lock. I darted behind the closest chalkboard, groping for a hidden exit, a button or a panel, anything that might lead to escape, because in my experience, such rooms were built around secret doors.

The third lock ground open as a section of wall behind me popped wide and revealed a ladder. It marched down another granite tube into oblivion. I plunged into it, but not before I heard a bewildered voice announce an even more bewildering find.

"Why'd the alarm go off? There's nobody here."

What the hell was going on?

THIRTY-TWO: RICHARD

I didn't have time to find out what happened to Mr. Henry. Not when the room was filling up with uniforms. I shut the secret door and climbed down a steel ladder. Water drips formed icicles, but I sidestepped slick sections and surrendered to the caverns beneath West Point. At the bottom, I pointed my penlight away from exit routes, deeper into the mountain. Some of my classmates thought one of the routes led all the way to hell, the center of the earth or some such. I guess it was a fair assertion.

My bizarre encounter with Mr. Henry changed the stakes. I broke his damn neck, and he was gone. What the hell happened to him? And who was General Wilkinson?

It wasn't the first time my circumstances with Mr. Henry veered toward the weird. I still couldn't shake the visions from his damn piece of flint. Maybe I wasn't caught up in arms races and cold wars. Did this whole thing belong in the realm of something bigger and older, something more powerful than spies like me?

I knocked my forehead with one hand. Spies didn't have time for superstitious shit, you know?

I felt my way along the passage and came upon a blocked doorway riddled with rust. I crept past this doorway a hundred times, never knowing where it led. The suits were using that room for something, and they didn't want it to be seen. When I threw my shoulder into it, I knew it would open. A couple of whacks, and the door yawned into another underground domain, the caverns and crevasses of my cadet life.

I shined my penlight around the space, noting flags we set out to mark our way. One tunnel led to our poker den. Another led to a stash of booze. But I chose the third tunnel, because it led to my secret domain.

I switched off my penlight and settled into smothering darkness. Claustrophobia passed if I pretended I was an ancient pharaoh, and the mountain was my afterworld dominion. Brain tricks, you know? I had a million, stuff I learned from George and his crew in case I was captured and tortured. Who knew simple pretending would save me from so much real life?

I shifted my attention to uneven rock and counted out steps. Twenty. Seventy-five. Two hundred and thirteen. I slid my fingers underneath a boulder, pulled a lever, and stepped aside as my hidden doorway sprung open, wide enough for me to slide through with an inch to spare.

When the entrance boomed shut, I put my penlight on the floor and flipped on an ancillary flashlight I kept stashed in my hidey-hole. Between the two of them, I had enough light to examine my hidden compartment, my top secret haven, a hole the mountain forgot. Five-by-eight was bigger than a coffin, right? And easier to check for signs of unwelcome visitors. Took me a whole month to scope it out and secure it freshman year.

All of this because spies got the best toys. I didn't want to leave them all behind in Europe. I needed a secret place to save some junk from my former life, because who knew when something might come in handy, you know? I brought back gadgets and my handy kit of sleeping potions and truth serums. They gave us a vial to swallow if we were ever captured, and I saved it, even though I didn't plan to use it. I kept my own stash of poisons, too. Arsenic, mainly. And cyanide and snake venom. And of course, a cavern was the perfect dark room. Photos hung like flags along one side of the space.

I set about emptying film from my Petal camera. On this trip to my haven, I sought a place to think, and nothing relaxed me like teasing images to life.

Before I got to my photography supplies, a murderous hand pressed against my pulse and choked off oxygen to my brain. I struggled against my attacker's grip and fought off waves of unconsciousness.

The bastard whispered next to my ear, disguised-like. "I'm like this rock to you. Look like one, too, if you could see me. Shame that can't happen."

My assailant knocked the flashlight from my hand and kicked my penlight into the far wall. When it flickered out, my world became a sarcophagus, oppressive and asphyxiating. I gripped his stranglehold and fought to breathe against the crush of darkness. "Somebody told me you couldn't handle the dark, Cox."

I struggled to force words through swollen lips, but they wouldn't form. Even small sounds were screams, encased in a buried cavern.

His fist whacked against my temple, and I tumbled through darkness. I guess I blacked out. When I came to, I tasted blood on my sticky lips. A flashlight illuminated my circumstances. I hung from the rocky ceiling, hands and feet trussed to a metal hook I didn't put there, rigged while I was unconscious. I screamed as my limbs stretched in four different directions. Muscles and sinew fought a losing battle to keep me together. After what may have been an eternity or thirty seconds, the rope went slack. Sweat ran into my eyes. I blinked and sent my mind elsewhere. One must endure torture to overcome an opponent.

I fixed my thoughts on staying alive.

"What do you want?"

I coughed. The intruder was somewhere behind me. I sensed him toying with the rope and preparing to tear me apart.

"I want to know about your friends. One friend specifically. This fellow called George. Where is he?"

"I don't know anybody named George."

The rope tore my limbs in four directions. I endured almost a minute of agony before it went slack and my oppressor snarled, "You're lying. I saw you with him. First, in his truck at Garrison station."

"I don't know what you're talking about."

"He offered you a job. Well, forced it on you is more like it."

Who the hell was this guy? I decided to shift gears. "I'll give you the dirt on George. But first, tell me. Who's Theo, really?"

"Theo? Why are you interested in her?"

"I think she may be working for George or somebody like him."

Did he snicker? "I don't know who she's working for, but it doesn't matter. She may as well be dead to you."

"Who the hell are you?" I twisted, trying to see the bastard's face. The rope tightened, and I struggled through another session on his makeshift rack. Torture never evolved. Men returned to the same tactics. Cruelty was an evolutionary constant.

The tension broke. I hit the floor hard. Man, was he on me. I tried to shield myself while he kicked me.

"You" Kick.

"Do not." Kick-kick.

"Get to." Kick.

"See me."

I plummeted into blackness once again. When I came to, I writhed on the stone floor and tried to force air into my lungs. His voice wafted from different parts of the room. Every sentence came from an unexpected place, adding to my dizzy desperation.

"I know you slept with Theo."

"Slep—" I couldn't finish for coughing.

"That's right. Don't deny it."

I balled my body into fetal position and fought to stay conscious. I had to keep him talking. "Is that what this is really about? A jealous tantrum over a woman?"

"Why should I care if you nail my castoffs?" His footsteps tapped against rock. "I s;ept with her, too. Don't worry. It's been a while."

The flashlight beamed inches from my eyes. They teared from the frontal assault of light and heat. His mouth moved next to my ear. "Your friend George is a real asshole."

"He's not my friend."

"I need to know where he is."

"Look, if I knew where he was, I'd already be rid of him." My thoughts tripped into an idea. "But I'm meeting him tonight."

"Where?"

"Know the island upriver? Pollepel?"

"I know it well."

I gritted my teeth and rasped, "He'll be there at midnight. I'm supposed to give him an answer."

At least, I spoke truth.

"This better not be some kind of trap."

"I think I hate George as much as you do."

He picked up my big flashlight and kept it trained on my eyes. "I'm going to leave you now, and because I'm a nice guy, I'll let you keep your stuff." The ball of light moved toward the exit. He turned a lever, and the access stone rolled away.

"Tell me one thing. Please. Who are you?"

"Doesn't matter."

"Then who is she?"

"Theo?"

"Yes. Please just tell me she's not on George's team."

"George's team?"

His laughter hammered my ear drums, yet another form of torture. His voice hurt my ears. "Theodosia Burr Alston hates that guy."

"Why?"

"Story's complicated."

"I need to hear it."

"You won't believe it."

"Try me." I writhed against my shackles and tried to kick toward the direction of his voice, but the damn things further hog tied me.

"I've wasted enough time. Just forget Theo, all right?"

"Who are you?"

"I'm nobody. But let me give you a piece of advice. If you follow George, you'll disappear. You might still be alive somewhere on this round rock, but everybody'll think you're dead, and in some ways, that's worse than dying."

"Why? Because I'll be George's stooge?"

I counted several heartbeats before he spoke. "I'll try to get to George before you see him at midnight."

"But what do you mean, worse than dying?"

The bastard hit me on the head and left me battered and alone in the dark. Just where I planned to leave him if he showed up at midnight.

THIRTY-THREE: THEO

I lost track of how long I sat outside in the snow. I couldn't summon Richard again, but I had to convince him the General was our mutual enemy. I needed to knock him sideways, do something he wouldn't expect. But what?

I could tell him the truth about me. The truth was all I had, and Richard would call it insanity. He'd never believe Nowhere was real.

I studied the icy Hudson below, tinted blue by cold and twilight. Rock and water, ice and sky, landscapes were elemental if we stripped them of humanity. I leaned into arctic air and hoped it would lend me a fresh perspective, some other way to accomplish my Nowhere assignment. How could I help Richard if he wouldn't let me?

Realization blew in with the wind. Merry was right. We had to kill Wilkinson. I resisted, because I couldn't imagine revenge as Nowhere motivation, especially not when I recalled what the Spanish pirates said. But if we eliminated the General, we also got rid of whatever threat he presented to Richard, and that was in line with my assignment. He might never know how it happened, but he could pursue the life he wanted.

It was the only way.

My heart twisted. However his life played out after I was gone, I hoped he'd remember me, remember *us*.

But what came next? I spent a lot of time worrying about accomplishing my Nowhere assignment. My Conductor warned me against failure with good reason. I didn't want to end up a forgotten soul, trapped in some menial Nowhere job for all eternity.

But if I could see my son again, I didn't care about being remembered. I wanted to see my son one more time. If that was what awaited me, I couldn't wait to find the General and finish him.

Resolved, I hurried across campus. I still had money in my room at the Thayer. Cash gave me options, time to regroup. A uniformed cocktail party spilled from the bar into the lobby. I wove through the obstacle course without being splashed by alcohol. At the top of the stairs, overhead lights strobed near the end of my hallway. I was a shade of myself, but I still worked my key into the lock. As soon as the door opened a crack, a hand shot through it. I recoiled into the opposite wall and charged the intruder.

"Theo. It's me. Merry."

"Lewis!" I elbowed past him and reclaimed my room. When I wheeled on him, he was still in the doorway. "I told you I never wanted to see you again, but of course, you take my words as an invitation to move in."

His blue eyes flamed. "Wilkinson. I know where I can find him at midnight."

"How did you get this information?"

"I can't tell you that."

"Then, how do I know it's of any use?"

"All right. All right. You're not the only person who can charm the concierge."

"How much did you bribe him?"

"Her." He winked, and I didn't mistake his subtext.

Did he bring her to my room? Take her on my bed? Could he still touch a woman and make her forget things like loyalty and responsibility? Meriwether Lewis was the most intelligent man I ever knew, even more educated than my father. Everything about him confounded me.

He cleared his throat and brought me back from memories we made.

"Hard as my charm is for you to fathom, people like me, women especially."

I moved to slap him, but he stopped my hand before it made contact with his face. His fingers squeezed my wrist, and I hoped he couldn't feel my pulse, the despicable man. My eyes burned into his until he released me and looked away.

"So. Where can we find Wilkinson come midnight?"

"We? You're going to join me?"

"Maybe. If you tell me you didn't screw your way to his whereabouts."

"Sounds like that bothers you."

"No, it doesn't."

He stepped close enough for me to count his eyelashes. "Why don't I believe you?"

I gulped and stepped backward. I came back to the Thayer to clear my head, not further muddle it. "Look, Lewis."

"Merry."

"All right. *Merry*. Let's stop talking in circles. You want me to help you get rid of the General. I'm willing to accept it as my assignment."

"You are?"

"Yes, but what happens at midnight?"

"The General is supposed to meet Richard out on the island. Remember, the one where I was hiding out when I fished you from the river and saved your life?"

Why did he always have to lord over me with his heroics? The man drove me mad. I walked to the window to put some space between us and threw back the drapes. Snow fell like flour through a sifter, rough weather to be outdoors. "How soon do you want to head that way?"

"We've got a couple of hours. Might as well go down to the bar and have a decent meal before we spend a night in the cold and end our mutual Nowhere."

"I don't want to spend that much time with you."

"Come on. It's either that or try to find something to do while we're stuck in this room."

I shoved him into the hallway and rattled the deadbolt in a bid to lock him out of my room, but he forced his way back inside. "Come on, Theo. You may as well join me."

"Dammit, Lewis! You leave me here and go eat without me. I'll meet you in the lobby in time to leave."

Merry took a step toward me. His visage radiated the confidence I imagined he displayed on his western expedition. He was one of those people who were always certain of the right way, who didn't dither even when they doubted themselves. "I'm not letting you out of my sight again."

"But I said I'd meet you."

"And I'm not taking any chances. I want to be done with this place. My Nowhere ends tonight."

"What do you think happens, Merry?"

"After Nowhere?"

"Yes. What's the point of this, this punishment, if it doesn't lead to something we want?"

"Where do you want it to lead?"

I turned my head to keep him from seeing my eyes tear. "I want to see my son again."

When he stood behind me and put his hands on my shoulders, I didn't flinch or shrug them away. We stood together at the window, watching snow slather on a fresh coat of white. After a few minutes, Lewis muttered, "I hope that's what awaits you, Theo."

"What about you? What do you want when this is over?"

"Me? I don't care what happens after Nowhere."

"Really? You don't want to see your mother again? Maybe reunite with Clark?"

"Nah, I just want to be remembered for what I accomplished in life."

"Why wouldn't you be?"

"You tell me. You lived over three years longer than I did. What did people say about my death?"

"Right after it happened, you mean?"

"When I pulled you from the river, you told me you thought I committed suicide. At the time, I dismissed it as you not being happy to see me, but now I wonder…is that really what people think?"

"Yes."

He stalked across the room and leaned into the dresser. In the mirror, I watched his eyes flame. "Tell me exactly what was printed at the time, what people said. Spare me nothing."

"You were buried in an unmarked grave. As far as I know, there was no investigation. Jefferson circulated the story that your suicide didn't surprise him, because you always suffered from melancholy."

"He said that?"

"Yes, and Clark agreed with him."

"I don't believe it. He was my best friend. Do you recall exactly what he said?"

"He repeated something about how upset you were when you left St. Louis. Everyone construed it to mean you were suicidal." I took a couple of steps toward him, but he simmered too much to touch. "Why does this matter now?"

He pounded his fists into the furniture and reeled on me. "Because the winners write history. You should know that better than anyone. With me conveniently crazy and dead by my own hand, who stood to take credit for everything I accomplished in life?"

"Jefferson," I whispered.

"That's right. My beloved godfather. I can even guess what history books say."

"My God, Merry. You're right. Even in my lifetime, your whole expedition was used to show Thomas Jefferson's brilliance in buying Louisiana from Napoleon. Everyone praised him for organizing a party to explore it. A lot was given over to how you and Clark were led to the Pacific by a native woman."

"There's nothing about my catalog of new plants and wildlife, nothing about my scientific discoveries, nothing about Clark's artistry with maps? Maybe if I'd published my journals before I died, I might've gotten my story out there. I had most of them with me at the end. Were they ever published? I bet they disappeared when I died. The whole thing wiped away my life's greatest accomplishment. It's no wonder I'm forgotten instead of revered."

He stood there, spent and sucking in air. When I was sure he wouldn't push me away, I went to him and took his hand. "If you complete your assignment, how do you want people to remember you?"

"My death happened too fast, and I was young. Only thirty-five. My world was unraveling at the end. The Madison administration refused to reimburse me for expenses I paid on the nation's behalf. As a result, I was bankrupt, and I was desperate to keep it a secret long enough to get to Washington and convince the bastards to pay me. I wasn't crazy or unstable or suicidal. I wanted my journals to be the official scientific record of the expedition. If completing my assignment rewrites my story, I'd like to be remembered as America's first scientist, because I was. Dammit, I was."

I took him in my arms and held him while his body shook with sobs. The Great Explorer was human. He cried, and I let him. When he quieted, he pulled back and looked at me. "I'm sorry, Theo. Nobody needed to see me that way."

We stared at each other for two lifetimes, until I closed the one remaining inch between us and tasted Merry Lewis.

Again.

More than a century fell away, our passion no longer doomed by political expediency. My fingers clawed at Merry's buttons and tore into his leather pants, desperate to feel his skin on mine, and he responded like merging our in-between bodies might bring us both to life.

Goosebumps radiated along the back of my neck when he nibbled my earlobe and breathed, "Theo. You were always the only woman I wanted."

I slipped my hand between leather and the skin of his thigh, reaching for him, the feel of him familiar and welcome in my hand. When he started to undo my dress, I released him and stepped beyond his touch. "Watch me," I whispered.

"Theo," he groaned, but he stood still, alight and waiting.

I walked my fingers along the front of my dress, teasing buttons open and baring bits of flesh. With a groan, I closed my eyes and imagined him entering me as I slid my dress and slip over my head and flung them across the room.

I didn't have to open my eyes to know Merry was captivated. His breath was ragged and feral. Enjoying my power, I arched my back and ran my hands over my breasts. My nipples groaned against the scant fabric of my bra, and I let the pressure build until I couldn't stand it. I slipped my hands behind my back and opened my eyes as I undid the clasps and cast my bra aside.

While holding Merry's gaze, I ran my hands along my bare breasts and teased them down my stomach. I quivered everywhere, and I didn't care if he saw it. His eyes followed my fingers to the triangle of fabric shielding my womanhood, but they bounced back to my eyes when I spread my legs and touched myself.

Before I could order him to undress, he pushed my panties aside and entered me. I wrapped my legs around him and rode him while he squeezed my bottom. His tongue licked my breasts, and in response to my building need, I undid his shirt and rubbed myself against his bare chest. He moaned, his thrusts building, and I ground into him until the world buzzed with light. Together, we tumbled into the white hot world of ecstasy. For a few minutes, our bodies truly lived again.

When we were spent, we fell onto the bed and lay tangled together. Merry's voice was raw when he whispered, "I never dreamed you'd honor me again, Theo. God, how I wanted you. I spent my life wanting you. I hope you believe me."

I kissed his nose. "I do."

He sighed. "As much as I'd like to, we can't stay like this. We've got to kill Wilkinson."

I wanted to rest, to savor my time with Merry, but instead I groped for my dress. I never basked in much during my too-short life. I always thought I'd have more time. Wasn't that always the way people in their twenties saw life? Everybody thinks they'll win the life lottery, a full-and-complete existence with a death at an old age. My life ended too soon. I would've done so many things differently had I known death would claim me at twenty-nine.

Nowhere gave me my opportunity to get something right.

I shrugged into my coat and followed Merry through the door. It was time to complete my assignment. To be finished with Nowhere. To get on to Forever.

THIRTY-FOUR: RICHARD

I didn't have time to decipher the intruder's barked revelations. Too bad I couldn't snap his photo, but I'd remember his voice. It sounded like it was from another time. Maybe that was the knock on the head talking.

Before he left, he took me off the rack and tied me up, hanging upside down, the bastard. I passed out that way. When I came to, I worked my way through the knots and freed myself. The Army taught me how to escape from most situations. The aftermath was the problem. I collapsed on freezing rock, but my wrists and ankles burned. Funny how the body responded to fear.

I didn't move until my pulse stopped racing. I patted my hands around my immediate space. Lucky me. It didn't take too long for my fingers to hit the butt end of my penlight.

I clicked the thing on and fixed my eye to the glowing dial of my pocket watch. Less than two hours. I had less than two hours until I was due to meet George and do what I needed to do. Frank would be there, too. I could only fire one bullet at a time. What would I do if Gudrid didn't come through? I'd be screwed for sure.

My muscles protested when I stood, but I shook it off and dragged myself into the tunnel. The ground was familiar as I felt my way toward the surface. It was up to me to get to George's meeting spot without being recognized. Even in my dress grays, I knew how to stick to the shadows. I left spying, but I never stopped seeing the world like a G-man, you know? I'd never be a normal college student, an attentive husband, or a loving father, not while various spooks wormed into my life and insisted I snoop for my country. George and his higher-ups trained me well. They thought I'd walk off campus any time they called and embrace whatever life they spelled out.

Who cared if it was a life I didn't want? In trying to out-spook a fellow spy, I'd prevail, or I'd die.

Outdoor air wafted against my face. I crept along a corridor I knew. Its curves climbed toward the grate in my barracks basement. I crawled through it and waited for a clear path to my room. A comforting hush hung over the bank of showers. I stopped in front of a mirror and assessed the damage, but I shouldn't have worried. The guy didn't inflict wounds where anyone could see. Besides, I didn't have time to get clean. Water couldn't fix how the dirt of my past stuck to me. It seeped into my pores and blackened my soul. Nobody ever walked away from shit like that. Even when they tried, it lived in memory.

If I chose to walk away from everything and start a new life, what would happen to me? People in my former business disappeared all the time. They died in the line of duty, a fact we couldn't disclose to the outside, or they immersed themselves in a new identity and sacrificed their previous lives to protect their country.

I crept up the back stairs, glad the place was always emptiest the hour before evening mess. Over-scheduled cadets didn't often take time to change for dinner, unless a dignitary's visit required a dress uniform. Plus, I'd been AWOL all day. Making up a story would be a pain in my ass, especially if my S.O. decided to investigate. He'd plant himself next to my bed and make sure I didn't move until morning, and that would be a problem.

But I made it to my room without encountering a soul. Joe wasn't there. I took advantage of the time to change into my dress uniform, ignoring the bruises and abrasions blooming purple along my rib cage and shoulder blades. Brass buttons eradicated my beating and made me look smart, and my gun added confidence. When I assessed myself in the mirror, my image was perfection, but my insides tumbled with froth. A life of looking over my shoulder wasn't exactly a life worth living, you know?

My roommate breezed into the room and threw his satchel on his bunk. "Hey, Cox, you're in some deep shit, man. You've been AWOL since lunch. The S.O. is pissed. He told me to send you down there as soon as I saw your ass."

I stood taller and watched myself in the mirror. One last glimpse of Cadet Richard Colvin Cox. He smiled and gave me a thumbs up before I lost him in the search for my hat. "You never saw me, Joe."

"If the S.O. or the sentry or pretty much anybody but me catches you here, my pretending not to see you won't matter."

"Just cover for me, okay? If you do, I won't ask for anymore favors the rest of this year."

"Yeah. Right."

"You've gotta cover for me. I'm meeting that George character again. It's the last time."

"I thought you said you didn't like that guy."

"Can't stand him."

"Then why're you risking your entire stash of demerits at the beginning of term? He's not worth it. Just tell him to get lost."

"He's leaving town after dinner. I'm meeting him to make sure he loses my number."

"Why not stand him up tonight and come clean to the S.O.? That'll send the same message and maybe preserve a few demerits in the process."

"Nah, he'll keep coming back unless I tell him I'm done face-to-face. I know the guy, remember?"

Joe took a step toward me. "You in trouble, Cox? I mean, besides the

AWOL thing?"

"Nothing I can't handle if you'll cover for me. Please?"

Water dripped in the sink. He cut his eyes toward it and moved to tighten the tap. "You probably ought to go out through the basement. I'll create a distraction, maybe help you get down there undetected."

I offered my palm, and when he shook it, I avoided his eyes and wondered if his handshake was the last warmth I'd ever know. "Thanks. I owe you."

Joe nodded and left the room. Thirty seconds later, shouts revved in the hallway. Before I changed my mind, I hightailed it down the stairs, buttoning my overcoat as I went. On the ground floor, five or six cadets clustered around the sentry's table, taking turns signing out for mess. I timed my approach and slipped past the sentry as the group left. My destination was opposite him, the stairs leading to the basement, the showers, and the tunnels. I was on the middle landing by the time the door closed, out of view of the sentry.

I breathed deep and tiptoed to the bottom. One bank of showers separated me from the grate that would allow my escape.

I waited until I heard the last cadet start his shower. Water mingled with his off-key rendition of *Mule Train*. I plugged my ears and bolted through the space, not stopping until I replaced the grate and climbed down the ladder into the tunnels.

The mountain groaned. Ice slithered into cracks, the way the government turned honest men and women into spies. Any spook would say he was more honest than the next guy, though. No action was illegal or grotesque if it protected our country.

At least, nothing was illegal or immoral until one had to live with it.

"Here's to taking my first stand," I whispered and pushed through a crevice on the rocky ledge above the river and hunkered down to wait for time to pass.

* * * * * *

Invisible icebergs bumped past the docks. An hour before midnight,

I hiked toward the spot George outlined. Given the murky light, I felt my way to the end of the dock furthest from shore. I couldn't take my own craft, because somebody could connect it to me. George didn't want anyone to find a trace of me when I vanished, which meant he had to provide my getaway ride. Convenient for my purposes, you know? On the side facing away from campus, I found it: A small motorboat, registered to no one, nameless and probably stolen. The keys were in the ignition, and the ice was cleared away from the hull.

I jumped aboard and unmoored the thing. With a grunt, I heaved away from the dock and steered into the current. Toothy ice streaked around the jut of West Point. I hunkered behind the wheel and hoped I wouldn't pass any boats headed upriver. If I wanted to remain hidden, I couldn't risk using my lights until I cleared West Point, but I probably wouldn't use them at all. On such a bitter night, somebody'd take note of a boat on the river, you know?

More ice knocked against the sides of the boat, but I drifted with it. Downriver, I could start the motor without drawing anyone's attention. Last thing I needed was someone saying they heard a motor boat crank up at such-and-such a time. Besides, if all went well, I'd be up with revelry, ready to stand for inspection and take my S.O.'s heat for defying his orders. A few weeks of punishment wasn't a high cost for the life I wanted, right?

I crouched in the bottom of the boat and mapped the heavens. I didn't believe in shooting stars. Superstition was useless horse shit. But if I glimpsed a falling star, I'd still make a wish.

I wanted to live the life I chose, and I didn't care how I made it happen. Like I said, nothing was wrong when it led to something right.

Clouds blocked the moon. I waited until I was well downriver to toggle the key. The boat shuddered into the upriver current, pointed toward a destination beyond West Point. My life would begin again on the shores of the most haunted site on the Hudson. When I got there, where would George be waiting? Would Frank show up? Maybe they'd kill each other and save everybody the trouble. No star fell on that wish, though.

THIRTY-FIVE: THEO

I streaked along a snowy path, buttoning my coat as I ran. A few stars winked through clouds, giving light to the field of ice between the mainland and the island. Wind howled around its ruined crown. I pulled up and pointed. "It looks like we can walk that way."

Merry touched the small of my back. "When I give the signal, follow me across the ice."

"I can lead as well as you. I don't need you to protect me."

"Look, Theo. If anybody is going to fall through the ice, I want it to be me, all right?"

He walked across the frozen river. About halfway to the island, he motioned me forward. I hurried across the ice and joined him. In response, he wrapped me in his arms. Merry's breath stirred my hair and pricked the skin along my spine. We would vanquish Wilkinson. We would save Richard. We would find our way out of Nowhere together.

Merry whispered close to my ear. "Ssshhh. We don't know who's out there, and it's about an hour before midnight. I'll keep you warm for a while, and we'll move a bit at a time, okay?"

I nodded and spooned into him. The river moaned and creaked beneath us, but the ice held. Who knew hearts could thaw? Besides, my father wasn't here to accuse me of betraying him.

Merry broke the spell. His breath sent chill bumps down the side of my neck. "Oh, and thank you."

"For what?"

"For letting me love you again. For a long time, I resented you for picking your father's political career over my love, but it's time to let that go. Whatever comes next, I know I'll take you with me. Somehow."

Wouldn't that be something?

Before I acknowledged Merry's admission, he released and rolled on his stomach. "We've got to get out there. Use your elbows to scoot across the ice. Follow my example, all right?"

It took thirty minutes or so, but we made the north side of the island just as Wilkinson's truck dove off the mainland and thudded onto the ice. It struck with such force. I couldn't believe the ice held. The headlights were off, but I watched it spin in the starlight.

Merry's lips moved against my ear. "Don't move. Let's see where he goes."

I let him watch Wilkinson, because as my last minutes of Nowhere ticked past, I didn't care what the General did. Instead, I buried my face in Merry's leather coat and gulped him in. His scent teased hints of other expeditions. Where did Nowhere take him before he showed up here and dragged me from the river? Like me, he wouldn't remember, but I hoped we'd wake up in some new reality and remember this. I concentrated on the safe weight of his arms, the hardness of his body, and whispered a silent plea. *Please. Let us save Richard from the General and be finished with this place. Let me remember I forgave Merry for rejecting me in life. And let me cross the membrane between Nowhere and what's next and walk into my son's awaiting arms.*

Wilkinson gunned the engine and skidded toward the open channel. Merry's arms tensed around my midsection and whispered, "He can't see where he's going. He's driving the truck into the river. Has to be."

Before I could stop him, he sprinted from our hiding place and tore across the ice. What was he doing?

"Merry! Wait!" I started after him, but his voice stopped me.

"Stay hidden. I don't want the bastard to disappear in the river. We need to make sure he's vanquished and gone."

I crouched behind some rocks and watched the scene play out. Merry sprinted toward the truck, his footsteps sure on the uneven terrain. Wilkinson's truck careened toward the channel. When it reached the outer edge, the ice cracked, and the front wheels dipped into the swift current.

Merry mounted the back of the truck, opened the door, and disappeared inside. I squinted to make out what was happening. My stomach lurched when the ice yielded a little bit more. The frigid river was about to claim the truck and everyone within it. Merry got out through the back door and brought Wilkinson with him. He had one arm around the General's neck. I stayed behind boulders and inched to within earshot, determined to be close enough to help.

Merry hauled the General onto the ice sheet. The truck teetered when they were clear. Wilkinson's words choked through Merry's grip. "Meriwether Lewis. What the hell are you doing here?"

"I'm ready to even the score, Wilkinson. A life for a life. Isn't that what you did when you sent one of your stooges to follow me along the Natchez Trace?"

"Quit choking me. I'll talk."

Merry released the pressure but still kept his arm around the General's neck. "Go on."

"You lost your mind at the end of your life, and you're still crazy."

"Who did you send to kill me?"

Wilkinson clucked his tongue. "Still delusional. I'm sorry your time in Nowhere hasn't rewired the circuits of your brain."

"I always knew what I was doing, you murderous bastard."

A gunshot pinged along the quiet shoreline. I stifled a scream when Merry fell to his knees, but he was still there. He didn't disappear into his next Nowhere life. My Great Explorer was still alive. He lost his hold on the General and rocked back and forth on the ice, fighting to stand again.

The General slithered beyond Merry's reach and kept his gun leveled.

He took his time on the approach while Merry writhed in pain. "You shot me in the hip."

"I was aiming for your ass."

"I wanted to be the one to kill you. Damn, I should've let you drown."

"You never were very good with tactics."

"Why don't you go ahead and finish me one more time?"

"Oh, I plan to." Wilkinson hooked his hands under Merry's armpits and dragged him across the ice. A bloody swath marked the ice as they moved toward the truck. They were beyond my range of hearing, but it didn't matter. I was frozen in place.

He hoisted Merry into the truck on the driver's side and fired five more rounds. When the gun was empty, he reared back and shouted, "Too bad you never learned to drive."

From behind, he heaved the truck into the channel. It tipped into open water and listed to one side. Ice-clogged river rushed in sideways. Wilkinson didn't stay to watch Merry vanish. Instead, he tromped across the ice, headed for the other side of the island.

I had to save Merry.

I bolted from my hiding place and ran across the ice. The truck was marooned on its right side with its roof sinking into the river, and I couldn't see inside. Ice shattered, and water poured into broken windows. The truck flipped upside down, its wet wheels gleaming in the moonlight. Merry was trapped, and I couldn't just let him die.

Without thinking, I dove into the ice-clogged water. I tugged at the doors until my fingers turned numb. In a rush of adrenaline, I crashed my fists through the windows and cleared giant daggers of glass. Still, I didn't find Merry inside.

Merry.

I swallowed part of the river with my scream and kicked against the truck to escape my own watery grave. I dragged myself onto firm ice and lay there, frozen and panting. Merry's disembodied voice shuddered through me. "You can't save me, Theo. It's too late. Try to remember how much I've always loved you and everything we were willing to forgive."

He wouldn't remember our time together, but it didn't stop me from grieving. I was still alive.

The weight of his voice swatted me face-first into the ground. Merry was gone, back to his New Orleans bar and his stingy bartender. I was left to finish my Nowhere assignment alone, and I was certain of two things. I had to kill the General and show Richard the path to his best life. It had to be why I survived.

Wilkinson wouldn't be surprised to see me. When I dragged myself across the ice and confronted him, I would be ready to kill.

THIRTY-SIX: RICHARD

There it was: Bannerman's Island. I remembered riding to Newburgh on the bus, staring at the spot in the river from my perch on Storm King Mountain. A rocky oval, it resisted the Hudson's pull for ten thousand years, but I was partial to the old castle ruin. Natives called it Pollepel, place of ghosts and ancient spirits, but I always thought of the story of that old Lenape witch-woman. It was a romantic notion, being able to come to the river and see the spirit of a dead loved one a final time. In the end, those stories were bull, but for the living, it was a comfort to believe they were true.

I gunned the boat's engine and turned away from the current, looking for solid ice to ditch the boat and walk ashore. I figured George was already there, and maybe Frank too, but I wasn't worried about them. If Gudrid delivered a strike team or even a sniper, George wouldn't be my problem. Maybe they'd pop Frank for good measure, and I'd ambush her and her team. I was determined enough to blow every mother fucking one of them away. I didn't care about what was right anymore. I was willing to kill for the life I wanted.

I bumped the boat against an ice sheet and threw one leg over the side. When I tested it, it crackled underfoot but held me. I scanned the wavy line where land began.

Bannerman's didn't really have a beach. It was a stubborn outcrop the glaciers couldn't scrape free. The approach was tricky, because the terrain offered nowhere to hide. I slipped on uneven ice, but I didn't bother to muffle my step. I smelled George's cigar before he stepped from behind a boulder near the frozen waterline. Orange embers wagged between his lips. "Dickie-boy. Glad you joined me."

Tobacco tickled my nostrils, but I faced him head-on. "Yeah, George. Or is it Wilkinson?"

He stepped toward me and blew smoke rings in my face. "Wilkinson. Haven't used that name in years."

"But it's your name, right?"

"In this business, you'll learn to forget old names and given monikers. Who I was doesn't matter, because I can be whoever I want."

"You're talking in circles without saying anything. Are you really a general? And if you are, why can't I find any record of you in the library?"

"Once we're out of here, you'll look back on your old life the same way. Who we were doesn't matter. We're on this planet to protect Americans, those living today and those yet to come."

Not this again. Where was Gudrid's promised team? How long would I have to stand in the cold and keep George talking before they showed up and shot him or took him away or whatever it was they needed to do? And where was Frank?

With my mission going to hell, I puffed out my chest. I had to keep him talking and buy some time. "If you expect me to go with you, at least tell me who you really are."

"Who I am is irrelevant. Come on, Dickie-boy. Embrace the possibility of who you can be."

"Is that why you kill people? To embrace possibility?"

He threw his cigar across the ice and sighed. "I kill people because it's necessary. My job keeps the American people safe. I don't like it, but I'm a good soldier. I do the job I'm given."

"So that's how you live with yourself. You believe you're a good soldier, doing the right thing."

"I'm doing the only thing, the best thing. Do you understand that? We're up against a threat to our very existence. And you and me? We're on this earth to make sure the right side wins."

"I'm not the soldier you think I am, George. I can't be like you."

"You don't have to be me to grasp the stakes. We could be nuked to bits any second by the Soviets. We're being overrun by enemies intent upon robbing us of our freedom bit by bit. I want to nail those bastards before they make it to our shores. I'm a patriot and a soldier when most guys in the organization still don't want to do what it takes to be free."

"I'm one of them, George. I don't want any part of this business. I walked away from West Germany because I saw where that life would lead. I kept secrets from my mother and cheated my future in the name of world peace, and for what? When we blow one enemy away, ten more rise up in their place."

"But you have the satisfaction of knowing you made a difference."

"I don't give a shit about that kind of difference. I want a life without regrets, George. Don't you have somebody who loves you? One person who wants you to come home? Someone who'll remember you when you're gone?"

George's lips wavered. "I had a wife. Once."

"What happened to her? She divorced your ass because you were always lying?"

Before I could react, George covered the ice between us and grabbed me by the neck. His ashtray breath wasn't enough air to sustain me, but if he kept squeezing, it wouldn't matter. Spittle rained down one side of my face. "My wife died. She died, you son of a bitch. An incompetent took my job, and they banished us to a climate that didn't agree with my wife's condition. I was working on a way to move us to a better place when her body gave up." I didn't realize he was crying until his fingers relaxed. "You're too young to know what it's like to watch your world die."

I rubbed my neck and pushed away from him. When I spoke, my voice rasped. "Is that why you're so good at this game?"

"I'm so good because it's what I know. Spying's all I've ever done. I keep thinking if I'm thorough enough, maybe I'll see my wife again. She begged me to find her. She believed I loved her enough to reunite with her soul someday. She's the only person who's ever mattered. I look for her everywhere, all the time. Just like I promised, and I'm willing to kill anyone who gets in my way."

Where was Gudrid's team? I couldn't keep George yapping much longer. If they didn't show up soon, I was going to have to take him out on my own. Or go with him. I shuddered. Going with him wasn't an option.

I rubbed my neck and kept talking. "What's wrong with my finding a love like that? With rejecting the world of the spy for a picket-fence kind of life?"

"Nothing's wrong with it until it breaks you. Trust me. I'm offering you the chance to avoid my heartache."

"But what about Frank, huh? He wants me to stay stateside. Work with him here."

"Higher-ups'll never stand for that, Dickie. Frank's a damn renegade, and you know it."

"He says you're a double agent, switch-hitting for the Soviets."

"Bastard sells guns to the Soviets, so he's a fine one to accuse me of duplicity."

"Duplicity is such a relative term." Frank stepped from the trees. "I'm one of those people who can honestly say I've always been true to myself."

George stalked across the ice and shook his hand. "I thought you'd never show up. I'm freezing my ass off out here."

"You know I had something to take care of. It took longer than we planned."

I ratcheted my head between the two of them. George *and* Frank?

George was working with Frank?

Fuck me. They were working together all along.

Frank talked like we were at a Sunday picnic, pleasant and warm and maddening. "Killing Gudrid was easy. She gets around a bit slower these days."

I was afraid to move. Instead, I whispered, "Gudrid?"

George's face didn't alter while Frank talked. "Rest of the team were a challenge. Proper tool for the proper job, though. And you know I've got some proper tools."

Frank paced around me, warming up to his story. Bastard must've been laughing at me all week. Hell, they probably both were. And they thought I could be a decent spy?

A worthy spy didn't wind up in the middle of a frozen river in January without any backup, because Gudrid and her team clearly weren't coming. I should've scoped out the rendezvous point earlier. I could've picked the best hiding place and set up my own sniper stand. It would've been fun to pick them off one by one.

Instead, I marched into an ambush with no team covering me. My smart ass would soon be a dead ass.

I concentrated on Frank's voice. "Gudrid gave you up, Cox. She and her guys aren't coming to save you. And they aren't going to assassinate George and me."

George laughed. "Ah, just like Alice, Dickie-boy. She also tried to get out by forcing the system to shut us down. You already know how that worked out for her."

Frank piped up. "When Alice figured things out, she got really unhinged, unreliable. She tried to close all the doors and reached out to all her contacts…our contacts. She started to undo things at exactly the wrong time, as things were already getting really hot. She tried to reach out to you, Cox. She contacted me to get to you."

Frank turned towards George and raised his Walther. "What I'd like to know is how she found out about me. When she got manic, she got sloppy. This was going to be my biggest arms deal. I was selling the secrets to a hydrogen bomb. You told me she and Fuchs were golden, George. But now she's dead and he's just a finch…and he's going to fink on us at his trial."

A gunshot zinged through the tail end of Frank's accusations. I fell to the ground, eyes blinded and ears ringing. Was death an assault on the senses? But when I surveyed my surroundings, I only saw mangled meat where Frank's face used to be.

George wheeled on me. "Damn Frank was an idiot to trust me. And you shouldn't have gone to Gudrid. But then you and Alice were cut from the same cloth. And just like her, you have no idea how deep in it you are. You're a traitor to your country. That's right, Dickie, you've been a traitor for years now, and you never knew it. All the work you two were doing was not to protect the US of A. You worked for me, for my purposes." He laughed again. "You should've paid better attention in your history courses. I've been doing this for years, decades. Longer than you can imagine. The first time I tried it was with Theo's father. He was ambitious and eager and smart like you, Dickie-boy. But when he realized how I tricked him into treachery, he tried to undermine the deal. He threatened to throw it all away. My only mistake was letting him try to work his way out of it. He was a master in the courtroom, and he got himself off. But he was ruined, and all the publicity put me at risk. I never made that mistake again, and I won't make it now." He raised his gun. "You've only got one choice. Come with me now, or you're done."

I got up and faced George head-on. Frank was right about one thing: The only truth was truth to self. "I'm never going back, George. I don't care what you do. I'm done with that life."

"Wrong answer. I got you into this, and I'm the only one who could ever get you out of it."

"I would never knowingly use my skills to betray my country. Never."

George cocked the trigger. I balled my fist, ready to render him a mess of cartilage and bone, but another person streaked over a boulder and knocked him sideways. His mouth wide, he toppled and careened along the rocky shoreline. Bone crunched when his head crashed into a boulder. Maybe the impact killed him.

But damn, his attacker wanted to make sure. She slashed George's torso with shards of glass, opening bloody gouges in skin and wool. When her fury was spent, she pivoted and flashed crazed eyes toward me.

"Theo? What are you—"

"Doing here?" She threw glass daggers on the ground and waved her lacerated palms in my face. "I'm finishing my mission," she spat, oblivious to blood splatter on my uniform. "I lost Merry. I won't lose you, too."

"Who's Merry? Who are you working with?"

She advanced toward me. "I'm getting everything back on track."

I backed away from her. "I'm not spying. Not with you or George. Not with anybody, Theo."

"But that's why I'm here. That's my assignment."

"Assignment?"

"To keep you from going with George, yes, because the life he offers will require you to disappear. Believe me, you don't want to disappear. I'm here to help you choose your best life, which leads to the life I want."

"And what's that?"

"I want to see my son again. To hold him and tell him how much I love him one more time. Or as many times as I can, if the rules allow."

"What rules?"

She sank onto a rock and winced as she picked glass from her hands. Blood dribbled onto the snow at her feet. I fished through my inner pockets and handed her a handkerchief. She pressed it between her shattered hands and looked up at me. "You've only been right about one thing, Richard. I'm not who I said I was."

"Then tell me who you are and how you know George. How you really know him."

* * * THEO * * *

"Yes, Theodosia Burr Alston. Let's tell him how you know General James Wilkinson."

After what I did to him, I didn't know how the General materialized, but somehow he did. I tried not to flinch when he aimed the tip of his gun at my temple.

"From the moment you were born, Theo, I knew you held all the promise of the world. So beautiful, so intelligent, so ambitious. You were everything to your father, like your son was to you, like my wife Ann will be to me again. You will always shoulder the regret of not living up to all that promise. But me? My biggest regret is that I can only kill you one Nowhere life at a time."

The bullet seared like a red hot poker as it broke the thin white skin of my temple. I groped the torn edges of my skull and studied my fingers. How long would it take to die? The world already receded, its borders ripped and wasted, but still I clung to it. Richard. He could defeat Wilkinson. Maybe he could save me.

Richard leapt up with a gun in one hand, aimed at Wilkinson's black heart, but the General knew the rules of a duel. He turned his gun upon Richard. His narrowest profile was exposed when he took careful aim. My fourth Nowhere life melted into the ice, but not before I heard one final shot.

THIRTY-SEVEN: RICHARD

The Quartermaster was always my favorite person in the Army, because he always gave more than he got. He was the guy who handed out the supplies, after all. He thumbed through tan uniforms and gestured to a chair. "Richard Cox. Have a seat and let me see what I can do about rustling up some duds in your size."

I ignored his request to sit, unease building in my gut. "But I'm not in the Army anymore. I left that life a long time ago."

"And it seems to have chosen you again." He pulled out a pair of khaki slacks and threw them my way. "Slip those on, will you?"

"Wait a minute." I missed the pants on purpose. They landed near my feet. "What the hell is going on here? Because I'm done with the Army."

The bastard pulled out a couple of brimmed hats to match the pants I refused to touch. He eyed my head and held up the one on the left. "I think this one will fit. Try it."

"No. I'm not touching a thing until you tell me what I'm doing here." I strode toward the door. "In fact, maybe I'll just walk."

"Oh, you can't do that, Cox. You have a mission."

I reached toward the doorknob, but I couldn't make my fingers touch it. No matter how I strained, the door remained a few inches away. I gave up and whirled on him. "What the hell?"

"Welcome to Nowhere, Richard Cox."

THE NEW YORK TIMES
JANUARY 17, 1957

West Point, New York - Richard Colvin Cox was officially declared deceased today. The West Point sophomore was last seen leaving his barracks on the evening of January 14, 1950 and disappeared without a trace. During the investigation, his roommate reported that Cox planned to meet someone for a meal at Hotel Thayer. Cox never signed in at the dining room. Campus logs indicate he never officially left West Point. No clue to Cox's whereabouts was ever found. He was twenty-one years old. He is the only cadet to ever vanish from West Point.

THIRTY-EIGHT: THEO

My Conductor approached along the train's corridor and stopped next to my seat. One word would erase my last Nowhere life. I clung to memories of Richard, of Merry, of everything I learned. Did Wilkinson trick my father into committing treason? Did he kill me? Could I find my son again? Was it true?

I gazed into my Conductor's dead eyes and willed him not to say it. My wishes didn't matter. He uttered it anyway.

"Theodosia."

When a person stands in front of a mirror, she clings to the vision she sees. She is the sum of her memories. But when someone cracks the frame, takes a sledgehammer to the glass, and throws the shards into an unknown heap, she is left with one certainty. Somewhere on the wall, she used to see a mirror. She doesn't recall what it showed her, but she's certain it was there.

Metal squealed against track, and a patchwork of steel beams knit muddy water to sky. Bridges punctuated my return to the Nowhere landscape. Where did I come from? How did I wind up here?

"Conductor."

"I'm sorry to see you again."

I gripped his lapels and shook him. "Tell me how to get out of this place. Please."

He sat next to me and took my hands. "Why do you think you failed again?"

"Don't answer me with questions. I didn't complete my assignment."

"Which was?"

"You know I can't recall specifics."

"Be general then."

"To help someone navigate a crossroads and choose their best life."

"You're here for the fifth time. Why is this task so hard for you?"

"If I knew the answer, I wouldn't be here, would I? I'm begging you. Stop talking in riddles. I'm not a patient, and you're not my therapist. I need you to tell me how to get out of here this time."

"I'm not omniscient. I lead you to an assignment, but the rest is up to you."

"I don't believe you."

"Anything more is against the rules."

"Fuck the rules."

"I'm sorry?"

"You heard me. I said fuck the rules. You have to help me complete my assignment and escape this place. I know I can find a better life."

He rested his hand on my stomach. "Use what you're given. You won't be alone to fight your worst enemy this time."

"My worst enemy?"

"I've already said too much." He stood and straightened his jacket. "I have other Nowhere tickets to punch. Remember what I said."

My Conductor left me as the Nowhere train shuddered across a bridge. Without heed to propriety, I unbuttoned my blouse and fanned my soaked camisole. So hot. So humid. I once endured the pestilential South, the place that robbed me of my son. Nowhere mocked me, sending me anywhere near there.

"Last stop. New Orleans. New Orleans, Louisiana is the train's last stop. Everyone, please exit the train to your left."

I balanced my leather handbag on my knees and chuckled.

New Orleans. Hell finally claimed me.

Smokestacks belched filth into the soupy atmosphere. Heat baked low rooftops and streets. When we chugged toward the bend in the river, I expected to find it a boiling cauldron.

My father once described New Orleans through the veil of his world view. "The gateway to our family's future," he called it. Since he was arrested, I always imagined New Orleans as a hell bulging with vice. A place where a soul was forced to commit its gravest sin, over and over and over for all eternity, but without the desired result. A drinking binge that never yielded the stupor. Promiscuous sex that didn't result in climax. Gluttons who were always hungry. Or in my case, I would relive the feverish attempt to save my son and watch him die, because my greatest sin, my defining regret, was losing a child I should've saved. I disappeared when I should've died, and Nowhere was my eternal punishment.

I mopped my cheeks with a scrap of fabric. "ML" was stitched in red along one corner. When my hand fell open, I read faint words in my handwriting. *My son forgave me.*

When did I see my son?

Salt stung my eyes. I strained and failed to remember who or what it meant. Clues were useless. They never jogged my memory. I was a cipher.

I heaved myself sideways and scanned my compartment. But for a solitary man in uniform, I was alone. He flicked through a newspaper, its headline blaring something about war in Viet Nam. The place was a southeast Asian backwater when I disappeared I-didn't-know-how-many-years ago.

Was America always at war? No matter the decade, regardless of the generation, human beings would kill for money and power. I'd never forget that detail, because the next crop of people would always be there to remind me.

The soldier was younger than I first imagined, perhaps even a new recruit. When he glanced in my direction, I waved, just a little flutter. He lowered his newspaper a few inches. His eyes were welcoming in a way that emboldened me. "I'm sorry to trouble you, but I seem to have misplaced my calendar. What's today's date?"

"Uh. Says here it's November 15."

"And the year?"

"1967."

"Thank you."

He nodded and dove behind a wall of events, things that were already history, while I scratched my stomach. Fresh sweat ran into my eyes. Air shifted, and I whirled to find the soldier standing next to me. He still grasped the newspaper. The seal of the United States Army rested on the crest of his hat. "Thought you might like to read up, Theo. You know, before we head into whatever's next."

"How do you know my name?"

"You don't remember me, but it doesn't matter. I'll never forget you."

He stepped through an open door before I organized my thoughts, swallowed by an atmosphere laden with steam and debauchery. I strained to read the tag on his jacket, but he was already too far from the train.

I lurched toward the door and called him, but he was lost in the frenzied activity along the levee. My head spun with it all. Steamboats disgorged people, and trucks laden with goods zipped in and out of warehouses. In my lifetime, New Orleans was an important port. Why should it be any different in 1967?

Newsprint crinkled between my fingers. I flipped through the pages seeking something, anything to give me a clue. On page five, I found it. Black-and-white accentuated the folds of James Wilkinson's face. A triangle of shirt-and-tie peeked from the neck of his black robe. Wilkinson, a judge? Of all people, he was the last person worthy of judging others.

I tore the paper with shaking hands, but I managed to preserve the story.

The Conductor called out from the back of the car. "Why are you still here?"

I lumbered down the aisle and grabbed his stiff arm. "Please. Tell me how to avoid becoming like you. I'm running out of chances."

"I'm giving you one forgotten memory. Use it well."

Before I could beg him for more, my Conductor pushed me through the door, banged it closed, and left me on a platform outside an empty rail car.

As I turned toward the city, my belly lurched. I couldn't remember who planted her inside me, but I knew she'd be a girl. Mothers often know.

I only wanted to stare into her eyes and compare them to my son's. Would she look like him? Could she ever fill the void he left? Would Nowhere try to force me to let her go?

I thwacked along the train platform to the tune of zydeco. "Judges aren't immune from judgment," I whispered. "I'll do anything to defeat you, James Wilkinson. Anything."

THIRTY-NINE: THEO

I stood along the frozen shore of the river of my birth. Confused, I blinked into the kohl eyes of a woman. Her tanned skin betrayed her heritage. She was a layer of the Hudson Valley's ancient history, one I peeled away when I was a girl.

"I remember you," I murmured. "You're the Lenape woman. The spirit who lives in the river. The one who reveals the souls we miss most."

She brought one slender finger to her lips. Her *shh* fluffed tree branches and rearranged clouds on high. Through low haze, I thought I glimpsed the north star, but it melted into her face, cheek-to-cheek with mine. She touched my hand, and I floated on her skirt's hem and followed her to the river. We crossed the glittering ice field and flew above the channel to the imposing base of Storm King Mountain.

I used to picnic there with my son. We watched sails billow around the edges of Pollepel.

She shook her mane, and water droplets streamed along my face. Or were they tears? I hovered between earth and sky, waiting. Her hand plunged into the water and revealed what she came to show me.

Her watery arms held my son. He was still ten years old, perfect and whole. I reached toward him and strained to touch his cheek, to feel his fingers twine with mine. When I opened my mouth, I could only whisper, "Do you remember me?"

His little face didn't alter, but water clogged the corner of one eye. He mouthed the words, "You don't need to say you're sorry, Mommy. I know you loved me. I'll always know it."

I moved to take him in my arms and fell into the abyss, the tunnel of madness that led where Nowhere always did. Down and down, through icy river and granite until the margins tore away the layers of time. A train whistle echoed through the void. When I turned to face it, light was day.

My boy was gone, but I wasn't alone. I carried the light of his words inside me as I trudged along the platform.

Nowhere might erase everything about my last experience, but it wouldn't rob me of my son. I clicked open my purse and scrounged for a pen. Before my Conductor spoke my name and claimed my memory, I carved four words into my left palm.

My son forgave me.

Want more stories like this?
Be first to know about new books from Andra Watkins!

Subscribe to her newsletter for new releases, instant freebies, and more!
andrawatkins.com

ACKNOWLEDGEMENTS

This isn't a history book. And it is. History is far more than facts and figures; it is also flesh and fervor. While I endeavor to adhere to historical evidence, I'm a fiction writer. My narrative is driven by a desire to breathe in the people and places of the past, and to exhale their essence beyond the bounds of time. I use historical passion and conflict, both documented and rumored, to construct afterlife stories for real people whose deaths remain unresolved, mysterious. Readers eager to learn more about the characters in this story can explore the list following these acknowledgements.

Theodosia Burr Alston was the ill-fated daughter of Aaron Burr. History remembers him as the man who shot Alexander Hamilton in a duel, but he also allegedly conspired to invade Mexico with General James Wilkinson. Their intentions for that venture remain shrouded by history. Burr was tried for treason when Wilkinson reported their scheme to President Thomas Jefferson as Burr's alone. Aaron Burr was acquitted, but he spent several years in exile. Less than a month after he returned to America, his ten-year-old grandson, Theodosia's son, died of malaria.

A grief-stricken Theodosia boarded a ship in Georgetown, South Carolina. She was bound for New York City to reunite with her father when her ship disappeared. While historians assume she drowned, her disappearance fueled sensational rumors. Did pirates force her to walk the plank? Was she captured by the British and taken to England? Did her ship sink in a storm? We will likely never know, but I used those elements to craft her afterlife story.

Did Theodosia Burr have an affair with Meriwether Lewis, captain of the Lewis and Clark Expedition to the Pacific? They certainly knew each other and even corresponded in life. While they were considered the most eligible bachelor and bachelorette of their era, we have no proof of a romantic liaison. Amorous rumors swirled around them, however. I used those unsubstantiated stories to craft my own.

James Wilkinson has been accused of assassinating numerous people, including Meriwether Lewis. We have no evidence that he was involved in the deaths of Theodosia and her son.

As stated in the novel, Richard Colvin Cox is the only cadet to ever disappear from West Point. Harry J. Maihafer's book *Oblivion* attempts to solve that mystery, though no one will likely ever know whether he succeeded.

In addition to using historical conflict to weave a new story, I also explore the layers of a landscape to populate my novels with ancillary characters. The Hudson Valley is full of worthy people to feature. It was hard to winnow them down to the ones readers met on these pages.

Both Henry Hudson (Mr. Henry) and Jane McCrea (the ferry captain) are Hudson Valley fixtures. In 1611, Hudson's crew mutinied and set him adrift in Hudson Bay. The exact details of his death remain a mystery. While no one knows exactly who killed her, Jane McCrea's 1777 death became the stuff of lore. In the most prevalent story, she was murdered by a native tribe loyal to the British.

Frank Banner is drawn from the life of Francis Bannerman, the Scotsman who built an arms empire and started construction of the castle on Pollepel (Bannerman's Island.) He died during routine surgery in 1918, leaving the building unfinished.

The Lenape woman of the river is part of Hudson Valley legend, and I tried to incorporate her in a way that would honor the native peoples there.

Gudrid is drawn from Icelandic sagas. She is known as the first Viking woman to give birth in North America. While nothing indicates she ever visited what was to become New York state, a lone rock with Viking-like carvings exists in the Hudson Valley today.

Alice is part of Richard Cox's mystery. Witnesses claimed he cried out for her a few nights before he vanished. No one knows why she mattered to him or even if that's what he actually said, but it was fun to imagine a story for her.

Though Cox had two roommates when he disappeared, I streamlined them into one character for simplicity.

Of course, Theodosia's Conductor is a figment of my imagination.

I have a few people to thank.

Amber Deutsch, thank you for continuing to be my long-suffering beta reader. You take these stories when they're garbage, and you somehow highlight the glimpses of what they could be. My books are always better because you read them first.

Nicole Leigh Shaw, thank you for lending this story your editing wizardry. For the first time, I enjoyed plowing through almost 4,000 edit notes. Your keen observations and unfiltered criticism made this a better book.

Brian PJ Cronin, thank you for allowing your Hudson Valley photography to be used throughout this story. The imagery contributes to the novel's atmosphere.

Word Hermit Press, LLC, thank you for bringing another Andra Watkins title to readers everywhere and for nominating this book for the 2016 National Book Award.

Smith Publicity, thank you for taking a chance on this story. From the first time you heard about it, you believed this book deserved a broad reach, and you worked to make it happen.

Jendi Pagano, thank you for tending to the dirty details of my author life. As my assistant, you help me make more words than I otherwise would. I can't imagine a career without you.

Veronica Calarco and Stiwdio Maelor in Corris, Wales, thank you for selecting me as writer-in-residence. The quiet atmosphere and plentiful walks helped me polish this story.

Linda and Roy Watkins, thank you for believing in me. I couldn't ask for better parents.

Michael T. Maher, thank you for saying hello, for giving me another chance when I stood you up, for marrying me, and for backing me in this crazy journey. You never give up on me. I love you.

And thank you, Dear Reader. I wrote this story for you. I didn't create it to be yet another book for your exploding to-be-read list. I promise not to bug you (much) to write reviews and share it a billion times on social media. In the twenty-first century, we've turned reading into a chore, when it was supposed to be a relaxing escape from reality. It's a world to live lives and visit places we might not otherwise get to experience. Stories top off the well of our lives when we're dry. Thank you for giving me a few hours and your imagination. If you have something to share, I'd love to hear from you at readme@andrawatkins.com.

Interior photo credits:
Brian PJ Cronin: frontispiece, pp. 11, 17, 29, 117, 157, 163
Andra Watkins: pp. 49, 69, 81, 95, 101, 129, 135, 171, 181, 187, 201, 213, 221

LIST OF ADDITIONAL READING

Burr by Gore Vidal
Oblivion by Henry J. Maihafer
Theodosia Burr Alston: Portrait of a Prodigy by Richard N. Cote
Meriwether Lewis: The Assassination of an American Hero and the Silver Mines of Mexico by Kira Gale

QUESTIONS FOR READING GROUPS

1. How complicated was Theodosia's relationship with her father? How does it compare with your relationship to your own dad? Do you think their bond was healthy? Why or why not?

2. Richard Cox wants to restart his life after a stint as a Cold War spy. Do you think it's ever possible to walk away from such a life? Why or why not?

3. Theodosia disappeared at sea in early 1813. After reading this story, what do you think happened to her? Do you think anyone will ever solve the mystery of her disappearance?

4. Do you think Richard is immediately attracted to Theodosia, or is he grasping at anything to establish a normal life? Do you think his feelings change over the course of the book? If so, how?

5. The General believes his nefarious actions are justified because he's keeping America safe from the Soviet threat. Is it ever acceptable to commit a crime to protect people? Why or why not?

6. Theodosia blamed herself for her son's death. As a mother, is it ever possible to accept that some events lie beyond the bounds of parenting? Why or why not?

7. Do you believe Theo really saw her son? Or was it an illusion caused by her death?

8. Meriwether Lewis never married. Theodosia married in 1801 at the age of eighteen. We have no concrete evidence they ever met, let alone fell in love or had a passionate affair. Since their day, stories about their romance are unsubstantiated hearsay. However, other unsubstantiated stories, like the Viking sagas, have been proven true through modern archeology and science, at least in part. Do you believe historical rumors present lost bits of history, details skewed by the winners to reflect badly on their enemies or tarnish their legacies? Or do you believe historical rumors are as fictitious as the story woven in this book? Why or why not?

TO LIVE FOREVER:
AN AFTERLIFE JOURNEY OF MERIWETHER LEWIS
(excerpt)

EMMALINE

A New Orleans Courtroom

Thursday

March 24, 1977

A drop of sweat hung from the end of my nose. I watched it build, cross-eyed, before I shook my head and made it fall. It left wet circles on the front of my dress.

"Emmaline. Be still, Child." Aunt Bertie fanned her face and neck with a paper fan, the one with the popsicle stick handle.

A popsicle would be so good.

The waiting room of the court in New Orleans was full. People were everywhere I looked.

Reporters in stripey suits talked with some of Daddy's musician friends. I loved to watch their fingers play imaginary guitars or pound out chords on their legs. Once or twice, Daddy's band members came over to squeeze my arm or pat my head. "In spite of what they's saying in that courtroom, we all love your daddy, Kid."

Everybody loved Daddy. Well, everybody except Mommy.

My nose burned when I breathed, because the whole room stank like sweaty feet. My face was steamy when I touched it, and my lace tights scratched when I kicked my legs to push along the wooden bench. I left a puddle when I moved.

I snuggled closer to the dark folds and softness of Aunt Bertie. She turned her black eyes down at me and sighed before pushing me away with her dimpled hand. "Too hot, Child. When this is done, I'll hold you as long as you want."

I slid back to my wet spot on the bench. The wood made a hard pillow when I leaned my head against it and closed my eyes. Wishes still worked for nine-year-old girls, didn't they?

I thought and thought. If I wanted it enough, maybe I could shrink myself smaller. It was hard to be outside the courtroom, imagining what was going on inside. Behind the heavy doors, Mommy and Daddy probably shouted mean things at each other, like they used to at home. Both of them said they wanted me, if they had to fight until they were dead.

I watched Mommy's lady friends go into the courtroom: Miss Roberta in her drapey dress with flowers, Miss Chantelle all in white against the black of her skin, and Miss Emilie in a red skirt and coat that tied at her waist in a pretty bow. They all went in and came out, and they always looked at me. Miss Roberta even left a red lipstick kiss on my cheek, but I don't like her, so I rubbed it off.

Aunt Bertie took her turn inside the courtroom, leaving me to sit with a reporter. He watched me from behind thick black glasses, and he asked me all kinds of questions about Daddy and Mommy. I didn't understand much. I knew Daddy was famous, at least in New Orleans, but I didn't understand what the word "allegations" meant.

My daddy was Lee Cagney. People called him "The Virtuoso of Dixieland Jazz." He played the upright bass, and when he sang, his voice made women act silly in the middle of Bourbon Street. They cried and screamed. Some of them even tore their clothes.

I understood why women loved Daddy. I adored him, too. But some grown women sure did act dumb.

Anyway.

None of the lawyers asked me who I wanted to be with.

The Judge said I was too little to understand, and Mommy agreed. But if they asked me, I would shout it all the way to Heaven: I wanted to be with Daddy.

When he sang *Ragtime Lullaby*, the sound of his voice put me to sleep.

He always splashed in the fountain with me in front of the Cathedral and gave me pennies to throw in the water. Thursday afternoons before his gigs, he sat with me at Café du Monde, sharing beignets with as much powdered sugar as I wanted. He didn't even mind my sticky fingers when he held my hand. He wasn't always there when I had nightmares, but he came to see me first thing in the morning.

People around me whispered about Daddy's "adulterous proclivities." I didn't understand what that meant, but it had something to do with his loving other women besides Mommy. No matter what they said, Daddy didn't do anything wrong. When he wasn't playing music, he was always with me.

Wasn't he?

A skinny reporter held the courtroom door open. "The Judge's ruling." He whispered, but his voice was loud enough for everyone waiting to hear. He kept the door open, and I saw my chance.

I struggled through all the legs to the door. Mommy's red lips curled in a smile as the Judge addressed Daddy. The Judge's face was loose, like the bulldog that lived in the house around the corner, and his voice boomed in my chest. When he stood and leaned over his desk, his hairy hands gripped the gavel.

"In the case of Cagney v. Cagney, I am charged with finding the best outcome for a little girl. For rendering a verdict that will shape the whole of her life. The welfare of the child is paramount, regardless of how it will impact the adults involved."

The Judge stopped and cleared his throat. I held my breath when his baggy eyes fell on me. I counted ten heartbeats before he talked again. "Mr. Cagney, I simply cannot ignore the fact that you had carnal relations with your then-wife's lady friends repeatedly, both under your shared roof and in broad daylight. The photographic evidence coupled with the testimonies of these poor women damns you, regardless of your expressed love for your daughter. From everything I've seen and heard in this courtroom, the evidence does not support your claim that you were set up. Justice demands that your nine-year-old daughter be delivered into the arms of the person who has demonstrated that she has the capability to be a responsible parent."

He looked around the room and sat up straight in his chair. "I am granting sole custody of Emmaline Cagney to her mother, Nadine Cagney, and I hereby approve her request to block Lee Cagney from any and all contact with his daughter until she reaches the age of eighteen. Mr. Cagney, should you violate this directive, you will be found in contempt of this court, an offense that may be punishable by imprisonment of up to 120 days and a fine of no more than $500 per occurrence. This court is adjourned."

He pounded a wooden stick on his desk, and everyone swarmed like bees. Daddy stood up and shook his fist. He shouted at the Judge over all the other noise. "Lies! Set out to ruin my reputation—my memory—in the eyes of my daughter! I'll appeal, if I have to spend every dime of my money. I'll—"

The Judge banged his stick again, lots of times, while my eyes met Daddy's. I ran from the doorway. The room was like the obstacle course on the playground, only with people who reached for me while the Judge boomed, "Order! Order! I will have order in my court!"

Daddy's lawyer held him and whispered something in his ear. It was my chance. I ran toward Daddy and his crying blue eyes. They matched mine, because I was crying, too.

Daddy elbowed his lawyer into the railing and reached out his hand. "Come to me, Baby."

I kicked at pants legs and stomped on shiny shoes. At the front, I stuck my hand through the bars and stretched as far as I could. My fingers almost reached his when my head jerked like I was snagged at the end of a fishing pole.

Mommy had the ties at the back of my white pinafore. Her glossy red lips fake-smiled. "I'm taking Emmaline now, Lee. Good luck to you."

She squeezed my hand. Her red fingernails dug into my skin.

"Ow, Mommy. You're hurting me."

Her high heels clack-clack-clacked as she dragged me through the chairs and down the aisle toward the waiting room. I planted my heels and tried to get one last look, my mind taking a picture of Daddy. Before we got through the door, I saw his shoulders shake. Three policemen held him back and kept him from following me. The world was blurry like the time I swam to the bottom of a pool and opened my eyes underwater.

Mommy picked me up and cradled me in her arms. Her blood-tipped fingers stroked my hair, but her lips whispered a different story, one the crowd couldn't hear. "Stop crying, Emmaline. You know this is for the best." She shifted me to the ground and adjusted the wide sash of her floor-length dress. Its sleeves fanned out as she pushed the bar on the door. I wished she'd take off and fly away.

Summer heat turned my tears to steam, and my eyes ached. Mommy struggled to pull me along through the reporters that blocked the path to the car. They shouted questions, but I didn't hear them. All I heard were Daddy's words. "Come to me, Baby."

Mommy smiled and pressed our bodies through the people. She kept her gaze glued on the car.

Aunt Bertie waited behind the wheel of Mommy's fancy red Cadillac Eldorado. Mommy always said the whole name with a funny accent. The engine was running. "There's Bertie. In you go, Emmaline. I'm ready to be done with this madness."

My legs squeaked across the hot back seat. Mommy ran her fingers under my eyes to wipe away my tears, but they kept coming. "Please. You're upsetting my daughter." She shouted over her shoulder.

The door slammed, and it was like a clock stopped. Like I would never be older than that moment. Everything would always be "Before Daddy" and "After Daddy."

Daddy.

His face appeared in the slice of back window. I put down the glass, trying to slip through, but Mommy ran around the car. She screamed and hit him, over and over. "You stay away from her, Lee! You heard what the Judge said!"

Her black hair fell out of its bun as she pounded him with her fists. He tried to move away from her. Toward me. He reached his hand through the window and touched my face. His mouth opened to speak to me, but a policeman came up behind him and dragged him away from the car.

"I'll write you, Emmaline! Every day. I promise," he shouted. "I'll prove these things aren't true! I'll give up everything to be with you!" The policeman pushed him through the courthouse door, and he was gone.

"I'll write you, too, Daddy." I whispered it, soft so nobody but God or my guardian angel could hear. "Somehow, I'll make us be together again."

THE JUDGE

I leaned my weight against an upstairs window, the ruckus of her daddy's court still unfolding on the other side of a bolted door. Breath ragged. White film on glass. Wet tracks trailed from my fingers, the record of my need.

My craving.

Had I waited too long to see her again? I used to watch her. How she played hopscotch on a broken slab of sidewalk. Colored chalk and creamy skin and sing-song. I stood in the shadows until I was sure. Until I knew it was her.

My little beauty. It was my name for her. Before. In another life.

She never saw me. All those times, I hid. I waited. I scribbled letters in cipher, that code we always used, but I never mailed them. Patience would yield to my desire. For as long as I could remember, all I had to do was wait for weakness to reveal the path.

That was before I saw her today.

Eye contact was electricity. It surged through my limbs and soared around my heart. She looked at me, and she knew me. I could see her there, behind those sea-like eyes. It was almost like telepathy when I heard her voice in my head.

What took you so long? She said.

MERRY

Thursday. March 24, 1977. New Orleans, Louisiana.

I always came to in the same New Orleans drinking place, my journal adrift in a puddle of stale booze. I couldn't recall what happened on those pages. A record of another failed assignment, the words faded before I could capture them. Fleeting images on stained paper, encased in leather. I colored in a few words here and there, before they vanished. Became nothing. A palimpsest of another job already forgotten.

But I always remembered my life.

Two shots should have finished me.

One through the head. The other in my gut.

Some folks said I killed myself in the early morning hours of October 11, 1809. Others were sure I was murdered. I couldn't remember what happened. Someone tore out those pages. Erased those images. Took the final moments that might have given my soul peace.

But the sensational nature of my death did more than destroy my life. It took my chance to finish my journals, to spin my own story, to ensure that Americans remembered me the way I wished to be. Death blocked my view of how people thought of me.

If they thought of me. I didn't know.

I feared my reputation was buried with my remains. As far as I knew, my rotted carcass was shoved into an unmarked grave in Tennessee.

Death led me to Nowhere, a place for shattered souls to perform a good deed for the living, to erase the negative impact of the end of my life and its potential consequences on my immortal reputation.

Could one good deed help me be remembered the way I wished to be?

But my Nowhere was a continuation of my downward spiral, the misunderstandings that haunted the end of my life. I couldn't salvage my name, but failure didn't destroy the urge to try again.

And again.

Until I just wanted Nowhere to end. I craved Nothing.

I blinked. Centuries of embers caught in my nostrils, and fuzzy outlines shifted in the dark. Like every time before, he was waiting on me.

I couldn't recall where I'd been, but I always remembered the Bartender.

"Merry. Knew I'd see you again. What'll you have?"

He showed me his back before I could reply. Me, I rattled the exits, one by one. My sweaty hands slipped off the door handles. Perspiration burned in my eyes. That's what I told myself it was. Tough men, real leaders, we didn't cry.

Just outside, the crowd swayed beyond the cracks in the shutters. Random glimpses of life mingled with my reflection in the wavy glass. Voices drunk with booze and the promise of mayhem. I shouted, but my voice dissolved in the heavy air on my side of the divide.

The Bartender rattled his fingers on the counter. "You know them doors won't open, Merry."

I rested my forehead on blackened stucco. Why did I always fail? Time after time after time? What was next for me? A man with my skills ought to be able to see the way through Nowhere.

How I craved the end.

Resigned, I dragged my fingers across the fog on the window and stumbled back to my seat. It was always mine. Every time.

The Bartender, he stayed in his spot in the back corner. The muscles in his arms worked as he poured the dregs of others down the crusty sink. I squinted into the murk of the place, hoping for some company, some other lost spirit to let me know I wasn't the only one stuck here, the only fool who made this choice.

Glass clinked on glass. "You just missed my last guest. She drank up my top shelf Scotch. Hope you weren't thirsty for that."

"Give me a beer. Draft is fine."

He stopped dumping wet remainders down the drain. Set his amber eyes on me. "Sure you don't want something stronger?"

I scanned the glittering rows of glass bottles on the shelf behind the bar. What mixture might dull the edges of another failure? Whiskey was reckless. Vodka was for the drinker who wanted to disappear into his surroundings. Gin fellows possessed a snooty sophistication I found repellent. Wine-drinking boys were prissy. Draft beer was Every Man.

Every Man wanted to be remembered.

I closed my eyes and imagined myself as an Every Man, not a Nowhere Man.

"Beer's powerful enough."

He made casual work of pulling a foamy pint.

"You want food?" Bubbles frothed onto the sticky wood in front of me as he slid the beer my way. They turned liquid, puddled around the bottom of the glass. I studied my drink and made him wait. Weakness meant letting the Bartender guess what I was thinking.

I picked up the slick glass and downed it in one long draught. Foam sloshed in the bottom when I set it down in a sloppy ring. "I think I'll just get right to my next job. You know I can't abide it here."

Firelight flickered behind his eyes.

"Suit yourself. You got any money left this time?"

I rooted around in my damp jeans, my shirt pockets. In the front slot of my black leather jacket, I found a single note. Crisp. Clean.

I unfolded it slow. Tasted bile. Thomas Jefferson studied me from the face of a two dollar bill. I stared back into those familiar eyes while the Bartender laughed.

"I got new tricks, too. You ain't the only one can change things up."

Glasses crashed into the flagstone floor as I leaped over the bar. When I grabbed him, the front of his shirt was soft in my fingers. "Why is it always damn Jefferson? You know he abandoned me, right? At the end? He was happy to let everyone think I killed myself. Never even sent anyone to try and suss out the truth. I worshipped him like a father, and he let me go down in history as the ultimate prodigal son." My voice caught in my throat.

He shook free of me and stepped back, his boots crunching through shards of glass. "I don't make the rules here, Merry."

"Rules. I'll never figure out the rules in this place."

"Hey, don't blame me for your predicament."

My nostrils flared against the stench of spilled alcohol and smoke. Even as I balled up my fist to hit him, I knew he had me cornered. Boxed in. It wasn't his fault I couldn't get things right.

His eyes softened. "You seem to be in a hurry, and I didn't want you to run off without your two. That thing is supposed to be your good luck charm."

"These scraps of funny money haven't made any difference the last seven or eight assignments."

"A dozen, Merry. You're up to an even dozen."

I slumped onto my stool. Thumbed through the pages of my journal. A word here. A scrap of letters there. No hidden message to guide me past the obstacles of Nowhere. To help me avoid the same mistakes. Every Nowhere appearance was new. I couldn't remember them once I failed. Who I met. What I saw. No matter how I arranged what I managed to save from my other outings in Nowhere, I couldn't make sense of the remnants of twelve times tried.

Twelve times failed.

"So, this is number thirteen. Can I just go ahead and skip this one? Have another drink?"

"You been around long enough to know that ain't how it works."

"Dammit. I know how Nowhere works. I just can't seem to make it work for me."

I closed my eyes and relived the moment Nowhere found me, when I looked into my own dead eyes being covered over with the dirt of a hole that was too shallow to hold me. It was a pauper's burial. An unmarked grave. I was barely cold.

That was when I saw it: a chunk of black leather. It stuck out of the ground at the head of my grave. I pulled it from the dirt, and when I opened it, I read these words:

Remembrance is immortality.

Make people remember your story your way.

Come to Nowhere.

My story was already in tatters. Newspapers trumpeted the supposed details of my apparent suicide. Two men who knew me best—William Clark and Thomas Jefferson—supported that tawdry version of events. Faced with a sensational story, no one cared about the truth.

With one muttered *yes*, I stepped through a portal. Woke up in a New Orleans bar.

The clink of ice teased me back. The Bartender stirred a sulfur-tinged cocktail and pushed it my way. "Seconds aren't allowed, but I'm feeling charitable today."

Liquid heat lit up my nostrils. "What is it?"

"A Thunderclapper. Of all my customers, I thought you might appreciate it."

An homage to the pills members of the Corps of Discovery took for every conceivable ailment. We called them 'thunderclappers' because they gave us the runs. Clark was always partial to them. I had to smile at the memory of him, running off to empty his bowels behind a rock. Afraid he wasn't going to make it.

I raised the glass and sucked the mixture down. Fire ripped through my gullet. Erupted behind my eyes.

The Bartender smirked while I coughed up smoke. "Think of it as a cleansing fire. Erases what's come before." He paused. Leaned his burly frame over the counter and touched my sleeve. "You know this is your last shot, right?"

"Thirteen is my last chance?"

"Yep. You fail this time, you get to be a bartender. Your life will be erased from human history. Nobody will remember you, and what's worse, you won't remember you, either. You get to live forever, though. Slinging booze you can't drink in a room you can never leave."

I looked at his weathered face and wondered who he'd been. What was his story?

How would it feel to forget oneself? To never again close my eyes and see the sun set over the Missouri? To fail to hear Clark's laugh whisper through the trees? To be Nobody?

I wiped my brow with the back of my hand. Whispered my plea. "Tell me. Tell me how to finish this. Please."

He pushed a button on the cash register, and the drawer popped open, a fat wad of bills on one end. He picked it up and tossed it from hand to hand. "I had my own failures, Merry. That don't mean I can remember them. I'm just here to do my good deed. To lubricate your ego a little and send you out again." He stopped and slid the cash across the bar. "This ought to be enough to see you to the end."

"Five hundred? That's too much."

He flicked his eyes to the door. A rattle crescendoed through wood and glass. "Not in 1977, it ain't." He swabbed the bar with a stained towel. "Look, Merry. I got another customer coming. Don't keep making the same damn mistake, all right?"

I grabbed his grimy t-shirt. "What mistake? Tell me."

But instead, he shook free of me. Leaned over and took something out from under the counter. "Here. You lost your hat, and you'll be needing another one."

I looked from it to the two dollars crumpled in my other hand. Jefferson's stare launched me into the streets, patrolling like a lunatic. Searching, seeking the unknown someone who could save me. Rewrite my story. Release me from Nowhere to find whatever was next for a broken soul like me.

And so it began.

Again.

THE THREE R'S OF 21ST CENTURY READING

- **Read** the book - Authors love to sell books, but they really want buyers to read them. If you've come this far, thank you again for reading. Your investment of time matters to me.
- **Review** the book - Amazon and Goodreads don't tabulate book rankings based on sales alone. Reviews weigh heavily into the algorithms for book rankings. Your review matters. More reviews mean higher rankings, more impressions and ultimately, more readers. Please take five minutes and write a review of this book. If you write the review on Goodreads first, you can copy and paste it into Amazon.
- **Recommend** the book - The people in your life value your opinion. If you enjoyed this book, recommend it to five people. Over lunch or coffee. At the water cooler. On the sidelines. Let people see and hear your enthusiasm for this story. Some of them will thank you for showing them the way to a good book.

CPSIA information can be obtained at www.ICGtesting.com
Printed in the USA
LVOW11s0726241016

509896LV00004BB/5/P